Jessica Huntley

HOW TO COMMIT
THE PERFECT MURDER

IN TEN EASY STEPS

ISBN: 978-1-916827-01-1
First edition
Website: www.jessicahuntleyauthor.com

Cover Design: GetCovers
Edited and proofread by: Jennifer Kay Davies

About Jessica Huntley

Jessica is, and always has been, a huge fan of psychological and suspense thrillers. Her favourite authors are Chris Carter and John Marrs. She loves the twists and turns and shocking reveals and uses the books she reads as inspiration to write her own.

Jessica wrote her first book at age six. Between the ages of ten and eighteen, she wrote ten full-length fiction novels as a hobby in her spare time between school and work.

At age eighteen, she left her hobby behind and joined the British Army as an Intelligence Analyst where she spent the next four and a half years as a soldier. She attempted to write more novels but was never able to finish them.

Jessica later left the Army and became a mature student at Southampton Solent University and studied Fitness and Personal Training, which later became her career. She still enjoys keeping fit and exercising daily.

She is now a wife and a stay-at-home mum to a crazy toddler and lives in Newbury. During the first national lockdown of 2020, she signed up on a whim to a novel writing course, and the rest is history. Her love of writing came flooding back, and she managed to write and finish her debut novel, The Darkness Within Ourselves, inspired by her love of horror and thriller novels. She has also finished writing the My … Self trilogy, completed a Level 3 Diploma in Editing and Proofreading and has worked with four other authors on a collaborative horror novel entitled The Summoning.

She is now working on a new novel in her spare time and reads every day (thrillers...obviously).

Other books by Jessica Huntley

The Darkness Series

The Darkness Within Ourselves
The Darkness That Binds Us
The Darkness That Came Before

My ... Self Series

My Bad Self: A Prequel Novella
My Dark Self
My True Self
My Real Self

Standalone Thrillers

Jinx
How to Commit the Perfect Murder in Ten Easy Steps

Writing in collaboration with other authors

The Summoning
HorrorScope: A Zodiac Anthology - Vol 1

Acknowledgements

This book is a weird one. I originally wrote a book called "The Way of the Road" back in the late 90s when I was a teenager. It had romance in it and was a cross between a thriller and a rom-com, so I wanted to bring it back to life. And this is what I came up with …

Thank you to the authors who agreed to read the book and provide an author quote (thank goodness you actually liked it!) J. Taylor and Abby Davies.

Thanks, as always, to my editor, Jennifer Kay Davies, who continues to edit my books and weed out all those small errors I always miss.

Thank you to my beta readers, who provided valuable feedback with regards to the plot, and characters and helped me iron out a few inconsistencies. Chelsea (@mylittlebooktique_x), Leanne (@leanne.loves.books), and Char (@theliteraryreviewjournal).

Thank you to all my amazing readers who keep me going through the tough times and remind me why I'm on this crazy writing journey to begin with. Receiving your messages and reviews about how much you enjoy my books is always the highlight of the day.

Connect with Jessica Huntley

Find and connect with me online via the following platforms.

Sign up to my email list via my website to be notified of future books and receive a twice-monthly author newsletter and also receive a **FREE thriller novella called My Bad Self.**

www.jessicahuntleyauthor.com

Follow me on Facebook: Jessica Huntley - Author - @jessica.reading.writing

Follow me on Instagram: @jessica_reading_writing

Follow me on Twitter: @jess_read_write

Follow me on TikTok: @jessica_reading_writing

Follow me on Goodreads: jessica_reading_writing

Content Warnings

Attempted rape.
Blood. Murder.
Inferred child abuse.

Prologue

ASHLEIGH

5 July 2022 – 02:32 a.m.

My tender eyelids flutter open like the wings of a newly hatched butterfly, but all I see is inky darkness; the type of darkness that swallows you whole, disorientating you so much you don't know which way is up and which way is down.

I don't know where I am.

I don't know how I got here (wherever here is).

And I don't know why my head is pounding like a steel drum.

It's strangely warm, but not a comforting warmth one gets from a log fire or a snugly duvet on a winter's night. It is a familiar warmth though; one that sets my heart racing and my teeth on edge. I've been here before and I think I've been here for some time because my body is trembling uncontrollably and my shoulder—

A scream escapes my lips and disappears into the darkness, then bounces off a nearby wall. The echo that hurtles back sends shivers down my spine.

I think my left shoulder is dislocated. My whole arm is numb, hanging lifelessly by my side. It may as well belong to someone else.

My shaky fingers grope around in the dark, desperate to find something, *anything*, to reassure me that I'm safe and secure, but I already know, by the way my heart's racing and the terror is creeping over my body like a spider, I'm far from safe.

My memory is foggy at first, but, after a few seconds, I remember why I'm here and everything that's happened over the past few days starts snapping into focus. Memory after memory pops into my head, playing out like broken snippets of a movie.

I remember everything ...

Oh God ... that means ...

There's a strange smell wafting through the air; damp and something else – something earthy. My nostrils scrunch up and I can almost taste the aroma in my mouth, putrid and vile. I lick my lips, trying but failing to moisten the cracked, delicate skin. After running my tongue over my top teeth, I realise, due to the thick film of plaque that's formed on them, it's likely I haven't brushed recently.

There's also blood in my mouth.

My head still pounds relentlessly. It's not a sharp or agonising pain, but a dull throbbing ache that's enough to cause discomfort and unease. I'm lying awkwardly on my back, so I slowly raise my body into a seated position and attempt to adjust my injured arm, but I can't ... because it won't move.

Pop ...

Another memory.

They start flooding my mind in nauseating waves.

With my right hand, I feel around in the dark again, prodding my left arm in a desperate attempt to wake it up.

That's when I touch the cool, solid metal encased around my wrist.

Handcuffs.

Pop ...

Another memory.

I gently pull on the cuff. There's a slight give, but no noisy sound to suggest I'm cuffed to anything metal or solid. But I'm attached to something ...

The cuff is tight and digging into my soft flesh. Blindly, I feel along the metal chain that links one cuff to the other and when I get to the end, I let out another loud scream.

There's a hand at the end that isn't mine.

'Hello?' I whisper, unable to control the trembling in my voice.

There's no response, so I summon up the courage and fumble around in the dark, feeling for the strange hand again.

I shudder when I touch cold, clammy skin.

The hand is bigger than mine, thicker; male.

I reach the other cuff and realise it's attached securely to the other person's wrist.

I call out again, but there's no reply.

I know the answer before I even check for a pulse.

I'm handcuffed to a dead man.

How to Commit the Perfect Murder
Step One

Be in it for the Long Haul

I want to be 100 per cent honest for a moment.

People who kill someone in the spur of the moment are more likely to get caught than those who plan the murder out meticulously beforehand.

It's surely a well-known fact of life. Google it.

You can't just kill someone whenever you feel like it and expect to get away with it.

That's why I've come up with ten easy steps to follow. Well ... I say *easy*, but if murdering someone was easy then we'd all be doing it, wouldn't we? Probably daily ...

My first step is this – if you want to kill someone then you have to be in it for the long haul, and what I mean by that is as follows:

You *must* do your research and you *have* to expect it to take time.

Nothing happens overnight; not fame, not fortune, not weight loss, not murder. Well, unless you happen to be really, *really* lucky. And those people who do become famous, get rich, lose weight or murder someone overnight are most likely faking it ... or cheating.

Me? I want to do things properly and work hard, be proud of my accomplishments.

Nothing worth having in life is free.

The point I'm trying to make here is that if you want to successfully kill someone and get away with it then you need to take your time and plan ahead and that requires, more than anything else, a great deal of patience.

Ask anyone who has built their own business from the ground up or written a novel and finally got that publishing deal after months or even years of rejection.

It all takes time, dedication, planning, heartbreak, and money.

Killing someone is no different.

Trust me.

Dear Diary

Date: 4 June 2000

Dear Diary,

A new boy started at my school today. His name is Bryan Matthews. He is, by far, the coolest boy I've ever met. I want to be like him so bad. My sister already has a crush on him. I think I do too, a little bit, even though I've never taken notice of boys before. He has this way about him that draws me in. He's like a shiny new bike to all the kids at school and he already, after only one day, has loads of friends. I'm sad that I'm not one of them. I want to be one of them. Maybe one day I will be his friend. Yes, one day I'll be his *best* friend.

Date: 5 June 2000

Dear Diary,

Sometimes I wish I could kill people and get away with it. It would be so cool, right? Just imagine it for a second ... imagine ending someone's life ... and getting away with it ... forever. It would take a lot of planning I think and a lot of self-sacrifice, but it would be worth it to see the life drain from their eyes as they realise that you'd finally bested them. Maybe I shouldn't think these things, but I do, so does that make me some sort of freak?

Date: 6 June 2000

Dear Diary,

Apparently, I'm not supposed to want to kill people ... so how come I do? *Apparently*, it's not a usual thing for a ten-year-old to want to do. I checked with the school counsellor. I made sure that she thought I was joking and only asking for a school research project. I'm pretty sure she believed me ... Does that make me different from everyone else, or is everyone else just lying to themselves? I bet everyone wants to kill someone deep, deep down, but they're too scared to go through with it.

Date: 7 June 2000

Dear Diary

Bryan Matthews is still the coolest kid at school, but he's a little bit mean. Like, today, he bullied a kid into giving him their lunch. He made them cry. I watched them sit in the corner of the playground and go hungry, but I did nothing to help. But it didn't make me hate Bryan Matthews. In fact, it made me admire him. He has about four friends now who hang around him all the time. I want to be part of his group so badly. I'll do anything ... *anything* ...

7

Chapter One

ASHLEIGH
1 July 2022 – 08:50 a.m.

My handbag is on the passenger seat, the contents haphazardly spilling out in all directions. I briefly take my eyes off the busy London traffic and rummage around for my bright pink lipstick.

I know it's here somewhere.

The car starts to swerve into the next lane, but I don't notice until a car horn blares and jolts me back to reality. I ignore the rude stare and hand gesture from the other driver and apply my lipstick, using the rear-view mirror. I pucker my full pink lips into a pout and smile, my teeth a dazzling shade of white.

Perfect.

My name is Ashleigh Elizabeth Alexandra Penelope Daphne Carmichael; sole heiress to my late-father's vast fortune, owner of his extravagant estate and current head of the Carmichael Foundation, a London-based, world-leading, pharmaceutical development and manufacturing company.

The foundation has grown organically over the past four decades ever since my father started it, and now employs over six thousand highly trained staff across twenty different facilities, including Europe, the United States and Asia. The London building is the head office and where you'll find me signing cheques and ticking boxes because that's pretty much all I do. I'm the attractive face of the company,

8

not the brains behind the operation. Can you imagine me learning about developing pharmaceuticals and how to run clinical trials? Ha! I barely scraped a C in Science, and I don't know what 'pharmaceutical' actually means. Luckily, my father's best friend and business partner, Sawyer Croft, handles the day-to-day business stuff that, apparently, I'm not qualified to deal with, which is fine, because I have far better things to do with my time … like shopping. I love shopping. Who doesn't, right? Especially when money isn't an issue.

My father tragically died in a freak car accident fourteen years ago on the Silverstone racetrack, during one of his track days. I barely saw the man. He left early in the morning before the sun came up and returned late into the night, usually when I was fast asleep. Sometimes he didn't come home at all, deciding to spend the night sleeping in his office instead. He was basically a stranger to me. Sawyer was more of a father to me in some ways. He'd taken his beloved Aston Martin for a spin and completed a few laps of the famous circuit at record speed — but then my father died when the brakes on his car failed. He crashed into a concrete wall and was burned alive in a huge explosion, like something out of an action movie. I didn't even know cars could explode upon impact. I was left an orphan at the tender age of eighteen (a mere three days after my birthday) and then, since I was technically a legal adult, I inherited everything.

And I mean … everything.

I turned into one of the youngest millionaires in the United Kingdom overnight. I was thrust into the spotlight and expected to know everything that was going on with my father's company and to make huge decisions that I didn't have the experience to make. It was never going to work. So that's why Sawyer stepped in, and I gratefully handed the reins over to him to deal with the daily business meetings, overseas phone calls and boring paperwork. I was told that I only had to show my face once a week or so, sign a few things and leave. It worked perfectly and still is working perfectly to this day. I have no intention of signing the business over to Sawyer for real though. It's *my* company, after all.

I am still a millionaire, but now I'm one of the most influential and successful thirty-somethings in the country. My Instagram page (@Ashleigh_Carmichael_Forever) has over 4 million followers and is growing hourly. My TikToks go viral every single day without fail and I receive a never-ending supply of free gifts, clothes, handbags and holidays from companies and businesses who want me to promote their products, and I'm more than happy to oblige them. I could easily buy all these things for myself of course, but why should I if they want to willingly give them to me? I'm doing them a huge favour at the end of the day.

In fact, that's what I'm doing at this precise moment. Yesterday, I was given a brand new white Mercedes to drive around for a week, with the request that I attend a few high-class functions, snap a few pictures for my socials and tell everyone how amazing it is. It is pretty amazing ... although I do prefer the new BMW, which I bought for myself earlier this year. It's purple and sparkly (a colour called purple fizz), a limited-edition shade that was designed and made especially for me, but I've barely driven it since I bought it. It's currently sat in my garage at my Kensington home gathering dust. Ah well, at least it looks cute.

I smack my Botox-enhanced lips together as I stare at my reflection in the rear-view mirror, taking one hand off the wheel and fluffing up my long blonde hair.

Oh, my goodness ...

Are my dark brown roots coming through already? It takes so much time, effort and money to stay a perfectly light blonde. I need to get my hair extensions redone as well; they are coming loose.

'Call Pam,' I say.

I ease my foot off the accelerator and squeeze the brake. Of course, this Mercedes is an automatic because, let's face it, it's physically impossible to use a clutch whilst wearing four-inch stilettos, which are so adorable by the way. I saw them in the window of Kurt Geiger a week ago and just had to buy them. They cost a small fortune, but I believe in having the best of everything.

Calling Pam, repeats the automated voice of the car phone.

So far, I am impressed with the level of technology this car has to offer. I must remember to say that line in my Instagram story and TikTok reel later.

'Pam's Cuts. How can I help?'

'Hi, Pam, babe.'

'Ashleigh, love! How lovely. Time for another touch-up?'

'Yes, please. The works. My extensions are a bit loose in places. I can almost pull them out.'

'We can't have that. I can fit you in tomorrow at noon.'

'Perfect. See you then. Bye, Pam, babe.'

'Bye, love.' The call disconnects.

'Add hair appointment with Pam to the calendar for twelve o'clock tomorrow.'

Adding hair appointment with Pam to the calendar for twelve o'clock tomorrow.

Pam is such a babe. Nothing is ever too short notice or difficult for her. Apparently, I'm her favourite client because whenever I walk into her salon everyone snaps pictures of me and posts them to their social media pages and then she gets an influx of appointments. She's booked up for months in advance, but always squeezes me in whenever I need my hair done.

I smile at myself in the mirror again. My life is awesome, if I do say so myself. I'm perfectly aware of how good I have it, how lucky I am to never have to worry about making ends meet, but, then again, I also have a substantial amount of pressure on my shoulders, something a lot of people don't realise or appreciate.

Let me put it another way …

If I so much as step a toe out of line, or post something online that is considered offensive to even one person, my name is dragged through the mud. I must be super careful what I say and how I say it, so now I have a social media manager who okays every post or story before I post it, which all came about because of a certain incident a couple of years ago, which hadn't even been my fault … Well, not really.

I was caught scoffing down a double cheeseburger during a week when I was supposed to be going vegan to promote a new plant-based diet that a health food company wanted me to try. Some random stalker snapped a picture of me mid-chew (which had not been flattering by any stretch of the imagination) and the next thing I knew it had gone viral all over Twitter and TikTok with the hashtag #VeganCheaterBurgerEater. It hadn't been one of my finest moments and the health food company had immediately dropped me as their promo girl. It's not like I had posted a picture of myself eating a burger. I'd just been very unlucky that some weirdo had seen the chance to humiliate me. I may have millions of adoring fans, but I also have a lot of haters.

The point is that my lifestyle is not for everyone, and I have learned to grow a thick skin; speaking of which, I must book another deluxe facial this week. My face is beginning to look its age and that is not good, not when you're the poster girl for the latest skin care product by Elemis, which promises to make you look five years younger with regular use (not that I use the product, of course. I just say that I do, and everyone rushes out to buy it).

I wear a lot of make-up and, when I say a lot, I mean *a lot*. On a regular day, like today, I apply it myself, using the latest and most expensive primer, foundation, bronzer, mascara, eyeshadow, blusher and lipstick there is on the market, all of which I usually get given for free. However, if I have a TV interview, or am attending an important business meeting, or know I'm going to be seen by lots of people, then my make-up artist comes over to my house and applies it first thing in the morning. Carl is amazing. He even does make-up for celebrities like Emma Watson and Emily Blunt. I met Emma once at a film premier and we hit it off straight away, although I haven't heard from her since. I gave her my number so we could meet up and go for drinks, but she's never replied to any of my messages. I think she's blocking me ... what a cow.

My short blue dress is riding up my thighs, which are, in turn, beginning to stick to the black leather seats. I dial up the air-con and tug my dress down, wiggling my bum as I do so. I'm on my way to a meeting with a brand new clothing designer. She's, *apparently*, the new up-and-coming fashion designer in London, but having looked at a few of her items online, they aren't really to my taste. I like light and bright colours such as pinks and purples and blues and yellows, which highlight my tanned skin (I must remember to book another spray tan this week), but her clothes are very dark and dark colours tend to completely wash me out and make me look like a corpse, no matter how brown my skin is. However, she's offering me a good deal and full coverage on her website, so I can't complain. I do dabble with modelling from time to time, but it always causes me severe anxiety because I feel like I need to constantly compete with all the other models. If I'm too thin then I get hounded by the media for being anorexic, and if I happen to put on an extra pound then I'm labelled as *unhealthy*. I'm much happier being my regular size ten, 34C and being able to eat a cheeseburger whenever I want, thank you very much.

Finally, the traffic starts moving again. As I mentioned, I live in Kensington, London, and I'll whole-heartedly admit that it is a very posh and expensive neighbourhood. My house is worth over fifteen million pounds and is within walking distance of the Natural History Museum (not that I've ever been). It's a Grade II listed building and was built in the 1840s by some well-known architect and designer (I forget his name) and has seven bedrooms and four bathrooms spread out over seven floors, including a basement and a lower basement, which always terrifies me. I've only been down there once when I was drunk as a bet. Never again. It's creepy, just like the basement in Sawyer's house …

The point is that I'm a city girl through-and-through and have never set a toe in the countryside, but I do hate the constant drone of traffic and how densely populated it is. Sometimes I feel as if I'm suffocating. As soon as I step outside my front door there are swarms of people all around me and buildings taller than the trees. What I wouldn't do to take this car (or my own car) out onto the open road in the country somewhere and really open her up, put my high-heel flat to the floor and get the speedometer over ten miles-an-hour. But that would mean I'd have to *go* to the countryside … and eww … *mud*.

I inch to a stop at another set of traffic lights.

I over-exaggerate a sigh and slump back into the seat, both hands gripping the wheel tighter than is deemed necessary. It's almost nine, which means I'm going to be late for my meeting. Then again, I'm almost always late. It's kind of inevitable living in London.

Ed Sheeran's 'Shivers', one of my favourite songs, comes on the radio so I press the volume button on the steering wheel and crank it up, singing the chorus at the top of my lungs. I do a few hair flips for good measure, closing my eyes to fully embrace the moment. My foot slips briefly on the brake pedal, so I readjust it.

A loud BEEEEEEEP! interrupts my singing.

My eyes fling open and I slam my foot against the brake as I realise, too late, that I've been easing out into traffic and am now half-blocking the road. More beeps and shouts erupt around me as cars attempt to get past.

'Sorry!' I shout, even though all the windows are up and they, more than likely, can't hear me due to the hustle-and-bustle of the London streets.

'Fuck … wank … bitch!' I hear someone shout. 'Learn … drive!'

I shudder violently, unable to control the waves of nausea that ripple through my body. Within seconds, the lights turn green, so I floor it, revving the engine hard. The wheels scream in retaliation. The Mercedes lurches forwards, faster than I expect, and, in my panic and frustration, I squeeze the accelerator down further.

My heel gets caught on something on the floor as I attempt to pull it away. I look down for a split second to try and sort it out and that's when the front of the car collides with a large, black monstrosity.

The airbag deploys.

My head snaps back and I see stars.

There's a lot of shouting and commotion.

I think a woman is screaming.

The next second a lorry slams into the side of my car.

I'm sent skidding across the road like a tin can and straight into a concrete bollard.

That's the last thing I remember ...

Chapter Two

June 2000

At ten years old I liked to think I was more mature than everyone else, especially the other kids in my year. Their idea of fun was to throw wet toilet paper at each other and giggle at dirty words.

So stupid.

The bell rang and, right on cue, all the kids in the classroom ran out screaming to go and play outside and chase each other around until one of them fell over and grazed their knees.

Again ... *So stupid.*

I waited patiently for the commotion to die down and then rose from my seat, clutching my book to my chest like a shield and walked into the hallway. My classmates chattered loudly, laughing and screeching like banshees as they rushed outside, barging past me into the blistering sunshine. I followed them begrudgingly, parked my bum on a wooden bench, which overlooked the playground, and opened my current read: *The Witches* by Roald Dahl.

I was a huge bookworm, and I didn't care everyone knew it because I was miles ahead of every other kid, intellectually. I often read a book in a day and could easily read more grownup books, like *Pride and Prejudice* or *Moby Dick,* but my teacher said I should stick to reading books designed for my age group, most of which I had already read. I'd devoured everything the school library had to offer. The librarian, Mr Lowe, often let me into the more advanced reading section so I could browse. He was the only teacher I liked. All the others were determined to squash my enthusiasm to read or always told me off for speaking my mind and telling the truth.

A few days ago, I punched the new kid, Bryan Matthews, in the face for calling me a retard because I'd given the correct answer to a complicated Maths sum without having to use a calculator. I pointed out he was wrong calling me a 'retard' because it was actually a derogatory term either for someone with a mental disability or for someone who was stupid and slow to understand, of which I was neither because I could do the sum in my head, and he couldn't. He kept shouting 'retard!' at me and encouraged the entire class to join in, so I got up from my seat and punched him in the face. Then I got detention. He hadn't passed out or anything. He had cried though ... and his nose had bled a teeny, tiny bit. He then got loads of attention from the teacher and the girls in the class, who said he was so brave ... *Yawn*.

Annoyingly, Bryan Matthews was pretty cool, and I found myself daydreaming about him a lot. I liked him, but I hated him too. I found it oddly confusing.

'Hey, freak!' Bryan's voice echoed across the playground.

I didn't look up, attempting instead to finish the page I was reading.

'Hey, I'm talking to you … freak.' He stood right in front of me. His looming shadow blocked out the sunshine, which had been gently warming me and my book.

I looked up, squinting. 'Oh, hi, Bryan. What's up? How's the nose?'

He sniffed loudly but ignored my last question. 'What's up is that you're a freaky bookworm. Go on. Say it.'

'I'm a freaky bookworm.'

'Now say that you're a freaky bookworm who wants to have sex with books.' Bryan laughed way too hard and gestured for his fellow cronies to join him. All five of them began swarming around him like flies on a dead body. How he'd managed to form a tightly knitted group of friends so fast was beyond me. I'd been at this school for years and had yet to make one good friend. He showed up and had a cult following seemingly overnight.

I sighed as I closed my book. It seemed that I wouldn't be able to finish this book today after all. 'I'm a freaky bookworm who wants to have sex with books.' My voice was low and monotone.

Bryan and his cronies howled with laughter, slapping each other on the backs and high fiving.

'Say something else!' shouted a boy who had ginger hair and freckles. Even the ginger-haired kids picked on me. I was, *apparently*, considered the lowest of the low at this school because I was so smart.

Bryan smirked. 'Now say … say you're a stupid freak who wants to lick my shoes.'

I sighed again. 'Bryan, have you ever heard the phrase *sticks and stones may break my bones, but words will never hurt me*?'

Bryan stopped laughing. 'Are you saying you want me to break your bones, freak?'

'You really are an imbecile,' I muttered.

'What did you just call me?' Bryan stepped forwards and knocked the book out of my hands. It clattered to the floor and the bookmark fell out. That made the little hairs on the back of my neck stand to attention.

I rose to my feet, staring at him. 'I said you're an *imbecile*. It means you're stupid.'

Bryan cackled as he watched me bend down and pick up my book. I also picked up a nearby rock, hiding it behind the book as I straightened up. I was still several inches shorter than him, but I squared my shoulders, breathing in as deep as I could. I read once, in a textbook, that some animals puffed out their chests to make themselves look bigger and more aggressive to predators that wished to do them harm, but it seemed my attempt was futile.

'You know what, freak? I'm going to test that theory of yours.'

'What theory?'

'That sticks and stones thing. Boys ...' Bryan stepped to one side as dozens of sticks and small stones came flying towards me, seemingly out of nowhere. They kept on coming, and I used my book as a minuscule shield, but it wasn't big enough to be of any help. Besides, Bryan grabbed it off me and chucked it behind him as his cronies continued to throw their missiles. A stone hit me square in the nose. A large stick slashed across my right leg. I yelped as I attempted to make myself as small as possible this time, all the while clutching my own rock in my trembling hands. I squeezed it so tight that it hurt, focussing my energy and strength into it.

Finally, the attack came to an end.

My ears rang and my heart pounded as Bryan crouched beside me. 'You're nothing but a freaky loser. Your mummy and daddy don't love you. You're ugly and fat and deserve to die. Now ... tell me what hurt more? The stick and stones, or the words?' Bryan made a horrible gargling sound and then spat on me before standing up, laughing as he stepped away. The horrible globule of spit slid down the side of my face as I stared after him.

And that was when I decided I was going to smash open his head one day.

Chapter Three

HANNAH
6 July 2022 – 22:50 p.m.

The big toe on my left foot feels like I've been stung by a nettle, and I want nothing more than to reach down and tear apart my skin; anything to relieve the itch. But I can't move – not even a little bit. Also, my nose and eyes are burning. What the hell is going on? Where am I and why do I feel as if my whole body is on fire? Everything hurts, everything aches …

My eyes fling open. A piercing light sears my eyeballs, but now I can't close my eyes in order to shield them. My body isn't responding to even the most basic of commands. I try and open my mouth to shout for help, but, of course, I can't move, so I stare at the ceiling of whatever room I'm in and start to count the black spots that are dancing across it. The single bright light bulb high above my head swings back and forth like a pendulum. Why is it moving? I don't understand what is happening …

Wait …

Not only do I not know *where* I am, but I have no idea *who* I am either.

I search my cloudy brain for an answer, but it's as useless as trying to find one particular star in the night sky when you have no idea what star you're looking for. What is going on? A cold slap of fear hits me across the face.

I'm in a hospital … or am I?

My eyeballs finally react to my brain signals, allowing me to see certain aspects of the room. I'm lying on a bed and there's a metal table nearby laden with medical equipment, including a scalpel and pieces of bloody padding and tape. I can't see any windows, so I have no idea of the time of day or even which day it is. It looks like a hospital, but a very cheap and dirty one ... possibly a make-shift medical room. Have I been brought here by someone? Kidnapped?

One by one my muscles start to switch on like light bulbs, allowing me to wiggle my toes first, then my fingers. It's a monumental effort, but I eventually manage to sit up and take in my close surroundings.

Despite there being no windows, I can feel a light, cool breeze from somewhere and hear the gentle hum of traffic. There's a blue curtain pulled around my bed which is blowing gently. I shudder as goosebumps appear over my pale, naked arms. I gently run my fingers over my pimply skin, hoping for some sort of memory to appear, but there is nothing.

I'm an empty shell.

Another breeze makes me turn and look over my shoulder. There is a door and it's open, revealing nothing but darkness ahead. My exhausted and confused brain immediately conjures up the worst possible scenario – a man walks in and attacks me and is holding me hostage for some unknown reason. Does he want my organs for the black market? Am I to be sold as a sex slave? I fight against the bile that rises in the back of my throat and turn my head away from the door, blinking away the hallucination.

I reach up one hand and touch my head, wincing when I find a large swelling and what feels like stitches embedded in my skull. Limp, dark brown hair dangles on either side of my face; I don't recognise it. My vision begins to distort as my surroundings zoom in and out of focus.

I call out for help in a weak and croaky voice, waiting a few seconds in between to see if anyone comes; no one does, and I feel relieved at that. My tongue is sticking to the roof of my mouth. I need water, but there is none by the side of the bed, so I gingerly pull back the thin bed sheet and attempt to swing my legs over the edge of the bed, but they refuse to move. Stubborn, stupid legs.

Patiently, I wait until the blood supply returns, then slowly lower my feet to the floor, gasping as the cold tiles touch the soles, which tingle at the sensation. First, I need water, and then I need to find help. Why is no one coming to help me? Does anyone know I'm here?

I don't understand what's happening ...

Ignoring the tingling that's creeping up my legs like a million tiny spiders, I inch my way across the floor towards the open door; my only means of escape and finding the answers I crave. My body feels weird, like it doesn't even belong to me. I wish I could kick-start my brain into remembering something ... *anything*, but there is nothing but a foggy mess inside. My poor brain can barely comprehend putting one foot in front of the other, let alone figure out how and why I'm in a hospital-type place, having seemingly just woken up from a coma.

I don't even know what day it is ...

I poke my head around the side of the door, peering timidly into the corridor beyond. It is dark, but I can just about make out a faint, flickering light ahead at the end of the narrow hall. My stomach performs numerous flips, the kind of nervous fluttering one gets before making a life-altering decision or when faced with a terrifying leap of faith.

My head pounds so hard I can hear it as clear as a drumbeat. Maybe I should hold up on trying to summon any long-lost memories for the time being … not that my brain is remembering anything anyway.

Why are there no hospital staff around? What the hell is going on?

'Hello?' I call out, my voice cracking after only one word. I cough, gasping as I attempt to regain control of my breathing. 'H-Help.'

I shuffle my bare feet across the cool floor, feeling my way along the corridor with my hands, grasping at the walls for some sort of stability. The walls are moving. It probably hadn't been a good idea for me to get out of bed, but no one had come to help me.

I have an overwhelming urge to keep moving forwards. There is something about this place that's stirring up an unwelcome feeling inside. It almost feels like …

A strange clicking emanates from behind me.

I freeze as all the tiny hairs on the back of my neck stand to attention. A cold shiver runs down my spine as a soft breeze blows against my neck. Where is it coming from?

I bite my lip to the point of pain as I turn my head and glance over my left shoulder. The corridor I've just walked down is empty, but the light from the room I woke up in is flickering ominously, casting dark shadows on the walls.

I push myself away from the wall and stand on wobbly legs. It's then that I glance down at what I'm wearing; a pair of baggy trousers and a t-shirt that I assume had once been white. My underwear feels damp, and I clearly haven't showered for several days, as the smell of my own body odour makes me grimace.

I shiver again as my feet continue to shuffle forwards. I don't even know what I'm doing. All I know is that I must get out of here before ... before *what*? Surely a hospital is the best place for me, but I don't want to be here. I just want all my memories to come back.

I try again to walk, but my body and brain are still not communicating exactly as they should. Everything inside me is telling me to go back to the bed and lay down before I cause myself an injury, but I can't ...

I have to keep trying to escape, but who am I escaping from?

I freeze again when I spot a hazy figure standing in front of me, highlighted ominously by the flickering light. My muddled brain can't seem to differentiate between whether it's a man or a woman. It's merely a human form and it's walking towards me, its arm outstretched ... a large object grasped between its fingers ...

I scream.

Chapter Four

ASHLEIGH
1 July 2022 – 15:02 p.m.

'Can you hear me? My name is Doctor Tomkins. Can you open your eyes for me?' A polite female voice stirs me from unconsciousness as I wrestle with my eyelids, forcing them open. The glue holding my fake eyelashes in place have fused them together, reminding me of the state I often wake up in after a heavy Friday night. A beaming white light shines into my eyes the second I manage to crack them open.

'Arrgg!' I shout, desperately trying to shield my eyes. I bat my arms around. 'What's going on? Where am I? Who are you? Get that light out of my face!' I shove the doctor's hand away, still flailing around frantically as if trying to get rid of a pesky wasp.

'I'm sorry, but I just need to check you aren't severely concussed.'

'Excuse me? Why would I be concussed? What is going on?'

'You were involved in a car accident several hours ago and have been unconscious since you arrived in the ambulance. You have a minor head wound, but otherwise appear uninjured.'

'I … really? Where am I? The last thing I remember is driving my car in Kensington.'

'You're at Chelsea and Westminster Hospital. I am just going to ask you a few simple questions to ensure you don't have any memory loss. Do you know your name?'

'Of course I do.'

'What is it?'

I look at her as if she's just spoken another language. 'Surely you should know that. Don't you recognise me?'

'I'm afraid not, no.'

I sigh in annoyance. 'Ashleigh Elizabeth Alexandra Penelope Daphne Carmichael.'

Doctor Tomkins raises her overgrown eyebrows. Is that judgement I see in her eyes? She asked me what my name was, so I gave it to her. I don't care for her snide attitude or her cheap hair dye job; the black does absolutely nothing for her skin tone. Her teeth are white and straight at least. If there's one thing I can't stand it's wonky, dingy teeth, which is why I paid thousands to have invisible braces fitted at age twenty and have my teeth professionally cleaned four times a year.

'Date of birth?' she asks as she makes a note on her pad. I notice she only writes one or two words down, probably not all four of my middle names.

'Seventeenth of February 1990.'

'Address?'

'Three St George's Gardens. Wait ... you said I was in a car accident?'

'That's right.'

'When?'

'Earlier this morning just after nine.'

29

'What time is it now?'

'Just after three.'

Six hours.

I've been unconscious in a hospital for six hours.

I don't remember a single thing about the accident. It's all a massive blur. One minute I'd been singing to the radio and then I woke up here. Did I crash into someone? Did someone crash into me?

'Miss Carmichael ... Are you all right?'

I shake my head, but then abruptly nod. 'No. Yes, I'm fine. When can I leave? I need to leave.'

'I have a few more tests to run first. Your head injury doesn't appear to have caused you any long-term damage, but you may have a headache for a few days. If you begin to experience any dizziness, nausea, confusion, sensitivity to light or memory loss then you are to come straight back, do you understand?'

I nod slowly, even though I pretty much have all those symptoms right now, but I want to get out of this place as quickly as possible. I hate hospitals.

I'd just turned seven when my mother was diagnosed with breast cancer. Unfortunately, despite having some serious symptoms for several months prior, she didn't go to the doctor until it was too late. She refused to admit that she was sick and, although the chemotherapy slowed things down, ultimately, it was like trying to apply a plaster to a gunshot wound. She was gone within two months of being diagnosed.

I spent a lot of time with her in hospital because my father dumped me there while he went to work. Apparently, looking after his dying wife didn't rate highly on his to-do list. According to him, she still had a job to do – look after me. It didn't matter if she was sedated or vomiting most of the time. The nurses looked after me, but mostly I stayed in the room with my mother and watched her die. I'll never forget the moment she took her last breath—

'Can I get you anything, Miss Carmichael?'

I shake my head, dispelling the bad memories.

That's quite enough of those. I didn't pay a private psychiatrist two hundred pounds an hour for eight years for nothing.

I watch as the doctor leaves my room and then shudder as a cool breeze floats in through a nearby open window. I instinctively reach for my phone because my hands feel naked without it, but it's nowhere around me, not even on the side table next to the hospital bed. I don't see my bright pink Fendi handbag either, which basically holds my entire life in its supple leather interior, including a very important book. The bag itself cost over three thousand pounds. I bet someone's nicked it.

A nurse wanders in so I immediately snap at her. 'Where's my Fendi bag?'

She freezes and looks at me as if I've just asked her to answer the million-pound question. 'I'm sorry?'

'My bag? Where is it? It's bright pink with Fendi written across the side.'

'I'm sorry, but I haven't seen it. Everything that was on you when the paramedics brought you in is on the chair over there.' She points to the flimsy plastic chair in the corner. I follow her finger and see that there's a single white envelope resting on the blue seat. She picks it up and hands it to me. I snatch it away from her, tearing it open. My eyes soak up the words at lightning speed, despite the handwriting being almost illegible.

If you want your stuff back, then wire £100,000 to the account below and then meet me at Skegness Beach Resort at 8 on Saturday morning. Don't be late or you'll never see your bag again.

22-43-56   78654376

My head snaps up. 'Who left this here?'

The nurse shrugs her shoulders. 'No idea.'

'I need you to find out … now! My bag has been stolen and is being held for ransom.'

I see the nurse's mouth twitch, as if she's fighting the urge to smirk at me. 'I'll see what I can do.' Her words are laden with sarcasm.

'Has anyone called the hospital asking about me?'

'No, no one. Sorry.'

I screw up my nose, resting back against the overly soft pillow. She's not sorry, not even a little bit. The snooty cow. I glare at the back of her head as she leaves the room. My hands begin fidgeting. I'm so lost without my phone. When I hadn't turned up for my business meeting at nine, they must have assumed I was being my usual self by being late, but it's gone three in the afternoon, so surely someone would have flagged it to my agent or my managing team. Someone would have noticed I wasn't answering my phone ...

Anyway, that's beside the point because someone has stolen my bag and is now holding it to ransom! I *need* my bag. There are things in there that ... let's just say that they are very important and if they happen to fall into the wrong hands then my life would get *very* complicated *very* fast.

My hands fidget again beside me, constantly looking for something to do. I grasp the bed sheets and squeeze my fists together. I *always* have my phone within arm's reach and without it, I feel as if I've lost an actual limb. If I had my phone with me right now, I'd be Tweeting and Instagramming and TikToking all about my stay in hospital to the world, but no one even knows I'm here. It's very disconcerting.

I need to get home or back to the office and tell everyone I'm okay. They must be worried about me. I can just imagine my housekeeper and agent fluttering about the place, calling everyone to ask where I am and why I didn't turn up for the business meeting. Even Sawyer must be worried about me.

I fling back the bed covers.

I've made up my mind.

I'm getting out of here ... now.

Chapter Five

1 July 2022 – 13:30 p.m.

Curtis was not happy. Not only had he lost eyes on his target for the past three days, but some blonde-haired rich girl, who'd looked a lot like a doll, had crashed into the back of his beloved 1967 Chevrolet Impala while he'd been stationary at a set of traffic lights. Luckily, his Impala was a pure, solid beast of American muscle and had only succumbed to a minor bump, whereas Blondie's flimsy new Mercedes had practically been written off on the spot, thanks to the front-end crumpling like a tin can. Then a huge lorry had smashed into the side of it, shoving it into a concrete bollard, so that had pretty much finished the car off.

He had got out of his car, ready to shout all the expletives under the sun at her for damaging his baby, but Blondie had been knocked unconscious by the impact. At first, time had stood still while he wondered what to do, mulling a dozen scenarios over in his head at lightning speed. He hadn't seen a lot of blood, so he could assume she was still breathing. He hadn't been able to open the driver's side door to rescue her as it was fused shut due to the crumpled metal, but he'd managed to open the passenger side door. He'd had to act fast because he knew he couldn't afford to waste time waiting around for the police to show up and start asking questions, so he'd quickly grabbed her pink bag, which was on the floor of the passenger footwell, then stuffed a hastily written note down her dress while he'd pretended to check her over. Someone must have called an ambulance because one showed up within minutes after that, so he stepped away and allowed them to do their job. Next, a police car had shown up and that had been his cue to leave.

He chucked the pink bag in his car and then he'd driven away, never once looking back to check if the police were following him. He knew it was an offence to drive away from the scene of an accident, but she was the one who'd crashed into him, so he'd done nothing wrong. Plus, she was in safe hands and he had a potential lifeline. He was safe ... for now.

That had been several hours ago. He'd managed to drive out of the busy streets of London and was now parked in a lay-by just outside of Peterborough. He'd taken the country roads as much as possible because an Impala belonged on the open road, not bogged down by heavy traffic. He drove wherever the road took him, which was basically wherever his target went. But sometimes, like now, he lost them, and he'd spend a few weeks tracking them down, inevitably finding them again. It was all about patience and being in it for the long haul. He would eventually win; he always won.

Curtis leaned against the warm bonnet of the car as he rifled through the contents of Blondie's pink bag. Anyone in their right mind could clearly see that she was wealthy, and he praised himself for thinking of such a clever idea so quickly, all whilst trying not to overreact at his precious car being slightly dented. It would have to stay dented for a while because he couldn't risk taking it into a garage to be repaired in case someone recognised it. The car stood out like a whore in the middle of a pack of nuns with its chrome finishes and metallic black paint job. Not to mention its sheer size and domineering presence on the road. Often, he found that other road users gave him a much wider berth than was necessary when passing him. He liked the thrill of owning a car like this.

Well … technically he didn't *own* it, but it was close enough.

Delving his hand into the plush leather bag (which smelled like some sort of fruity perfume; not exactly unpleasant, but not something he was used to), he pulled out the following: a purple, sparkly smartphone (worth over a grand), a pink Gucci purse (with several credit cards and over one hundred pounds in cash, which he pocketed without a second thought), a small bag of make-up, Christian Dior perfume (most likely, he determined, the culprit making the bag smell fruity), oversized, gemstone-encrusted sunglasses, a folder with a load of papers, a packet of chewing gum (which he helped himself to) and lastly, a small red notebook.

He loosely tallied up the items, knowing they were worth a small fortune due to the designer labels alone. He reckoned, once she read his note, she'd easily transfer the money. He knew exactly the type of girl she was: spoilt and rich and addicted to her worldly possessions, too attached to her phone and obsessed with posting online. Then, when she arrived tomorrow morning (which she would, there was no doubt about that) he'd be able to blackmail her out of a few more quid too. Or maybe he'd hold her to ransom and demand millions for her release, but, then again, when had that idea ever gone to plan? It certainly hadn't the last time he'd tried it.

Why did he know so much about women like Blondie? Because he had first-hand experience of dealing with them; his twin sister, to be precise. Mia had always been far too wrapped up in her own world to care what was going on in reality. Back in their hometown of Milton Keynes, he would always see her posing for photos as a teenager, taking numerous snaps of the same shot to get the perfect angle. This was even before social media became a huge thing, and they had phones with decent cameras. She'd been too hung up on her looks, brain-washed into thinking she had to look perfect.

In the end, it had killed her.

Or had it?

Mia often crept into his thoughts; his memories of her face would haunt his dreams. She had been so beautiful, even without the layers of make-up. What would she look like now had she survived past her eighteenth birthday? Seventeen years, three-hundred and fifty-five days. That's how old she was when she'd died and all these years later, he could still see her perfect face every time he closed his eyes; the way her naturally dark hair used to curl over her ears, her slightly crooked teeth when she smiled, her light brown skin.

Gone.

All because of *him* ...

Curtis shook his head violently, unwilling to let his mind become distracted. The vision of his sister disappeared in a haze.

He attempted to unlock the smart phone. Of course, there was a password and, of course, Blondie had a vain picture of herself as the screensaver, posing in a barely-there string bikini on a boat. He rolled his eyes in disgust as he attempted the usual passwords (1234, 4321 and password1), but eventually the phone locked him out. He tossed it back in the bag and sighed, picking up his own, much less expensive phone, to check if a notification had come through regarding the transfer of the money.

It had not.

Maybe she was still unconscious in a hospital. Maybe he should have given her more time.

He glared ahead into the distance and counted a few passing cars. His body vibrated with hatred and loathing. People like Blondie, people like *him*, didn't deserve to live. He wanted to eradicate them all, every last one of them. That was why he was here after all, why he'd waited all these years to get revenge.

It was time to hit the road.

Dear Diary

Date: 15 June 2000

Dear Diary,

I haven't been able to write for a few days because I've been so busy with schoolwork and whatnot, but also something very exciting has happened, so I've been a bit distracted. I'm in! I'm friends with Bryan Matthews and part of his gang. It's all very exciting and I can't quite believe it. How did I manage it? Well ... I caught him smoking round the back of the school, so I asked if I could have one. It's amazing what can cement a friendship, isn't it? Oh yeah ... then the cigarette made me sick, but it was all worth it.

Date: 16 June 2000

Dear Diary,

My mum has a nose like a bloodhound. She could smell the smoke on my clothes and now I'm grounded for a week. Again ... worth it.

Date: 17 June 2000

Dear Diary,

Bryan told me today that his dad likes to get drunk and hit his mum, which is quite sad really when you think about it. I feel like Bryan is confiding in me. I'm not sure why, but I think we might be friends forever. Unless something really bad happens, but I can't imagine it will. I want to be with Bryan all the time. He makes me feel better about myself by picking on the weaker kids, which means I must be strong, right? Sometimes I don't agree with what he does, but as long as he doesn't do it to me then I don't care.

Date: 18 June 2000

Dear Diary,

Today I watched as Bryan beat up a kid in the playground and then threatened to kill them if they told anyone it was him who hurt them. I felt bad, but then another part of me was relieved that it wasn't me. I'm not sure why Bryan is full of anger. Maybe it's because of his dad. Maybe he thinks it's okay to hit and hurt people. Maybe he isn't such a good guy after all, but he's still the coolest kid in school and I'm glad to be his friend.

Chapter Six
June 2000

After I survived the attack from Bryan Matthews and his cronies, my face looked awful. The bruises and cuts on my body I could hide with clothes, but not my face. I tried to wear a hat which I found in my locker and pulled the cap low over my face, but the teacher said I wasn't allowed to wear a hat in school, so when she saw the state of me, I was sent straight to the nurse's office to get cleaned up. I didn't tell her what had happened. I said I'd fallen in the playground, like the last time. I'm not sure if she believed me because she gave me a funny look. Kids always fell, right?

They fell down the stairs too ... That's what my dad said happened to me last year. I fell and broke my arm, which really hurt, and I had to have a plaster cast on for weeks. I don't remember a lot of what happened ... But yeah, I must have fallen.

Anyway, my left eye was swollen and black, but at least I could still see out of it so I could read. I started reading *Moby Dick* today. I borrowed it from the school library.

But then the next day Bryan Matthews stole my copy of *Moby Dick* and tore out all the pages and scattered them over the playground. I tried to find every page, but I think some went missing; they blew away in the strong wind. No one stopped to help me.

Over the next few days, my mind was filled with vivid images of killing Bryan Matthews. I even had dreams about him. In one dream, I sliced his throat open with a sharp knife.

There was blood everywhere and I woke up in a cold sweat and felt sick, yet it also filled me with excitement.

Then I thought about stabbing him with a knife instead.

Or maybe I could torture him for a while ... make it really hurt ... decisions ... decisions ...

By the end of the week, I'd practically thought of nothing else. Even my reading had begun to take a back seat. My plan to kill Bryan Matthews was simple. I was going to smash his face in with a rock or a hammer. Brutal, right? There would be blood everywhere and his head would look like a smashed pumpkin at Halloween by the time I'd finished with him.

Then again, maybe that might be a bit too messy, and I'd have to hit him hard in order to kill him instantly. I'd have to have an advantage over him somehow. What if I couldn't knock him out with the first hit? What if he fought back and overpowered me? I'd be toast.

Maybe I should just plan to run him over instead; a much easier and surer way to end someone's life. But then ... I'm too young to drive now, so I'd have to wait nearly a decade. Plus, then there would be lots of blood and brains all over the car, which I'd need to get rid of somehow.

I guess murdering someone wasn't so simple after all.

Pushing him down some stairs seemed like a good option. Maybe he'd break his neck or maybe he wouldn't and then would escape somehow. Or he'd be so severely damaged that he'd need constant care for the rest of his life, which he didn't deserve. Although, the thought of him being trapped inside his own broken body was quite appealing.

As a ten-year-old, I wasn't exactly equipped to kill someone right this second. Even now, he was much bigger and stronger than me and could easily overpower me if I attacked him. Plus, he had lots of friends who were also much bigger and stronger, so I'd need to kill him when he was alone and vulnerable. Maybe I should just—

'Hey, loser.'

I looked up, not because I answered to the name of *loser*, but because it was more of a reflex and, to be perfectly honest, the loud voice startled me. I was sitting alone and eating my lunch in the corner of the playground, as far away from the other children as possible. I was disappointed to see that it wasn't Bryan who had approached me and decided to end my happy solitude, but one of his cronies; the small, ginger-haired one.

'What?'

'That's some black eye you've got.'

'Yes, I'm very proud. What do you want?'

'I'm just giving you a warning, that's all.'

'Oh yeah?'

'Yeah. It's for your own good. Stay away from Bryan. He's mine.'

I sniggered as I put down my chicken sandwich; a pathetic-looking thing that had been squashed at the bottom of my school bag all morning. 'Trust me, I'd love nothing more than to stay away from him, but he insists on coming up to me all the time and making my life hell. Maybe he's obsessed with me or something. I think it's *him* who needs to stay away from *me*.'

Especially as what I'm eventually planning to do to him will put an end to his miserable life.

Ginger-haired Boy slammed his hands down on the bench next to me and my body jumped in fright. 'This isn't a joke. If you don't stay away from him, then I'll kill you, you understand?'

'Are you in love with him or something?'

Ginger-haired Boy curled his top lip into a snarl. 'No.'

'Then why do you care so much about him? Why do you like him so much when he's clearly nothing more than a big bully?'

'We have a connection.'

'Sure you do.'

'Look, you've seen what he does to some other kids in the playground. You got off lightly the other day. Consider this a warning … He's dangerous.'

'Got it.'

'I'm serious.'

'So am I. I'm not afraid of Bryan Matthews. If anything, he should be afraid of me.'

Ginger-haired Boy and I began a staring contest. His left eye twitched several times whereas mine remained motionless, not even when an annoying fly buzzed around my head. Ginger-haired Boy finally succumbed to my death glare and sighed. I continued to stare at him as I ate my squashed sandwich.

'Fine,' he said, 'have it your way, but don't say I didn't warn you, loser.'

I glared at the back of his head as he walked away, silently wishing I could make it explode and watch as brain matter splattered across the tarmac. He was no better than Bryan Matthews.

I think there might be something wrong with me.

Normal kids my age didn't dream of blowing heads up, did they? Maybe everyone had that dream, but it was one of those things that no one spoke about, like menstruation or erectile dysfunction. I wasn't too sure what those were exactly (I had an idea, but nothing concrete), but I often overheard a lot of things and, apparently, you weren't supposed to talk about those things openly, which was sad really because if someone had a problem then why couldn't they talk about it? I'd love to be able to talk about the fact that I had the urge to kill people (or at least one person in particular), but if I did, I feared I might be locked up in a crazy house for the rest of my life and then I wouldn't be able to kill Bryan Matthews. At least, that's what I assumed would happen from watching a few TV shows. I didn't watch a lot of TV; I'd rather read books, but sometimes the gentle drone of a TV show was enough to quiet the thoughts about killing Bryan Matthews.

I turned back to my lunch; it tasted like feet, but it was better than going hungry. My dad was always too busy with his new business so didn't have the time to make me a proper packed lunch.

I could see Bryan and his cronies hanging out by the fence on the other side of the playground. They kept glancing over at me one by one, trying to be subtle but failing miserably. I often wondered what I'd done to deserve their unwanted attention. Bryan picked on a lot of kids (and I really mean *a lot*), but he seemed to have an unhealthy obsession with me. Sometimes I wondered what his home life was like, whether his mummy and daddy loved him, or if he was one of those kids whose parents beat him or argued all the time. I considered myself lucky in that respect because my dad was hardly ever around, which didn't mean he didn't love me. It just meant that he had better things to do than raise his child. I spent a lot of time with my uncle instead, which was worse in many … many ways.

Now that I'd thought about it a bit, I didn't think I could kill someone right now. I was too weak and pathetic. I had no power. I was basically a nobody, but maybe one day I could be a somebody; I could amount to something if I worked hard.

Maybe one day I would be in a better position to kill someone. Or maybe one day I'd snap … and Bryan Matthews would be there to see it all unfold.

That was it; that was the new plan.

I must be patient though. *You can't rush perfection.* I was pretty sure I read that somewhere in one of my books.

I'm coming for you, Bryan Matthews …

How to Commit the Perfect Murder
Step Two

Adapt and Overcome

Let's be real for a moment. The plan you originally thought up in order to kill someone may change. Shit happens. Life gets in the way. Obstacles block the path. People butt their noses in where they don't belong. These are all perfectly manageable situations if you're adaptable, can think on your feet and can come up with a way to overcome these obstacles and changes.

Because if you can't then you will fail.

End of story.

Sometimes you may have to put up with a lot of crap, but that's okay as long as you keep your eye on the end goal. Nothing else matters. Remember that. And by adapting and overcoming every barrier, you will become a more precise and dangerous individual. Yes, you may have to suffer along the way, but that's all part of the process.

So, when you plan out your murder make sure you take note of where things can go wrong. Maybe jot a few ideas down of how to overcome any issues, but at the end of the day, you can't plan for every situation, so don't stress too much. Just stay focussed.

Think of these changes and challenges as learning curves; the more you learn the more qualified you become.

I'm a professional.

Trust me.

Chapter Seven

ASHLEIGH
1 July 2022 – 15:30 p.m.

To my surprise, the nurse doesn't put up much of an argument to get me to stay in hospital. She does threaten to call the doctor in a half-hearted manner, but I tell her that if she does, I'll scream and get her fired (perhaps a tad over-dramatic and harsh on my part, I admit, but I'm desperate … and besides, it clearly works). She gets me to sign a form to say I'm discharging myself of my own free will and that I won't hold the hospital accountable if anything bad happens to me as a result of my injuries and leaving the hospital early. Blah blah blah.

I literally couldn't care less right now because all I can think about is getting my bag back from the scoundrel who's stolen it. I know that may sound shallow to some, but my whole life is in that bag. I cannot survive or function without the items inside, especially my phone. My fingers need something to do. An annoying itch spreads all over my body at the thought of the multitude of messages and notifications I must be getting that are going unanswered. All those little red notifications popping up is enough to make my skin crawl and feel a little bit sick.

I get dressed back into my blue mini dress, thankful to be out of the hideous hospital gown that does nothing to compliment my figure, and stuff the ransom note into the band of my Victoria's Secret bra. I carry my heels instead of wearing them as I walk on the shiny hospital floors because I feel wobbly on my feet and don't trust that I'll not go flying.

I stumble through the front double doors and out into the glorious sunshine. That's the moment when the reality of the situation hits me like a tonne of bricks ... I have no money to get a taxi, nor a phone to call one to get me home. I don't think I've ever been in a situation like this before, not even on one of my random nights out when I've stumbled around London so drunk I can barely remember my own name. I *always* have my phone and money on me.

Without attempting to kick-start my brain into thinking of a Plan B, my body automatically sets off along the road, my heels swinging from my left hand. I must look a right state. I haven't even seen myself in a mirror yet, but my hair feels tangled and flat.

I manage to make it outside of the hospital grounds, but then stop and take a deep breath, reassessing the situation. The pavement is warm under my feet, the searing light of the day making my headache worse; it's now so bad I can barely keep my eyes open. What I wouldn't give to be able to curl up in a ball and close my eyes and sleep forever. A few painkillers wouldn't go amiss either. Maybe a G&T to wash them down.

Urrgg, I feel sick ...

I cough and lunge towards the side of the road, dry heaving into a bush. I have nothing in my stomach, but it still contracts and rolls as it attempts to get rid of something; anything. A small bubble of bile comes up, which I spit out.

Yuck ... who am I?

Maybe this isn't such a good idea after all. I've been by myself for less than five minutes and already feel like giving up.

'Are you okay, Miss?'

I wipe my mouth with my hand and straighten up. A woman with a toddler is hovering nearby, a frown on her face as she watches me right myself. The toddler is strapped into his pram, sucking on an ice lolly, which is melting in the heat and covering his hands in sticky, red juice.

'I ... No, not really. I need to get to Kensington Gardens. Can you point me in the right direction, please?'

'Yes, of course. Turn left here and it's about a mile or so down the road. Don't turn off and you'll be fine. Or you can take the number two bus, which should be along any minute.'

I nod and smile as relief floods my body. 'Thank you.' I keep quiet about the fact I don't have money for the bus. I don't want her taking pity on me. What kind of person wears a Dior dress, but doesn't have money for public transport?

'Are you sure I can't call you a taxi or something?' she asks, as she lowers her eyes to the ground, assessing my bare feet.

'No, thank you. I'll manage.'

The woman nods and proceeds to push the pram towards the hospital. I watch her leave for several seconds before turning back to the task at hand.

I can do this.

One mile.

I can walk one mile.

Easy.

I cannot walk one mile.

It's so far! It's the furthest distance I've ever walked … sober. I've walked two miles in tiny heels while drunk, but it had never seemed as bad and difficult as this. Plus, I'd had friends with me and one of the men had given me a piggyback for most of the way and I might have passed out on his back for several minutes.

I have no idea where I am. For all I know I'm in a different city completely. Is this even London? I never take notice of where I'm going when I'm in a taxi or I'm driving myself because my satnav always tells me the way. I don't have to worry about memorising street names or road signs because there's no need to. My hands keep searching for my phone because if I had it right now, I'd have used Google Maps already. How do normal people live like this? Seriously!

Several hours later (at least I assume it's been hours; it certainly feels that way) I drag myself up the stone steps to my front door. My breathing is erratic and laboured. I'm gleaming with sweat and my legs are about to collapse underneath me. I don't even have a key to let myself in, so I ring the bell, as embarrassment and fury simmer under the surface.

I stare up at my fifteen million pound house, imagining the chaos within the walls at my disappearance for the past several hours. It's taking an awfully long time for my housekeeper to answer the door. Maybe she's too busy answering phones and arranging a reward for my safe return, or maybe she's out searching for me herself, although I think that might be a tad too far for Mrs Brown.

The door finally creaks open and Mrs Brown stares down at me in her usual demeaning way. There are no happy, relieved tears in her eyes, no sudden gasp as she realises I'm finally home safe and sound. She merely runs her eyes over me, scanning me from head to toe and then sighs and steps aside, like it's perfectly normal to find me half-collapsed on the front steps, which, to be fair, does happen most Friday and Saturday nights, but hardly ever in the middle of the day. Maybe she thinks I've started on the cocktails and champagne early.

'What's happened now?' she asks as I stagger past her.

'I ... What do you mean "what's happened now?" Haven't you been wondering where I've been for the past—' I briefly glance at the enormous grandfather clock opposite the front door, an antique I just had to buy at a cute auction place I went to last year. It was a bargain too; only £215,000. '—eight hours?' I finish with a gasp. Gosh, it's gone five already. It really has taken me nearly two hours to walk one mile.

Mrs Brown raises her eyebrows at me. 'Drinking, by the looks of it.'

I clench my teeth together. 'I'm in no mood for you to have a go at me right now. I was in a car accident and was taken to hospital. My bag and phone have been stolen and I had to walk over a mile to get back home because I didn't have a phone or money for a taxi.'

'Couldn't you have asked to use a phone at the hospital to call home and get your driver to pick you up?' Her face barely flinches as she speaks. Mrs Brown always talks to me as if I'm a pathetic child and has done ever since I was one. She basically raised me because my father was hardly ever around, but I get the feeling she doesn't like me very much. However, I pay her salary so she's lucky I've kept her on this long and not kicked her to the curb without a reference.

'I ... I don't know my home phone number.'

'Of course you don't.'

'Well, I've never needed to dial my own number, have I? It's plumbed into my phone, which I've now lost.'

Mrs Brown reaches past me and pushes one of the numerous buzzers on the wall. We wait in awkward silence, eyeing each other every few seconds. She always looks pristine and elegant. Her greying hair is tied neatly in a bun at the back of her head and her yellow blouse is expertly ironed, not a single crease or line anywhere where there isn't supposed to be one.

A couple of minutes later, a maid scurries through the door from the lounge area and stands to attention, her back as straight as a rod. Mrs Brown clearly runs a tight ship here. The maid is shaking like a deer caught in headlights. She's quite pretty and I recognise her as the maid who brings me cups of tea in bed sometimes when I'm ill (or more usually, hungover). I don't know her name though ... In fact, I don't know any of the maids' names.

'Madeline!' snaps Mrs Brown. *I guess her name's Madeline*. 'Don't just stand there. Take Miss Carmichael upstairs and help her get washed and dressed into some clean clothes.'

'Yes, Ma'am.'

'No!' I shout, a little louder than I intend to. I take a breath. 'No, that's okay. I mean ... I'm perfectly capable of taking myself upstairs and getting washed and dressed.' At least I think I am. I've made it this far ... just about.

Mrs Brown snorts at me – *actually snorts* – and then dismisses the maid (whose name I've already forgotten). 'Do you need anything then, Miss Carmichael?' she asks. I've known the woman for over twenty years and yet she still refuses to call me by my first name.

'I need you to call ... whoever it was I was supposed to be meeting this morning and tell them I was in a car accident and that's why I never showed up. Tell everyone.'

'But no one has called asking for you.'

I stand and gawk at Mrs Brown, as if I've just been slapped across the face. 'Just tell them!'

'As you wish, Miss Carmichael.' Mrs Brown nods her head at me and walks away, her long black skirt swishing side to side. Snooty cow. I bet she's not going to tell anyone.

I stand alone in my huge entrance hall long after Mrs Brown has left. The expensive slate tiles are cool under my feet, which are now completely filthy from walking a mile through the London streets. I don't even want to think about what I could have possibly stepped in. I'm in desperate need of a hot bubble bath. Maybe I should have allowed what's-her-name to run me a bath because I've never run my own before. I don't even know where the expensive bubble bath is kept, the one that smells of lavender, or where the LUSH bath bombs are.

Feeling somewhat defeated and with my head and shoulders slumped forwards, I tip-toe up the extravagant spiralling staircase, clutching the gold-plated, ornate banister for dear life. The stairs have a luscious, crimson carpet running up the middle (because I wanted to feel as if I were walking the red carpet every time I came down the stairs, like they do in the movies) and it feels so comforting and soft against my sore feet. I must book myself a pedicure and foot scrub as soon as possible. I automatically reach for my phone and only find my heels.

I sigh, stopping mid-way up the first flight of stairs to catch my breath. Something sharp digs into my skin under my dress. I scoop out the note, removing it from its hiding place and scan it again.

There's no way I'm giving this person £100,000.

Yes, the items inside are probably worth close to that sum, but how can I possibly trust that they'll even give me my bag back once I transfer the money? Plus, they want me to go and collect it? Are they nuts? I suppose I could send my driver, but then I'd have to include other people in this ridiculous scam, and I'd rather not suffer through the embarrassment of losing my bag to a stranger who wants to extort me for money.

Without thinking, I practically fly back down the stairs, through the entrance hall, through to the back of the house and out into the vast gardens (yes, plural. I have a vegetable garden, a water garden, a tranquil garden and a flower garden). I run into the triple garage and flick on the lights, scanning the area for the wall safe where I know the spare sets of car keys are held (my actual car keys to my BMW are ... you guessed it ... in my bag).

I open the safe, grab the keys and slide into the front seat of my purple car, quickly plumbing 'Skegness' into my satnav.

Three and a half hours away! Are you kidding me?

The rational part of my brain kicks into gear and starts flashing alarm bells, like:

You have no money on you.

You have no way to buy food.

You've never driven more than five miles in one go before.

You're on your own and this is dangerous.

They are all very reasonable and practical warnings; however, the irrational part of my brain seems to make a lot more sense:

Once you get there, you'll get your bag and purse back, so you'll have money for food and petrol.

It will be an adventure.

You know self-defence because you took a lesson in karate five years ago, so you'll be fine.

I know what I *should* do.

I *should* get out of the car, run upstairs and get so-and-so to draw me a bubble bath and forget any of the past few hours ever happened. Then order myself a new phone, new bag and purse and forget about all the other items, but I don't ...

I turn the key, back out of the garage, pausing to wait for the automatic door, and then blindly follow the satnav out of London and towards God only knows where.

Chapter Eight

HANNAH
6 July 2022 – 23:01 p.m.

I scream so loud the walls visibly shake, and the floor vibrates like one of those machines at the gym that supposedly burns calories. I stumble sideways into the wall, grasping at it as if it's going to reach out and offer me a helping hand. The dark figure runs towards me, stretching out a hand and grabbing my left wrist. They squeeze tight; so tight that it hurts.

'Help! Get off me! Help!' I yank my arm back, but I have very little strength in my muscles, especially since my shoulder is still causing me significant pain. In fact, my whole body feels like unset jelly. How long had I been unconscious to lose all strength like this? My head aches; not from the large bump on the back of it, but from the sheer amount of effort it's taking to remain standing and conscious. I just want to go back to sleep.

'Cut it out or I'll never get you out of here.'

I gasp at the rough-sounding male voice. 'Who are you? What do you want from me?' I yelp as the lumbering man starts dragging me down the corridor towards the scarily lit exit sign. Where is he taking me? I have no idea what's out there.

'Are you fucking kidding me right now? After everything that's happened, you're playing dumb?'

'I don't even know you. Stop dragging me and tell me what's going on.' I'm finally able to yank my arm out of his grasp, stumbling as I do so. My legs manage to hold me up, but I'm dangerously close to collapsing.

The man sighs as he closes his eyes and tilts his head towards the ceiling, squeezing the bridge of his nose between two fingers. 'We don't have time for this, Hannah. Now that you're awake, we need to get on the road ... now.'

Hannah.

He just called me Hannah, but it means nothing to me.

'I ... I don't recognise that name.'

The man stares at me. 'You what?'

'I don't remember my name. How do I know you? Who are you?'

'Are you fucking around with me right now? Is this some sort of sick joke?'

'Do I look like I'm fucking with you!'

The man's eyes widen, but then he grins. I can't help but notice how perfectly straight and white his teeth are. 'Fine. Whatever. I'll play along, but can we just get the fuck out of here and then I'll explain everything, okay?' He holds out his hand, as if it's some gesture of goodwill.

I frown as I back away, shaking my head. 'I'm not going anywhere with you until you at least tell me who *you* are.'

The man rolls his eyes. 'Fine. Have it your way. My name's Bryan Matthews.'

Chapter Nine

1 July 2022 – 16:30 p.m.

Overall, the drive from London to Skegness had been uneventful. The one stop Curtis allowed himself had been merely to stretch his legs, rifle through Blondie's bag, which was now safely stored underneath the driving seat, and relieve himself in a hedge. His bladder had been on the verge of bursting, but he hadn't regretted the large can of Coke he'd downed earlier. The heat was bearable; he'd always had a seemingly unquenchable thirst and liked to keep himself hydrated, but not with water. Only losers and health freaks drank water. Beer and Coke were his staple liquids.

The gauge on the car showed that the tank was dangerously low as he pulled into the car park at the beach resort. He had seen a small petrol garage in the town, so made a mental note to stop by there once he'd scoped out the place and got his bearings. He had a little money left, but not enough to fill up the tank. This beast guzzled fuel like a thirsty camel and now he was heavily relying on Blondie to transfer that money into his account. That was the thing about living on the road a lot of the time; it required funds — funds which he didn't come by very often. Curtis didn't work, but managed to survive via other means, not all of which were legal or morally right. That was the price of commitment, he'd always told himself. He was in it for the long haul after all.

The beach resort was busy, too busy for his liking. He preferred it when places were quieter because crowds made him nervous. Anyone could hide in a crowd. Families milled about with their cranky, sticky toddlers, who were begging their exhausted-looking parents for more ice cream, more sweets, more juice. Large, noisy seagulls attacked every scrap of food that fell to the floor, squawking incessantly at holidaymakers, who performed a funny little dance to get away from the hungry birds. Sunburned teenagers surreptitiously drank beer or vodka disguised in a water or juice bottle while lying on the sand, laughing. Overweight men strolled around in swimming shorts that were far too small for them, having probably not fitted properly in over a decade. They still seemed determined to squeeze every inch of themselves into the stretchy fabric.

Curtis's lip curled in disgust as he scanned the crowds, thinking. Would his target be here as planned? Was he too late? Had he already missed them? His stomach twisted in knots from both hunger and anxiety, but he knew only one thing would settle it; one thing would put an end to his suffering. Soon ...

He sighed heavily as he leaned against the car, feeling the warmth of the metal through his jeans. He crossed his arms over his chest; a clear warning to anyone walking past that he didn't want to engage in conversation.

An attractive young woman in a neon-pink swimsuit glided past, throwing a wink and a smile at him over her shoulder. He watched her tight bum sway from side to side as she walked away, admiring her for a few seconds before getting back to the task at hand.

No distractions.

His eyes darted from side to side, scanning.

His target had to be here.

Maybe he should just accept the fact he'd lost his target and move on to the next phase of the plan. He was almost certain Blondie would come through for him with the money. He couldn't move forwards without it. Everything cost money these days. Maybe it would have been easier to mug someone again, but hardly anyone carried cash these days. It was becoming obsolete.

But what if Blondie called the police? What if she didn't transfer the money on time and she called the cops on him instead and sent them here to arrest him for stealing her bag? Would she really travel all the way to Skegness to confront him?

Curtis dipped his head as he ducked inside the car and took a seat. He began searching the crowds again. Nothing but tourists as far as the eye could see.

Wait ... what was that?

A police car driving at a snail's pace was approaching his parked car. It had just turned in from the main road.

'Shit,' he said aloud as he scooted down in his seat, cursing himself for being so stupid.

Were they here for him? Had that snooty bitch sent them here? He couldn't risk walking around, not with the police car nearby. He had to find somewhere to stay for the night, but a roadside hotel was out of the question, given his situation. He'd have to park somewhere and kip in the car.

Something brushed against his ankle. Shifting in his seat, he grabbed the item and held it up. It was Blondie's pink purse; it must have fallen out of the bag when he'd shoved it under the seat earlier. With nothing better to do, he ignored the police car and began looking through the purse again. He'd had a quick look before when he'd pocketed the cash, but he hadn't checked for her ID to find out her real name. He found her driving licence and held it up to the light.

Ashleigh Elizabeth Alexandra Penelope Daphne Carmichael.

He scoffed and rolled his eyes. Who the fuck needed that many middle names? His eyes focussed on her last name.

Carmichael ... *Carmichael* ...

He knew that name.

It lit a flicker of recognition somewhere in the back of his mind. The memory was there, trying to catch alight, but it kept dying out before becoming solid. This was when he could have done with his ex-girlfriend, Hannah, sitting next to him. She could remember everything, every little detail. He always thought she had a photogenic memory, or whatever the technical term was. There was a time, during their brief relationship, that they'd had a huge argument and she'd been able to recall exactly what he'd said months later, which had proven him a liar. Even he couldn't remember what he'd said, but she could, which was exactly why they hadn't been relationship material and they'd ended things eventually.

Well, *she* may have been relationship material, but *he* wasn't. He'd tried it, just to be like a normal person, but he wasn't normal, and he knew that. He had more important things to do than take women out to dinner, spend money on them which he didn't have and listen to their incessant whining. He had lied to her daily. He'd slept around with numerous women and hadn't cared if she found out, which, ultimately, she did. He'd tried the boyfriend thing with Hannah, thinking he might be able to change, but it had been a mistake and he regretted ever thinking that he could.

Then she went and got with *him* ... fuck her.

But Mia had liked her ...

A lump formed in his throat as Mia's name popped into his head. He forced it back out, but then it shoved its way to the front of his mind and stayed there. Damn it. Why was Mia haunting his thoughts? He didn't want to think about her anymore and that alone filled him with gnawing guilt. He knew he should continue to think about her, to keep her spirit alive, but whenever he did it made him reckless and angry. And now was not the time for recklessness and anger. He needed to have a cool head and be able to react quickly.

Enough ...

Curtis continued to stare at the ridiculously long name on the driving licence. Where had he seen the name *Carmichael* before? Why was it burning a hole in his mind? Blondie was pretty in her licence photo: blonde hair, green eyes, her lips too full and loaded with Botox, her skin smooth and flawless. Yes, she was attractive, but he didn't recognise her, which made the frustration in his gut even more annoying. Her eyes though … something in them threatened to light that spark of recognition inside his mind again …

A few minutes later, satisfied that his brain wasn't going to conjure up the answer, he grabbed his mobile and typed her name, minus the four middle ones, into Google. He raised his eyebrows when he saw the amount of search results that appeared. Jesus Christ, the woman was actually a famous heiress to a bloody fortune and owner of a million-pound pharmaceutical company. She'd been on the cover of *Playboy* magazine, was the face of dozens of beauty products and had millions of followers across social media. He clicked on one of her random TikTok videos, which had over 5 million likes, and watched it.

It was a video of her on a night out, surrounded by friends, drinking an enormous blue cocktail out of a fishbowl. She was dancing to a song, swishing her hair back and forth. The hashtags were *#drinkinglikeafish #cocktailhour #livinlavidaloca #yolo*.

Curtis rolled his eyes as he flicked through a few more of her videos, but they began to bore him, so he resumed his Google search, scanning the dozens of headlines which were mostly about her social media videos and various high-profile events she'd attended on the arm of some stuck-up rich bloke with quaffed hair.

Then a name jumped out of his phone and hit him in the face, causing his breath to catch in his throat. He stared at the screen in astonishment at a photo of her as a teenager, standing next to two men, only one of whom he immediately recognised.

The man with dark brown hair, dark eyes, dressed in a smart grey suit wasn't touching Blondie and wasn't smiling; neither was she. The other man had his arm around Blondie, squeezing her into the side of his body, a menacing grin on his face.

Sawyer Croft.

He knew her father's business partner.

Chapter Ten

ASHLEIGH
1 July 2022 – 17:03 p.m.

I solemnly swear I am *never* driving anywhere ever again. This car was sold to me with the explicit guarantee it would be 'the most comfortable car I'll ever drive and will feel as if I'm floating on a cloud'. Well, I can guarantee you *this*, Mr-Salesman-With-The-Pointy-Nose-And-Too-Tight-Trousers, this car is definitely *not* comfortable to drive, *nor* is it like floating on a cloud. What a load of utter ... rubbish. I've got a good mind to ask for my money back.

The shooting pain in my right leg started fifteen minutes ago and now it's all I can think about. I've been driving for just over an hour and, basically, cannot feel my left butt cheek. How do normal people spend hours driving all the time? Are their butts constantly numb? I'm driving barefoot because, of course, I didn't think to change my shoes before I jumped in the car. My feet are freezing because the air conditioning is on full blast so my toes may be at risk of hyperthermia. I could turn it down, but then my sweaty butt would stick to the leather seat. I literally cannot win. Leather seats are the worst. Oh yes, they look beautiful and expensive, but have you ever tried sitting in one whilst wearing a short dress in the middle of a heat wave? No? Try it ... I dare you.

After two hours of slow torture, rather than crying hysterically into the steering wheel, I admit defeat and pull into a service station somewhere along the M11, or possibly the A1(M). I don't know anymore. All the roads look and sound the same. My stomach is practically consuming itself, but I can't buy anything to eat because I don't have any money, so I scurry past the fast-food restaurants and straight into the toilets and come face to face with my worst nightmare and the exact reason why I don't use public restrooms.

I freeze at the doorway, debating whether I want to walk across the dingy tiles barefoot or run back to the car and fetch my heels. I choose the latter. No way am I risking picking up a random disease by having bacteria enter through the small cuts on my feet.

Once I've relieved myself and washed my hands a dozen times, I wander back to the car, ignoring the gurgle in my stomach as I smell hot McDonald's fries and sizzling burgers, and begin to perform a few static stretches and lunges by the car, psyching myself up for the rest of the journey. I'm clearly attempting to prolong the inevitable, getting back in the torture device. I take a few cleansing yoga breaths for good measure, channelling my inner calm ...

A group of young men, who appear to be on their way to a stag weekend (one of them is dressed like a bride – literally in a full wedding dress complete with a tiara), keep wolf-whistling at me and beckoning me to join them. Therefore, my calm evaporates. I expect they recognise me from somewhere. Possibly *Playboy* ... What an awful mistake that was. It's not like I'd needed the money. I'd just wanted to show the world how amazing my boobs looked after my enhancement surgery.

'Hey baby, fancy joining us?' says one of the party who's wearing a green leotard, which is leaving little to the imagination in the crotch department. I can see wispy dark hairs escaping out the sides. *Gag.* He starts staggering towards me.

I stop performing stretches and stand up straight, my body entering the so-called flight or fight response as my muscles tense and my heart rate increases. 'No, thanks,' I say. 'Do you have any water?'

'No, but we have vodka.' He holds out a clear bottle, Morrison's own brand. Yeesh, that stuff would probably taste like vinegar compared to the usual high-end Russian vodka I drink at just over £5,000 per bottle.

'Can't ... I'm driving.' *Not that I'd put that swill anywhere near my mouth.*

'Where you heading?'

'Skegness.' As soon as the word leaves my mouth, I regret it. Maybe informing a group of drunk stags where I'm travelling to alone isn't such a good idea.

'Skegness is a shit hole. Why don't you join us in Peterborough? Gonna be a wild one.'

'Can't ... I need to go to Skegness.' *And I'd rather be skinned alive than get on a party bus with you.*

'Why?'

I frown as the man stops in front of me. I automatically take a step back as my heart thuds in my chest, attempting to not react at the overwhelming odour emanating from every pore in his body and keeping my eyes firmly peeled on his face and not his bulging, hairy groin.

'I'm visiting my boyfriend.' Perhaps it's best I don't mention I have no phone and no money and am on my way to confront a stranger who stole my bag.

'I'm sure he won't miss you for one night. I can make you forget all 'bout him, baby.'

'Thanks, but I really should get going.' I reach behind me for the driver's side door and open it without looking.

'Nice car you got there.' He nods at it.

'Thanks.'

'Must have cost you a pretty penny.'

'Uh … yeah.' Probably more money than he'll ever make in a lifetime. I'm inching ever closer to the car door, using it as a shield against this guy, who is now dangerously close to being kicked in the crotch.

'Hey, Tony! Leave the skank alone. They'll be plenty of hookers for you later!' I have never been more relieved in my life to be called a *skank*. Tony grins at me; a few of his teeth are crooked and stained.

'Shame,' he says.

I jump into my car, slam and lock the doors. My body doesn't stop trembling until I watch the party bus full of stags leave the car park several minutes later.

Ignoring the severe hunger pains in my stomach and my dry mouth, I pull out of the service station and get back on the road. According to the satnav, I've only got another hour or so until I get there, but what am I supposed to do until eight o'clock tomorrow morning? I have no money for a hotel. I must not be thinking clearly because no sane woman would have done what I've done and put herself in this situation. Maybe I'm experiencing some symptoms from my bump to the head from earlier. Is it causing me to make stupid decisions or am I making them of my own free will?

Usually, I'd sing along to the songs on the radio, but I'm not feeling my sexy and confident self at the moment. I just want my bag back. It's all I can think about. Well, that, and the fact Mrs Brown said no one had called asking for me in the six hours I'd spent at the hospital.

I still find that hard to believe. I have dozens of people who work for me and loads of friends, but no one had wondered or cared where I was when I didn't turn up for the business meeting? No one had thought to call around and ask after me?

No one?

No one!

I don't buy it.

Mrs Brown has never liked me. Actually, that's not completely true. She used to like me a lot when I was a child, but the moment my father died and I inherited all his money and the business, she morphed into a snooty cow who turned her nose up at me, not afraid to show her judgemental eyes.

I sometimes get the feeling she blames me for my father's death. It's the way her nostrils flare whenever I talk about him; the way her postures stiffens. I know they were close and maybe Mrs Brown wanted to have a closer relationship than your average housekeeper and boss should have, but how could it have been my fault my father crashed his car on the race track that day? It was a freak accident that just so happened to have occurred a few days after I turned eighteen and, coincidentally, only a week after he'd changed his will so I'd inherit his whole estate and business. I didn't even know he'd done that until his lawyer told me afterwards. I'd been as shocked as everyone else. I'd heard the sniggers and the hushed voices behind closed doors. I'd listened as Sawyer and the legal team had discussed the future of the business. They wanted to cut me out, wanted to freeze all my assets and hand the company over to Sawyer.

'She's not mature enough to run the business.'

'She'll never be able to cope.'

'She'll ruin us.'

'Sawyer should be the face of the company.'

Well ... I proved all those idiots wrong, didn't I?

Dear Diary

Date: 11 September 2001

Dear Diary,

Today the world stood still and watched while terrorists flew planes into the Twin Towers in New York and the Pentagon. That's in America. Even at age 11 I know this is a huge moment and it will probably change the world forever. It scared me a little. My sister has been glued to the screen all day and has cried her eyes out, saying that the terrorists are coming to get her too. *As if.*

Date: 12 September 2001

Dear Diary,

Yesterday was the only day when I didn't think about Bryan Matthews, but today I can't stop thinking about him; the way his hair blows in the wind, his cute but crooked smile. I'm very excited because it's his 11th birthday party this weekend and he's basically invited the whole school ... except for a couple of the weirdos and the partially deaf kid. Even my sister got an invite, but I told her she can't go because otherwise she'll be all weird around him and expect me to introduce them. I know she's only 11, but she's quite pretty and I won't lie, I'm a bit jealous of her.

Date: 15 September 2001

Dear Diary,

Oh wow … Bryan's birthday party was amazing. He had a pirate theme, so we all dressed up in fancy dress. Although he did complain that the terrorist attacks in America stole his thunder because half the kids from school didn't show up because their parents wanted to keep them home for safety reasons. But I didn't mind because it meant there were less kids around to steal his focus from me.

Date: 16 September 2001

Dear Diary,

Bryan Matthews had his hair cut today. He just waltzed into school with a buzz cut. I can't believe he didn't even warn me about it. I'm feeling quite sad because I loved his hair so much, and now I can't fantasise about running my fingers through it … which I don't do … I just meant …
Actually, I think his new hairstyle suits him. It makes him look dangerous.

Chapter Eleven

July 2003

I was thirteen years old, yet I didn't act the way thirteen-year-olds were supposed to act. Not according to my dad anyway, and my teachers, and all the other kids. Apparently, it wasn't normal to want to read all day, to rather spend time conversing with fictional characters in books than speak to real people my own age. But here's the thing – if kids my age were worth talking to, then maybe I'd speak to them, but all thirteen-year-olds wanted to talk about was boring stuff, such as the possibility of so-and-so having a crush on them, or what's-her-face kissing thing-a-ma-jig behind the school sports shed. It was like, I turned thirteen, and suddenly I was supposed to be attracted to the opposite sex and expected to talk about it all the time. No. Not me. No.

I didn't know much about sex and, to be honest, I'd rather it stayed that way for as long as possible. I know it was what happened between two people who loved each other. I read about it in books, and it sounded gross and weird. My uncle explained a few things to me a while ago, but I didn't understand everything. Then he touched me and told me it was okay, so I believed him because he had never lied to me before, even though we didn't love each other in that way.

Girls my age were wearing make-up already and the boys were stealing their dads' beer, swigging it for a couple of minutes and then pretending they were wasted. Yawn. I had no interest in alcohol or drugs. I wanted to keep my mind sharp. Those things would all come in good time … when *I* was ready to experience them.

My dad forced me to go to the end of summer school dance because he said, and I quote, "It will be good for you". Even my uncle agreed. Well, they were both wrong. Wrong. Wrong. Wrong.

So far, it had been the most boring three hours of my entire life. Thank goodness I'd been able to sneak a book in under my clothes. I found a nice and secluded corner, away from prying eyes, sat down and started reading *Harry Potter*. The latest book was out, and it was the thickest one yet. I was so excited to learn about the *Order of the Phoenix*. But, of course, I got interrupted several times by shrieking girls and laughing boys all saying stuff like:

'I totally just saw up Kirsty's dress!'

'Anyone got any vodka?'

'OMG, I think Daniel likes me!'

'He keeps staring at me … should I kiss him tonight?'

I stayed in my corner and prayed to God I became invisible as their loud voices got closer to my hiding place.

'Hey, loser!'

I guessed my invisibility cloak hadn't worked then …

'Whatcha doing hiding in a corner? Got no other losers to dance with?' sneered Bryan Matthews as he leaned against the wall next to me. 'Whatcha reading that rubbish for? Just wait for the movie to come out.'

I rolled my eyes so far into the back of my head that it made me dizzy. 'I like reading,' I replied.

'Reading's for losers.'

'I disagree.'

'Reading's boring.'

'That's because you can only read at the level of a toddler.'

Bryan growled at me. Yes, he actually growled like a dog. Then he snatched the book out of my hands and held it above his head.

I slowly stood up, but I knew there was no way I was going to be able to reach the book because Bryan had shot up about four inches in the past few months and I'd barely grown one. I didn't even try to grab the book back. Instead, I lunged forwards and elbowed him in the stomach. He dropped the book straight into my outstretched hands and I ran in the opposite direction so fast I was certain I left speed marks, like in cartoons.

'Arrrggg!' I heard behind me.

I kept running through the swarms of teenagers dancing, through the empty hallways, through the front doors of the school, down the steps and out onto the street. I stopped, bending over at the waist to catch my breath, but I could still hear shouting behind me. They were chasing me.

I took off running again, not even considering the direction. I allowed my feet to take me wherever they wanted to go, my arms pumping at my sides, my precious book clutched in my right hand.

Loud footsteps echoed behind me for several minutes, but, eventually, they dropped off and all I heard was my erratic breathing, the thumping of my own heart, which felt as if it wanted to crash through my chest and flop out onto the pavement.

I stopped again and sucked in the night air, each lungful feeling as if it might be my last. I needed to get in better shape. I didn't play any sports because most of the sports at school were team sports and I didn't like being part of a team. Plus, all the other kids never picked me anyway. I was always the last one standing awkwardly, and I hated it. I really should try and work on my fitness though. There were some cross-country running events starting at school soon. Running was usually a solo sport, right? I didn't have to be a team player to run fast. Maybe I could start doing that and work on my cardiovascular fitness at the same time? It would help me in the long run.

Despite feeling like I might drop dead at any second, the exhilaration I'd felt just now as I was running was wonderful, or maybe it was the thrill of the chase I was enjoying. Either way, I made a mental note to sign up for the running events when the new term started in September.

As I glanced around, I realised I had no idea where I was. I didn't recognise any of the road signs or the houses on this road. The streetlights flickered randomly as the wind gently brushed the trees next to them.

I shivered, despite it not being cold. I had no choice but to turn around and try and find my way back to somewhere more familiar, but if I went back the way I'd come I risked running into Bryan Matthews and his cronies. But if I kept walking straight then I'd likely get even more lost than I already was.

I didn't want to go home. Not yet.

That's when I heard a noise to my left. It sounded like an injured animal, a horrible wailing, gargling noise. I clutched my book tighter in my hand, slowly turning to the left, and followed the sound. It stopped and started sporadically, several times, before ceasing completely.

'Hello?' I called out, knowing that if anyone answered me the first thing I'd do was spin around and run away. I wasn't particularly brave, but maybe I should be. Maybe I should start standing up for myself and others more.

I gulped back the solid lump in my throat as I approached a thick bush. I think that was where the sound had been coming from, but I couldn't be sure anymore because it'd stopped and all I could hear was the wind and the sound of cars in the distance.

I reached out my hand and pulled back some of the branches. A sharp stab of pain told me I'd cut my finger on a branch, but I instantly forgot about the pain when I saw what had been making that awful noise.

I gasped, stumbling backwards onto my bottom, as the horrible taste of bile formed in my throat.

I screamed and then ran all the way home.

How to Commit the Perfect Murder
Step Three

Get Your Priorities Straight

This is, quite possibly, the most important step of them all so make sure you pay attention. I'm only going to say this once.

Nothing else in your life should matter apart from your main objective; not kids, not relationships, not work, not anything. If you aren't 100% committed to ending someone's life, then you will fail. If you decide to let all the fun stuff cloud your judgement and distract you from your goal, then you will fail. I'm sorry to sound harsh, but it's true. If you find that hard to digest, then maybe you shouldn't be planning to murder someone in the first place.

Other people will try and persuade you otherwise. They'll try and make out like having a family and moving to a big house in the country is the only dream you should ever have. They are wrong. If you want to kill someone, then go ahead and do it!

Now, I'm not saying you should kill people just for the fun of it. Oh no, I'm not a psychopathic serial killer who enjoys slaughtering people like animals. I'm a normal human being. I only want to kill those who deserve it. Perhaps you could call me a vigilante, like that TV show *Dexter*, although granted he's a little bit messed up in the head. I'm not. I'm normal. I wasn't baptised in blood at three years old.

Anyway, I digress ...

The point is that you should only kill people who deserve to die and if you aren't the one to take them out then they'll just get away with it and never pay the price for being an evil human being. Every morning you should look at yourself in a mirror and repeat these words:

'I will accomplish my goal. I will kill (insert the name of your target here).'

Bottom line ...

You must get your priorities straight!

Trust me.

Chapter Twelve

HANNAH
6 July 2022 – 23:01 p.m.

Bryan Matthews.

The name jolts a familiar feeling inside me: anger. My jaw clenches as I step away from him, my arms becoming rigid at my sides. I may not fully remember who this man is, but there's an invisible force tugging inside my head, telling me one simple thing – get away from this man as fast as possible. He reaches out his arm again, offering me his hand.

'Hannah. Trust me. We need to leave. Now.'

'Why should I trust you?'

'Wow, you really have been messed up. Did you hit your head again?'

My hand automatically touches the injury on my head. The wound is sore to touch, but there's another bump near it that feels tender too. Have I been hit twice? And my shoulder still hurts so bad I can barely move it.

'How did I hit my head?' I ask, lowering my arm. 'And why does my shoulder hurt?'

'How did you ... are you fucking serious?' I don't even flinch at his tone of voice, despite it echoing down the empty corridors. Why are all the corridors empty? This is a hospital, right? Then again, the more I look around the more the answer jumps out at me: no, it is not a hospital. It is a strange, empty building with some medical equipment. We shouldn't be here ...

'I'm not going anywhere with you until you tell me how I hit my head and how I know you and why my shoulder hurts.'

Bryan rolls his eyes. 'I don't have time for this shit.'

Before I have a chance to react, Bryan lunges forwards, grabs my wrist, turns me to the side and then hoists me up onto his shoulders, as expertly and swiftly as a trained firefighter. I scream as he jogs down the corridor towards the exit, hitting his back as hard as I can with my clenched fists, like a toddler throwing an almighty tantrum. Pain erupts from my shoulder and head, but I fight against it.

It's no use. He is too strong, and my injuries (however they happened) are sapping the energy out of me, rendering me almost completely useless. I kick my legs as hard as possible, hoping I'll catch him in the groin, but he easily pins them down with only one arm, tucking them against the side of his body.

My first thought is – where is he taking me and how am I going to stay alive? But then, as we exit the building into the cool dark air, my muddled brain forgets about the fact I'm being kidnapped because there's a much more pressing issue to address now.

The building he's taken me out of is some sort of office building, complete with numerous windows, all of which are blacked out.

Not a hospital then.

I stop screaming as he plonks me down on solid ground, my legs buckling slightly. I shiver as I wrap my arms around my body. Bryan just stares at me with his eyebrows raised.

'You see? You aren't in a hospital. You're safe.'

'B-But … what's going on? Where am I and what happened to me?'

'Okay, I'm going to say this really slowly, so you'll understand … You need to trust me. Here, put this on.' Bryan turns to a nearby black car, opens the passenger door and brings out a black hoodie, which I take with shaking hands and put on, zipping it up high under my chin. Now I have several layers on, my body stops shivering from the cold.

'So … my name is Hannah?'

'Um … yes,' he replies. I frown at him. 'How about we get you some food first? I have snacks in the car. I'll tell you everything once we're on the road. It's safer if we keep moving. I don't like staying in one place for too long.'

'Are we hiding from someone? Are we wanted by the police?'

'Is that a trick question?'

'Why won't you answer any of my questions?'

Bryan laughs. 'I do hope your memories come back. I really can't be bothered going through everything.'

'Will you tell me one thing?'

'Shoot.'

'Why do I have a heart tattoo on my wrist that says *Bryan Forever* underneath it?'

Bryan throws his head back and laughs again. 'Oh, Barbie … you're gonna love this story. Get in, I'll tell you on the way out.'

Chapter Thirteen

ASHLEIGH
1 July 2022 – 18:45 p.m.

By the time I pull into the car park at Skegness Beach Resort, I'm practically on my last legs. Driving is hard, especially when dangerously dehydrated and, quite possibly, concussed. I'm not sure how I've managed it, but I've arrived ... albeit unscathed, but almost definitely mentally traumatised.

I lean my head against the headrest, relieved after eventually managing to parallel park for the first time since I passed my driving test however many years ago it was. Although, *technically*, I didn't pass my test because I bribed the instructor, but still ... Thank goodness for the remote parking sensors on this car otherwise I would have scraped it all along the left side. Why do they make parking spaces so small these days? This is why I very rarely drive around London because there's nowhere to park and, even when you do happen to find a space, it's so narrow that you can barely open the door to get out. Also, so I've learned, parking whilst other drivers are watching is one of the most stressful situations I've ever been in. My forehead and top lip are so damp I could soak a tissue if I had one.

Once I'm recovered from the parking fiasco, many questions and thoughts start racing through my mind, but as each one pops in, I immediately counter it with an answer.

Why am I doing this again?

I want my bag and phone back (amongst other things).

Do I know who it is I'm looking out for?

No.

Do I have any idea what I'll say to the man (I'm taking a huge leap here and assuming it's a man) when I eventually find him?

No.

Am I going to get murdered by a stranger?

Quite possibly.

Do I want to change my mind and go home?

Yes. But it's too late now. I'm here. I may as well attempt to locate my bag.

But here's the thing: I may have arrived, but according to the note, I'm not supposed to meet the person until eight o'clock tomorrow morning. What on earth am I supposed to do for the next thirteen hours? I'll starve to death by then!

Okay ... here's the plan.

Locate water and something to eat.

Then, park somewhere inconspicuous and try and sleep.

Get my bag back without getting killed.

Drive home, spend fifteen hours in the shower, douse myself in disinfectant, crawl under my satin-covered sheets, forget this whole fiasco ever happened, order a takeaway and drink a whole bottle of wine (maybe two).

Good plan. It's a solid plan.

I awkwardly swing my legs out of the car and stand up. My muscles in my butt and lower back groan in protest. I perform some more stretches against the car whilst scanning the immediate area for any sign of danger and/or free food and drink.

It might be nearly seven in the evening, but the temperature is soaring. Families with their kids are enjoying the beach, old men with leather for skin are strolling about in too-tight Speedos (eww!) and the ice cream van is consistently pulling in a roaring crowd. My mouth salivates at the mere thought of an ice cream.

Mental note: keep spare cash in the car for ice cream emergencies.

That's when I notice a couple of policemen, laden with paper bags full to the brim of chips, getting into a police car. They are dressed in their proper attire, complete with high-vis vests and holsters. One is short and one is tall.

On autopilot, thinking only of my stomach, I stumble across the car park on shaky legs and bang a little too hard on the driver side window of the police car.

'Hello! Can you help me?'

Tall policeman rolls down his window and peers out at me, eyebrows raised as he takes in my sparkly blue dress and bare feet. 'Can I help you, Miss?'

I slap on my most dazzling smile. 'Hi, yes, sorry. I've lost my bag and it's really expensive. I was wondering if I could borrow a couple of pounds for some food and drink. I'm parched.' I fan my face with my left hand.

Tall Policeman squeezes his lips together as he glances at Short Policeman then slowly back at me. 'You have no money on you at all?' I see them shift their eyes towards my BMW, which they've clearly seen me walk from moments before.

'No, I don't have anything. Everything was in my bag.'

'Where did you last see your bag, Miss?'

'In London.'

This receives another eyebrow raise from Tall Policeman and another glance at his colleague whose jaw is clenched so tightly (I assume to stop from laughing) I'm surprised it's not causing him a brain aneurysm. 'I see ... so how do you imagine your bag got all the way to Skegness?'

Is that sarcasm in his voice?

'It ... it got stolen,' I stutter stupidly.

'Did you see the person who stole it?'

'No. I was in a car accident.'

'Are you injured, Miss?'

'I ... no, but—'

'Is that your car?' Tall Policeman nods at my purple BMW.

'Yes.'

The two policemen swap glances again. 'It doesn't look as if it's been in an accident,' says Short Policeman, who's also at least three stone overweight in my opinion.

'That's because it wasn't that car I crashed.' I think there may be a hint of desperation creeping into my voice now. It's risen a couple of octaves.

'Miss ... have you been drinking?'

'I ... no! I'm telling you the truth!' My voice is super-sonic now.

'Then please explain how your bag got stolen in London, you crashed a car, but yet are driving an immaculate beamer, you're barefoot and are at Skegness Beach Resort begging for food?'

I stare at the two policemen and realise my mistake. I take a step back, wanting to retreat to the safety of my car as quickly as possible, but also wishing I could smash their faces into the windscreen.

'Are you going to help me or not?'

Tall Policeman sighs and gets out of the car. He's at least a foot and a half taller than me and skinny as a rake. I bet if I shoved him hard enough, he'd topple over. The thought does cross my mind. His name tag says 'PC Stevens'.

'Look,' he says, 'give me your name and address and I'll check things out, then see where we are, okay?'

I shake my head. 'Don't bother,' I mutter.

I scurry back to my car, feeling a bit like an unwanted puppy at Christmas. I hear Tall Policeman shout at me to come back, but I ignore him. I slam the car door a bit too hard, start the engine and drive away, the tyres skidding on the hot tarmac.

A mile or so down the road, I find another beach-side car park that appears to be free, so I park up and watch as some seagulls fight over a discarded bag of chips. I have a good mind to get out and fight them off myself ...

In fact ...

Screw it. I'm desperate.

I launch myself out of the car and run at the seagulls, flapping and waving my arms. They take off into the air, squawking and screeching. I bend down and pick up the bag of chips, ignoring the family of four who are staring open-mouthed at me from a nearby bench. The bag is about half full of chips, which are cold and have a sprinkling of sand for seasoning. I begin scoffing them as I walk back to my car, attempting to ignore the build-up of humiliation washing over me.

What I really need is some water because these chips are covered in salt and are already sapping my mouth of what little moisture it's holding. As I lean against my car, munching the cold chips, I glance around again.

The scenery is stunning here. This is the first time I've ever had chips by the beach. How sad is that? Even as a small child my parents never took me on trips to the seaside; they were always too busy. Then, when my mum died, there wasn't a chance in hell my dad would take me and the thought of Mrs Brown ever taking me on a beach trip is laughable.

The waves roll and crash against the shore. The seagulls are back and circling above me like hungry vultures. The family of four have now moved on and they've left behind—

No way ...

A bottle of water?

Did they leave that intentionally for the hapless woman they'd just seen stealing cold chips from a flock of seagulls, or are they litterbugs who don't care about the environment? Either way, I couldn't give two hoots.

I sprint across the tarmac, scooping up the bottle, and drain half the contents in one go. My body practically sighs with relief as the warm water hits my stomach. At least now I won't starve to death overnight.

I take my prized possessions back to my car and lean on the bonnet as I admire the ocean again. There's a prominent waft of hot chips in the air, coming from a nearby chippy, mixed with salt and something tangy. It's heavenly. And, for the first time since leaving home, however many hours ago it was, I feel content and, dare I say it, happy.

I breathe in deep, filling my lungs with the salty air, close my eyes and listen to the roar of the waves.

Then a seagull drops a huge splodge of poo in my hair.

Seriously!

Chapter Fourteen

1 July 2022 – 16:45 p.m.

Curtis clenched the phone in his hand, unable to stop the tremble. He stared at the photo, squinting against the fading glare from the sun, but the anger flowing through him was too much to control. He fought against the urge to throw his phone on the ground and stomp on it. Somehow, he restrained himself, quickly turning off the screen; even looking at the name made his stomach lurch.

Sawyer Fucking Croft.

The man who had indirectly ruined his life; yet he'd never met him.

But here he was … again … fourteen years later.

Was it merely a coincidence that Sawyer's old business partner, Alan Carmichael, had a daughter who'd crashed into him this morning or was it for some other unknown reason? Alan Carmichael was dead; died in a fiery car crash a long time ago, apparently, so why was his airhead daughter now sniffing around? Or was she? Did she know about her father's business partner and his sordid past? Was she connected to him in some way?

Fuck.

And she was most likely on her way here at this very moment to … what … confront him? About what? What had he done?

Ashleigh Too-Many-Middle-Names Carmichael was an unexpected liability and now he had to prepare himself for something he didn't want to have to do. If only he hadn't tried to bribe her for money, but how was he supposed to have known who she was? It had been a spur of the moment decision and he'd fucked up ... big time. Again.

Curtis watched as the police officers returned to their car, probably returning from a walk around the area, looking out for any trouble. They had smiles on their faces and freshly brewed cups of steaming liquid in their hands. No doughnuts. Although one of them looked as if he'd consumed one too many doughnuts and the other could do with fattening up.

There's no trouble here, Officers. Keep walking, you bunch of dickheads.

After a few minutes, the police car pulled out of the car park and drove down the road, heading towards the centre of town, which instantly lifted a weight from Curtis's chest. It wouldn't be dark for hours, but he needed to find somewhere to hide, somewhere inconspicuous where he could watch the world go by and hopefully find his target, or maybe they would find him. They had been playing a game of cat and mouse for a long time now, but Curtis wasn't tired of it; he never tired of the game.

He knew he had to try and forget about Sawyer Croft and Ashleigh Carmichael and just pray and hope that her rear-ending his car had been just a huge, unfortunate coincidence. After all, he had to get his priorities straight.

But Curtis didn't believe in coincidences. Not since Mia had died. The doctors and the police had told him it was death by suicide; that she'd jumped of her own free will from a ten-storey building in the middle of the day onto the solid concrete below. Most of the bones in her body had been smashed apart from the impact, her bodily fluids and organs smeared across the pavement and spattered onto nearby buildings and pedestrians. The only way she'd been identifiable was because she'd had her driving license on her and was wearing the same clothes he'd last seen her in.

It was no coincidence that she'd jumped from the same building where his so-called best friend had worked; a building which was part of the Carmichael Foundation. She'd been there to visit Bryan Matthews, who she'd dated briefly when they were both teenagers, but apparently Bryan had not seen her that day. She'd never made it to his office. The police had reconstructed her jump trajectory and deduced that she'd leaped from the office above Bryan's; an office belonging to a man called Sawyer Croft, who'd just so happened to be away that day.

Sawyer Croft.

Alan Carmichael.

Bryan Matthews.

They'd all been involved in Mia's death somehow and Curtis was determined to prove it.

And now here was Miss Ashleigh Carmichael, aka Blondie, who'd crashed into him and was directly related to two out of the three men he blamed for his sister's death.

No coincidence, indeed.

Mia had been happy. She'd had her whole life ahead of her. She'd been accepted into Oxford University to study

Law. Whenever Curtis had seen her, all she'd ever done was smile at him and say how excited she was about her future.

But then she'd supposedly ended it all …

He hadn't bought it then and he didn't buy it now.

It was why he was in fucking Skegness. He was going to get to the bottom of his sister's death whether it was the last thing he ever managed to do.

And that meant finding his target.

Several hours later Curtis was snoring in his seat, which he'd pushed back as far as possible to give him extra room to stretch his legs. It hadn't taken him long to drift off. He'd become used to sleeping in this car.

A strange noise stirred him from his deep sleep, but not enough to wake him completely. He adjusted his position but couldn't find a comfortable one. Annoyed, he opened his eyes.

The second his eyes opened the driver door was yanked open and he fell sideways through it. Rough hands gripped his jacket and dragged him the rest of the way out of the car and onto the gravel.

'What the fuck!' He kicked his legs to gain some momentum to throw the intruder off, but he'd been caught off guard.

Such a rookie mistake. Why didn't you lock the fucking door, Curtis?

'How the hell did you find me?' demanded the assailant.

Curtis was dropped on the ground. He lay there for a few seconds, catching his breath. 'I think it's you who's found me,' he panted.

'Bullshit. You've been following me for God knows how long now. I'm sick of it. It's over. You hear me?'

'It'll never be over. Plus ... we have a new problem now.'

'Which is?'

'Ashleigh Carmichael.'

'Am I supposed to know who that is?'

Curtis laughed as he got to his feet, brushing the dirt from his favourite jacket. 'She's trouble and she's on her way here.'

'Why?'

'Cos, I thought I could blackmail her into giving me money.'

'You're a piece of work, you know that?'

'I learned from the best.' Curtis winked, but he wasn't prepared for the fist that came hurtling through the air. It landed clean on his nose, breaking it.

Dear Diary

Date: 1 July 2003

Dear Diary,

I wish I had a special superpower. I don't even care what type of superpower it is. That's not true. I want the ability to read people's minds or to control their actions. That would be super cool because then I could make Bryan Matthews all mine. He has a stupid obsession with girls at the moment, but not with me, which is so unfair.

Date: 6 July 2003

Dear Diary,

Okay, so it's the summer holidays now and it sucks because I don't get to see Bryan every day. But he has invited me over to his place for some shooting practice. Apparently, his dad owns a rifle and wants to teach him how to use it. So, he's invited all his gang to come along. But I need to ask my dad first if I'm allowed to go.

Date: 7 July 2003

Dear Diary,

He said no.

Date: 15 July 2003

Dear Diary,

My dad never lets me do anything fun. I kept on and on at him to let me go round to Bryan's house to shoot the rifle, but he kept saying no. I went anyway. That was three days ago, and he never found out, so I think I'm in the clear.

Okay, let me explain what happened at Bryan's. Holding a rifle was so cool. I felt so powerful. I pretty much missed every target, but Bryan hit them all. He kept showing off and, I won't lie, I felt a bit of resentment towards him. Why is he always so good at everything? It's not fair. It's like everything comes so easy to him, but all of us other kids have to work hard to accomplish anything.

Although he did accidentally shoot out the top window of his house, which I found hilarious. His dad didn't though, and I saw Bryan look afraid for the first time. Maybe he isn't so tough after all.

Chapter Fifteen

September 2003

Finding that dying cat under the bush gave me nightmares for weeks. I felt so much gnawing guilt my stomach swam with nausea; not guilt about the fact I'd seen an animal in pain and covered in blood, but because I hadn't done anything to help said animal. I'd screamed and run away because that was what I always seemed to do. I never did find out whether the cat survived. It probably didn't. It had been badly injured, probably hit by a car and had crawled under the bush to die. I should have done more ... I don't know why I didn't. It would haunt me forever.

Thanks to me elbowing Bryan Matthews in the stomach at the school dance, I was now the number one target for him and his cronies at the start of the new term. I couldn't get away from them, even if I hid behind corners and waited for them to leave a room before entering it. They still found me and stole my things. I stopped bringing books to school because I was afraid they'd get stolen or destroyed. Something had to be done about him.

And something *would* be done.

One day ... I was still working on it.

I wished time would hurry up and pass. I wanted to be a grownup, like ... *now*. I wanted to do all the things grownups could do, like buying and owning a gun. I was aware in the UK people didn't walk around carrying guns, but they did in America. Over there, it was considered normal to carry a gun. Maybe I should move to America when I'm a grownup, or maybe I should become a police officer. Then I could arrest Bryan Matthews for merely walking down the street and lock him in jail for the rest of his life for the misery he put me through daily.

You know, that wasn't a bad idea about putting him in jail. Not for life though; maybe just for a few years so he'd suffer for a while. I wouldn't want him to get locked away forever, otherwise I'd have no way of getting to him.

I learned a valuable lesson last week. My dad had hardly been paying me any attention, like ... none at all. I was carted off to my uncle's house (he wasn't actually my uncle, but he was close) for the summer holidays, something he wasn't exactly thrilled about, but he was pretty cool. And he was never any trouble either because he was almost always drunk or smoking some sort of funky cigarette that smelled funny. He said it was a special grownup cigarette that made you feel happy. I wanted to be happy. So, when he fell asleep on the sofa one day, I picked up the special cigarette and took a few puffs. I started coughing and quickly put it back down on the side table in case he woke up, but he didn't, so I sat and smoked the whole thing. I'd never smoked before, but my uncle was right; it did make me feel happy.

I sat and giggled to myself for several minutes as I watched my hands go in and out of focus, listening to his snores. Then I picked up a nearby pen and drew all over his face. Then I ran to the bathroom and was violently sick. I woke up covered in vomit on the bathroom floor with my uncle standing over me, shaking his head, but with a wicked smile across his thin lips.

'Serves you right, you little shit,' he said before slamming the door and leaving me lying in my own mess. Things got pretty bad after that with my uncle, so I had to resort to daydreaming about killing Bryan Matthews just to get me through the long days.

The dreams became extremely vivid. I know it wasn't normal, but it felt so right, like I was meant to do it, like I was *born* to do it. The more I saw his stupid face the more I wanted to kill him. It consumed me and I spent a lot of my free time thinking of ways to kill him.

If I ever did own a gun one day, then I could shoot him in the face.

I could push him off a tall building or through a window.

I could run him over with my car.

I could stab him over and over with a sharp knife.

I could drown him, hold him under the water until the bubbles stopped.

I could choke him.

Honestly, there were so many ways in which to kill him. I was spoilt for choice. How was I supposed to choose? I didn't want his death to be fast. I wanted him to suffer as much as possible and for as long as possible. I was thinking that stabbing or bludgeoning was the way to go; much more up close and personal than pushing him out of a window, for example.

It was the third week back at school and I'd already been sent to detention four times. I was sitting by myself in a room and had to write, 'I will behave and listen to my teacher' 200 times. I got to fifty and my hand started cramping. It wasn't my fault that I hadn't listened. Bryan Matthews had been flinging wet tissue at the back of my head while the teacher had been talking and I'd been distracted and missed her question. Then I'd spun around in my seat, picking up the wet tissue stuck to the back of my head, and dumped it on Bryan Matthews's head. The whole class had burst into hysterical laughter.

And here I was ... in detention.

But Bryan Matthews got away with it.

Life sucked. I really should learn to control my temper. Maybe I should take up boxing as well as running this year ... you know, to let out my pent-up aggression. I had to be patient and not give the game away now. I was only thirteen after all. There was still plenty of time to hone my skills.

The plan had only just begun.

How to Commit the Perfect Murder
Step Four

Blend In

I'm not saying that you need to don a fake moustache and get plastic surgery or dress up like a fucking detective in one of those lame 80s TV shows. No, what I mean by *blend in* is you need to not draw attention to yourself, which means no social media, no getting arrested, no being the centre of attention. Just stay under the radar, keep yourself to yourself and be as inconspicuous as possible.

Or – and just hear me out for a second – you could go the opposite way. Throw those lavish parties, be an influencer on fucking TikTok and have millions of followers, get arrested by streaking across a football pitch, punch people in the face if you feel like it. I don't give a shit what you do, but whatever you do decide to do … blend in. You can still be completely invisible even if you're loved and adored by millions of fans because most people don't take any notice, nor do they really care about anyone but themselves. I bet you all the money in the world that the most influential and well-known celebrities are some of the most lonely and depressed people out there.

So, whichever way you decide to go, just stick to it.

Easy, right?

You probably think I'm crazy, but believe me, I know what I'm doing. I've been a pro at blending in for my entire life. Most people barely even pay me attention and, when they do, they don't really see me for who I really am because I'm an expert at pulling the wool over their eyes.

Blending in might mean you have to stand out, but blending in with the right crowd will set you up for the long haul.

Trust me.

Chapter Sixteen

2 July 2022 – 07:30 a.m.

He hadn't slept well after the fight; not well at all. It had nothing to do with the fact his nose was possibly broken or that he'd landed hard on the ground during the punch up.

Having finally knocked the man unconscious, he'd then bundled him into the boot, driven fifty miles, dumped him in a random back alley, and then driven back to Skegness for a couple hours of awkward sleeping. It wouldn't keep the man away for long, but hopefully, it would give him enough time to get his affairs in order. He was fed up with playing this game of cat and mouse.

And the whole thing with Ashleigh Carmichael was just a headache he didn't need.

He'd parked a few streets away from the beach resort upon his return trip. It was time to get some breakfast and then head to the supposed meeting point. Maybe she wouldn't even show up. He checked the phone; the money hadn't been transferred yet …

No, she wasn't going to be there.

There was no way.

After adjusting the seat back to its usual position, he put the car in drive and pulled out into the light morning traffic, muttering a few words of profanity when the engine groaned and spluttered. He needed to stop by a garage soon and get it checked out. He paid for a bacon roll from the breakfast café on the main high street with a crumpled five-pound note he found in the glove box and ate while driving to his destination. He licked his fingers clean of grease as he pulled into the empty car park of the beach resort. The place was empty, but he knew the crowds would arrive once the heat of the day settled in.

According to his watch, it was 07:58.

It was now or never ...

He watched as the time reached 08:06, but the only car that entered the car park was a beat-up old Vauxhall.

Five more minutes ...

The seconds passed slowly, but with each one the tension and knots seemed to disperse. His shoulders relaxed into the leather seat.

She wasn't coming.

Figures.

At 08:16 he drove out of the car park, filled up the tank at the petrol garage, grabbed a sandwich and coffee to go, and then made his way out of Skegness, using the smaller roads.

He breathed in the salty air as he drove with the window cracked open. The huge car handled the narrow roads and tight corners well, but it guzzled fuel at an alarming rate. He remembered his dad teaching him to drive this car. He'd struggled to adjust to the automatic at first, often slamming his left foot down on the invisible clutch, but now he couldn't imagine driving any other car. It was a part of him. It was more than just a car. It was years of spending time with his dad after his mum—

His eyes flicked to the rear-view mirror as he noticed a flash of purple.

Fuck ...

A purple BMW was tailing him and doing an awful job at that.

'Fuck's sake,' he muttered, slamming his palm into the steering wheel.

She'd found him, but instead of meeting him at the designated place, she'd resorted to tailing him. Why? Plus, the money still hadn't been transferred. What was her game? Well, whatever it was she was playing with the wrong man.

'Let's see how bad you want your fucking bag,' he said with a smug grin as he put his foot to the floor. The engine roared; the animalistic sound emanating from under the bonnet was music to his ears. The flash of purple disappeared within seconds, and he laughed as he kept the revs up while navigating the various corners.

The next town was coming up soon, so he eased off the accelerator and allowed the car to reach the proposed speed limit of thirty miles per hour.

Unfortunately, the traffic through town was heavy; everyone was attempting to get somewhere at the same time. It didn't help that the roads were narrow. Cars upon cars lined the streets and he had to slow down to a snail's pace as he approached a set of traffic lights.

Another flash of purple ...

The BMW was two cars back.

'Fuck!' he shouted. If he put his foot down right this second, he could possibly squeeze through the traffic lights before they turned red, and she'd be left behind.

He did just that.

It worked.

Yes, he received a few aggressive horn blasts from other drivers, but he made it through and checked his rear-view mirror, smiling as he watched the BMW crawl to a stop at the lights behind him.

He weaved in and out of traffic as best he could, praying he got through before she caught him up.

So far so good.

He exhaled hard as soon as he exited the town and was back on the coastal roads. The sun was slowly rising, the heat of the day creeping up with every passing minute. He clicked his neck from side to side; the stress of the past few days was catching up with him. He'd barely slept, constantly hovering on the verge of sleep, but never quite succumbing to it. He flicked his eyes to the rear-view mirror again and frowned when he spotted yet another flash of purple, which disappeared as he rounded a corner.

'Goddammit!'

She was beginning to get on his nerves. She had to go. He couldn't have her following him everywhere. He had shit to do and having her tagging along was not part of his plan. He blamed himself. He should have just left her and forgotten about the money.

He kept driving until he saw a deserted lay-by up ahead. He parked, immediately got out and jogged into the nearby trees, pretending to be going for a piss. The crunch of tyres on gravel behind him alerted him to the fact she'd done the same.

Stupid bitch.

She had to be the dumbest woman on the planet. Although, credit to her for having the guts to drive all the way here by herself and track him down. Whatever was in that bag of hers had to be worth risking her life. He walked in a large circle, keeping the lay-by on the right as he heard a car door open.

She was searching his car; he'd intentionally left it unlocked.

The perfect bait.

He appeared from the trees and there she was, bent over and searching the front of his car. She had a great bum. He watched her for several seconds, admiring the way her hips moved from side to side and how her thighs flexed slightly. He had an immediate flash of fucking her on the bonnet of his car, but quickly dispelled the vision as he walked up behind her.

He could easily overpower her, knock her unconscious, throw her in the boot and she'd be out of the way for a while, but he hadn't come here to kidnap a rich woman. Maybe he would just see what she had to offer, play with her for a little bit. She looked like a fun plaything. All blonde hair and blue eyes; kind of like a Barbie doll.

He cleared his throat and watched as Barbie froze, still with her bum in the air, leaning through the car door. He continued to enjoy the view of her pert little rear end.

'Can I help you, Miss?' His tone dripped with sarcasm.

Barbie took a small step back and straightened up, but she misjudged how low the roof of the car was and bumped her head on the way up.

'Ouch,' she muttered, rubbing her blonde head of hair.

He raised his eyebrows as he took in her bare feet and general condition. She looked like shit, like she'd been dragged through a hedge backwards and left for dead in a ditch. What the hell had happened to her? But, despite the grubbiness of her appearance and the strange brown stain on the top of her head, she looked ... cute. Too cute for his liking. He had an overwhelming urge to help her, to whisk her up in his arms and rescue her as if he were a brave, shining knight.

But he was no knight ...

'Okay, look, Mr ... whoever you are ... just give me my bag and I'll be on my way,' she said in a harsh tone, attempting to sound serious, but failing miserably on the last syllable as her voice cracked and wobbled. 'I don't know why you took it from a helpless woman who'd just been in a car accident, but I won't call the police if you hand it over right this second.'

He folded his arms and adjusted his stance, so his feet were slightly wider. 'Are you telling me you drove all this way just to get your bag back?' His face creased into a wide grin as he tried hard to hold back a laugh. It was ridiculous to think that she'd done it, but he found it mildly fascinating and hilarious. Was it really all about her precious bag and phone, things she could easily replace in a matter of hours? Or was it something else? What else was in the bag? What wasn't she telling him?

'Yes.' Barbie pulled her dress down her thighs, which looked clammy with sweat. He wanted to run his tongue over them.

'Why didn't you pay the money? That was part of the deal, wasn't it?'

Barbie threw her long blonde hair over her shoulder and laughed. She looked more relaxed than she had a few minutes ago. She had a certain air about her, clearly confident about herself, no doubt because she knew she looked like a runway model, but there was something else about her too; something that he couldn't quite put his finger on. She was oddly familiar.

'You think that just because I crashed into your stupid, ugly car that's justification to charge me a hundred grand to get my bag back? What kind of man are you?' Her accent was London upper class; posh, but not too posh like those reality TV stars he'd seen on a programme recently when he'd been flicking through the channels at a hotel.

'Excuse me, but this car is a 1967 Chevrolet Impala.'

'Is that supposed to mean something to me?'

'It's a damn sight better than that piece of crap you're driving around. Do you realise it glows in sunlight? I could see you coming from a mile away. You may as well have a red flashing light on it.'

She shuddered slightly as she said, 'Excuse *me*, but it's a brand new, state-of-the-art BMW M2 and no doubt cost a lot more than that monstrosity of yours.'

He raised his eyebrows. 'Is that supposed to mean something to me? It's clearly made of weak plastic and glitter. This Impala is a full-blown American muscle car.'

Barbie rolled her eyes, which reminded him of his ex-girlfriend, Hannah. She used to roll her eyes a lot too and it had bugged the hell out of him.

'The steering wheel is on the wrong side.'

He stared at her. Was she really *that* stupid? 'It's an *American* car! Of course it's on the wrong side.'

Barbie screwed up her nose in retaliation and then held out her hand, although he noticed it was trembling. 'Just give me my bag back and I won't call the police.'

'No.'

'No? I don't think you're in a position to negotiate here, Buddy. I could have you arrested for theft and extortion and driving away from the scene of an accident.'

'How? You don't have a phone to call the cops.'

'I—'

'Listen, Barbie, either you pay the hundred grand, or you'll never see your bag again.'

'And how am I supposed to do that without my phone? I can't magic cash out of thin air, nor can I transfer money wirelessly with my mind.' She folded her arms and leaned on one hip, glaring at him with raised eyebrows. It seemed she had him in a bind.

'You don't scare me, Barbie.'

'Don't call me that.'

'Whatever. I don't have time for this shit.'

Another shudder. 'Fine,' she answered with a pout.

'Fine … Wait … What the fuck are you doing?' His mouth dropped open as she strolled around to the passenger side door, opened it and slid into the seat, wiggling her bum around on the leather as if she were getting herself as comfortable as possible.

'I'm coming with you.'

'Like hell you are.'

'Where my bag goes, I go. You don't want to give it back to me? Fine, then I'm coming with you wherever you go until you do.'

He laughed as he ran both his hands through his hair, ruffling it and making it stick up. 'You have got to be fucking kidding me?'

Barbie closed her eyes and breathed in deeply. What the hell was she doing? Why did she seem to react badly in some way every time he swore at her?

'Do I look like I'm joking?' she asked quietly.

'I could be a serial killer, you know. You could be willingly getting into the car of a serial killer. Are you a fucking idiot?'

Barbie pursed her lips together, her jaw clenched so tight he could see the muscles twitching. He stormed around to the passenger door, stood to one side and pointed with a stiff arm down the road.

'Get out.'

'No.'

'Now.'

'Bite me.'

Chapter Seventeen

ASHLEIGH
2 July 2022 – 08:45 a.m.

The look the guy gives me reminds me of the look my ex-boyfriend used to give me right before he beat me. It unsettles me and, for a moment, I regret my choice of words and bravery, but then he sighs loudly, turns his back on me and runs both his hands through his hair. I watch as the large muscles in his back and shoulders flex and ripple under his tight shirt. His arms are nicely tanned, not fake either; it's real, I can tell. His black hair is on the long side, curling over his ears and down the back of his neck. I have an urge to run my fingers through it, like he's doing now. He's attractive in a rugged sort of way. The beard stubble suits him, outlining his perfectly chiselled jaw. Do I have a mild crush on the guy who stole my bag? Possibly. Don't judge me, I'm only human.

His back is still turned, and I can see he's taking deep breaths, as if he's attempting to calm himself. Then he shouts in frustration and kicks a nearby stone. It hurtles into a bush and a bird flies out in terror. I remain sitting in the car, waiting patiently for his temper tantrum to end.

I'd not parked at the meeting point on purpose. There was no way I was letting him hold all the cards, so I'd parked out of sight of the entrance to the car park and waited. I recognised the black American car straight away as the car I'd driven into. Then, when he'd given up and driven away, I followed him at a distance ... or so I thought. I guess he was right about the fact my car is instantly noticeable due to the bright colour and shiny chrome finishes. Yes, I'd lost him for a while, but his car isn't exactly inconspicuous either. It stands out among the crowds because it's huge and hideous.

Never mind. I'm here now.

He's still standing with his feet spread apart and now has his hands on his hips, staring down the road.

I should say something to break the tension that's hovering in the air like a bad smell.

'Look, if you just give me my bag back then you'll never see me again. I promise.'

He turns his head, looking up and down the road again and that's when it hits me – I'm completely alone with a strange man, in the middle of nowhere, on a quiet road. Not one car has passed us in the time we've been in this lay-by. What am I thinking? It's not like I can grab my bag and make a run for it and flag down a car to help or even get to my car and drive away in time. He'd easily catch and overpower me. I have to play along, catch him off guard and make my escape at the opportune moment. It's my only choice. My car will have to stay here. Once I have my bag back, I'll have the cash and means to call a taxi to drive me all the way back to London; back to safety. Then I'll arrange for someone to come and collect my car.

That's the plan.

Of course, I'm also secretly hoping he'll turn around and say, 'Sure, no problem, I'll give you your bag back. No need to pay me. Have a nice day.'

The man turns around and stares at me with a smug smile that does nothing to ease the butterflies in my stomach. 'Sure, Barbie, have it your way. You can come with me.'

I nod my agreement, but inside I'm screaming in annoyance. He rocks the car as he gets behind the wheel, grinning at me as he starts the car. He's calling my bluff. He thinks I'll back out and run away. Not a chance am I doing that. Where my bag goes, I go.

Dirt and gravel fly up behind the car as he accelerates out of the lay-by, covering my BMW in a thin film of dust. I watch in the side mirror as my car disappears.

The sun is high in the sky now, as a few stringy clouds drift across it. Panic rises in my chest as we speed down the road, but I'm safe in the knowledge that once I can get hold of my bag, I'll be safe. I have no idea where we're going.

'So ... what's with all the middle names?'

I gasp loudly. 'You went through my bag?'

'Of course I did. I'm not stupid.'

'Find anything interesting?'

'Besides tampons and lipstick?' I squeeze my lips together, rolling my eyes. 'I think I recognise you, you know,' he adds.

'That's nice. Most people do. I'm quite famous.'

The man snorts and something dark flashes across his face. A frown, a shadow ... something. His accent is indecipherable. I'm no good with accents, but he certainly doesn't talk like a Londoner. He looks to be travelling by himself; no hint of another person anywhere that I can see.

'What's your name?' I ask. 'I may as well know the name of my travel companion.'

He pauses for a few moments and then says, 'Curtis Redding.'

I lift my eyebrows in response but say nothing. It sounds like a posh name, but he's the furthest thing from posh. He looks and smells like a homeless person, but with better hair and straighter teeth.

I sit quietly for a few minutes, glancing over at Curtis every few seconds as if I'm expecting him to attack me. I stare down at my bare feet, which are filthy and sore. I left my heels in my car.

'Where are we headed?' I ask. I've never been good with silence, except if I want it to be silent and, right now, I feel as if I should get to know the man who's basically keeping me and my bag hostage.

'*We* aren't heading anywhere.'

'Okay, so where are *you* headed?'

'Anywhere the road takes me.'

'Are you being philosophical?'

'Huh?'

'Oh, I'm sorry. Do you not know that big word?'

'Fuck off.'

I shudder at his use of vile language and fiddle with my hands, picking at the pink gel on my nails, which had started peeling off yesterday. I can't stand having chipped nails. It makes my skin crawl.

'What was that?' he asks.

'What was what?'

'That shudder.'

'What shudder?'

'I just said *fuck* and you shuddered.'

I shudder again; this time attempting to hide it by scratching the side of my face. 'I don't like swear words.'

'No shit.'

Another shudder. 'Stop it.'

'Say fuck.'

Shudder. 'No.' I wish I'd never said anything.

Curtis laughs and thumps the steering wheel with his hands. 'This could be fun. Are you telling me you've never said a swear word in your entire life?'

'No, I'm not saying that at all.'

'Then why don't you swear? It's part of everyday language for most people.'

'Well, I can assure you that I'm not like *most people*. I don't *need* to swear. Unlike most people, I can get my point across by using language that is deemed appropriate. I have a vast vocabulary, I'll have you know.'

'Jesus Christ, you sound like a fucking robot.' I shudder violently and try and cover it up again by rubbing my arms up and down as if I'm cold. 'There must be another *actual* reason why you don't swear.'

'I can assure you, there isn't.'

Curtis stares ahead at the winding road for a while and I continue to shiver next to him. I'm not sure why I'm cold because it's blinding sunshine outside and the car temperature gauge says it's nearly twenty-five degrees.

Eventually, he shifts sideways, leans behind him to the back seat and drags across a leather jacket, dumping it on my lap without saying a word. I hesitate for a few seconds before putting it on, unsure if I want to put my arms through a piece of material that doesn't look as if it's seen the inside of a washing machine for nearly a decade. It smells a bit too. The brown leather is heavily worn in places, but as soon as my arms slide through the sleeves, I feel warmer.

'Thanks,' I mutter.

'What will it take for you to say fuck?'

For goodness sake. He's *still* on this. 'Why is it such a big deal to you that I don't swear?'

'Because it's fucking weird, that's why. I tell you what, I'll make a deal with you. I'll give you your bag back if you say the big C word right now.'

After shuddering, I turn my head to look at him. 'Are you being serious?'

'Totally.'

'Why don't *you* say the C word?'

'Because I'm afraid that if I do you might burst into tears or something and I don't like dealing with crying women.'

'You'll seriously give me my bag back if I say *that* word?'

'Yes.'

I sigh heavily and stare at the open road. How can I trust this man? He can't be serious about this, can he? I already know that I won't do it, but a small part of me is enjoying making him wait for my answer. I breathe in deep, pushing my ample breasts out in front of me. I notice his eyes drift away from the road for a second.

'No,' I say.

Curtis lets out a long breath. 'Suit yourself, Barbie.'

'Please stop calling me that.'

'No.'

My stomach grumbles loudly and I squirm in my seat. I'd been unable to find breakfast this morning and there'd been no further seagulls to fight with for scraps of food.

'There's a chocolate bar in the glove box,' he says with a nod.

I open it and pull out a Twix. It's squashed and melted. 'How long has this been in here?'

'Beats me.'

I sigh as I consider whether to risk my health by eating an old chocolate bar or continue to starve.

'Are you afraid it's going to kill you or something? It's chocolate. It doesn't have an expiration date.'

'Everything has an expiration date.'

'No, it doesn't.'

'Yes, it does.'

'Do you always have to argue over everything?'

'No, I'm merely stating a fact.'

'Are you going to be this annoying all the time?'

I hold my breath, open the wrapper and take a bite. I almost melt off the seat. Oh wow. It tastes like gooey, chocolate heaven. I've never been so hungry in my life, not even when I was locked in that room by ... you know what, it doesn't matter.

I nod and chew simultaneously and make some sort of un-ladylike noise in response to his question.

'That's what I'm afraid of,' mumbles Curtis.

Chapter Eighteen

HANNAH
7 July 2022 – 01:30 a.m.

I have the car window all the way down and my eyes closed against the rushing air, which is causing me to shiver, but it makes me feel less nauseous, less … afraid. Yes, I'm afraid. I've willingly climbed into a car with a strange man who I don't know, but, then again, I don't know who *I* am either, and it had been a better idea than standing around in the cold not knowing which way to turn and having no place to go.

At least this man – Bryan Matthews – has shown up and seems to know who I am. Maybe my memories will return the longer I spend with him, or maybe they won't, and I'll be forced to start a new life, and create a new identity.

Bryan told me about the heart tattoo. Thankfully, it's not a real one. The fact I allowed him to draw on me with a permanent marker pen at some point tells me that we must have gotten … *close,* but how close exactly did we get? I lick my index finger and then rub it over the 'Bryan Forever' inscription, attempting to remove the writing and heart, but all it does is smudge it into a crude blob.

My head throbs. Not a small, light throb like the beginnings of a headache, but a pounding, sickness-inducing, stampede-of-elephants-clambering-around-inside-my-head type of throb. That can't be a good sign. I don't know a lot about amnesia (just like I don't know a lot about anything right now), but I do know it usually occurs when someone has received a blow to the head or, in some cases, suffered through a severe trauma.

'How did I hit my head again?' I turn my face away from the cold air and wind the window up a little, but not all the way. I still need the fresh air. If I didn't have it, I know I'd start to feel claustrophobic inside this tin can.

'It's a long story,' replies Bryan, never taking his dark eyes off the even darker road.

'You keep saying that, but I'm sitting here now and we're driving to God-only-knows-where, so I think you'd better start explaining.'

Bryan sighs loudly, gripping the steering wheel tighter. He's been keeping his grip at the ten and two o'clock positions the entire time he's been driving, never once dropping his posture. 'A man attacked you. You fell, I think, and you hit your head, but that was before he attacked you. To be honest, I'm not entirely sure what happened. I wasn't there when you fell.'

'What man? You?'

'No, not me. Someone else.'

'Who?'

'You really don't remember?'

'No!'

'His name was Curtis Redding.'

I focus my gaze on the road ahead, only able to make out the dim cats' eyes and a few faded white lines in the middle. 'I don't recognise the name.'

'Are you sure?'

'Why do you keep asking me that? I've told you a dozen times ... I don't remember anything!'

'Fuck ...' Bryan mutters a few other words, which I'm not able to catch, and then indicates left, turning down an even narrower road, this one void of any markings whatsoever. My heart leaps in my chest at the thought of leaving the main road; the thought of leaving civilisation. It feels as if I'm being driven down the road to my certain doom.

I close my eyes and, without warning, the car jerks and comes to an abrupt halt. My body is forced forwards as the seat belt bites into my shoulder, and my head flops back and forth like a rag doll. Pain erupts in my head once more, almost causing me to pass out.

'What the—' My eyes open and I quickly realise why we've stopped. A lone sheep is standing in the middle of the road, staring at us head-on, stamping its foot.

'Fucking sheep,' says Bryan.

I roll my neck from side to side as adrenaline pumps through my body.

A flash—

Another flash—

A memory—

An image of a man throwing himself at me appears before my eyes. There is blood and a loud shout and then pain. I fall – he falls – but nothing else comes to me. The memory is still lodged behind a wall in my mind, but the wall has a large crack in it. I need to work away at that crack until it crumbles.

'I remember something,' I murmur.

Bryan looks at me briefly and then inches the car forwards towards the stubborn sheep, which is still standing its ground. Its eyes are glowing white in the headlights. Bryan beeps the horn twice, but the animal refuses to move an inch. Who knew sheep were so brave?

'Fuck this.'

I watch with mild amusement as Bryan puts the car in park, opens the door, gets out and marches up to the sheep. 'Fucking move!' he bellows.

There they are … man and sheep; both unwilling to back down.

I bite back a laugh.

Another flash—

My head explodes with pain.

Memory after memory piles into my brain one after the other as I recall how a man (presumably Curtis Redding, but I can't be certain as I still don't recognise him) grabs my hair and pulls me to my feet. He starts dragging me along the floor as if I weigh nothing more than a sack of potatoes. Then I get up and tackle him. We tumble and fall down a small cliff and then—

There is another memory after that which is on the cusp of appearing, but all I can see is a cloudy fog in my head. Something else happened after that, but what? Does Bryan know more than he's letting on? What isn't he telling me?

There is something else in my mind too …

A flash of blonde hair. A woman. But who is she? Where is she? And why can I not stop picturing her face?

I stare at Bryan as he finally manages to shoo the sheep off the road. I wish I could read his thoughts. Something doesn't add up ...

Dear Diary

Date: 27 May 2004

Dear Diary,

Being fourteen sucks for three reasons.
One: You're old enough to basically look after yourself, but still not classed as a legal adult, so you can't do all the cool stuff like drink, smoke and drive a car.
Two: Your body starts changing in weird ways and you have no idea what's going on. Some days you wake up and think, 'where the fuck did that come from?' or 'that's new'.
Three: You still get treated like a child by most of the adult population.

Date: 29 May 2004

Dear Diary,

I swore for the first time today. Out loud. I swear all the fucking time in my head and on paper. Bryan Matthews swears all the time, and everyone thinks it's cool (except for the teacher when she overheard him, and he was sent to detention). I thought I'd try and be cool like him, so I swore at a teacher. It was nothing serious. I only told her to 'go to hell'. It's not even a proper swear word for fuck's sake! Anyway ... long story short, I got sent to detention. Then the teacher called my dad. Then I got grounded for a week. Yep, being fourteen definitely sucks. But still, me and Bryan became closer because of it, so I'm taking that as a win.

Date: 2 June 2004

Dear Diary,

I'm still grounded. Can you believe it? I've read every book in my room at least three times. I'm only allowed to go to school and come back and that's it. I swear, when I'm grown up, I'm going to swear every fucking day ...

Date: 19 June 2004

Dear Diary,

I'm finally free! Yey! I was grounded an extra two weeks because I swore at a teacher again. I called her a whore, but, in my defence, Bryan called her that first, but he got away with it because he said it quietly. I said it a bit too loud. My bad. Come to think of it, Bryan is always getting away with shit and I'm always the one getting told off. How is that fair? Bryan bullied another kid today. We followed them on the way home from school. They'd just bought an ice cream. Bryan stopped them on the street and smashed the ice cream into their face. It dripped all down their front and onto their clothes. It was chocolate too and they were wearing a white top. Then he managed to smear some on their bum, so it looked as if they'd shit themselves. It was hilarious.

Chapter Nineteen

2 July 2022 – 09:00 a.m.

He was pleased she hadn't agreed to take his offer of swearing to get her bag back because the more he thought about it, the more he imagined there was something in her bag that was worth risking her life over. What sane woman would willingly get into a car with a man she'd never met after tracking him down over one-hundred miles away? Maybe she wasn't sane. Maybe she was completely crazy and deluded and would end up stabbing him while he slept. Why did he always attract the crazy ones? He still thought she might be fun to play with for a while though. Plus, what harm was she doing? He hoped those didn't turn out to be his famous last words.

He glanced at his passenger out of the corner of his eye, watching as she chewed noisily on the chocolate bar. She seemed to be savouring every mouthful as if she hadn't eaten for days. God, she was infuriating though. And now he was stuck with her until he could decide what to do with her. He had rope in the boot; at least he had the last time he'd looked. Maybe he could tie her up and leave her somewhere. She'd be perfectly safe until some unsuspecting bystander came along and found her. No, come to think of it, that was a bad idea because when she was found it would raise suspicion and she knew exactly what he looked like now. She'd call the police and have him hunted down like a dog.

Goddamn this fucking woman!

He couldn't make up his mind. He checked his phone, which was perched precariously on the dashboard.

'Are you expecting a call?' asked Barbie.

'No.'

'Then why do you keep looking at your phone?'

He sighed heavily. 'You don't miss much, do you?'

'Hey, I'm not just a pretty face.'

He scoffed. 'I'm just checking to see if a hundred grand has magically appeared in my account and then I can kick you and your stupid bag to the curb.'

'Just give me my bag back and I'll leave. This thing has gone on long enough now.'

'What thing?'

'This … whatever *this* is … this show of male dominance or whatever.'

He threw his head back and laughed. 'You're hilarious.'

'Why did you try and blackmail me? What do you need £100,000 for?'

He was silent for a while, pondering his answer. He couldn't let his mask slip, not now. 'I like money.'

'Everyone likes money. Why not ask for more?'

'I didn't know you were stinking rich at the time.'

'So, you do know who I am then.'

He shrugged his response, which seemed to irritate her somewhat as she pouted her lips at him as she spoke.

'So, you must also know how powerful and high profile I am. When word gets out that you've kidnapped me then—'

'I'm gonna stop you right there. Kidnapped? You think I've *kidnapped* you?'

'What else would you call it?'

'Let me remind you about something, Barbie. You're the one who went and tracked down a stranger. You're the one who willingly got into my car. The fact you're here right now is all on *you*.'

'Yes, but you started it because you tried to blackmail me.'

He clenched his jaw. 'I swear you're the most annoying woman I've ever met, and I've met a lot of annoying women. I have duct tape and rope in the boot and I'm not afraid to use them.'

Barbie bit her full bottom lip and stared out the window. It seemed he'd won this round …

'I need to use the ladies' room.'

'Can't you just say you need a piss, like a normal person?'

'I'd rather die.'

'I'll have you dropping your snooty rich girl talk soon and swearing like a sailor.'

'I highly doubt that.'

He smirked as he pulled off the main road and down a smaller, narrower road, full of potholes with grass growing in the middle. The car didn't have the best suspension, so he slowed down to avoid causing any damage. He stopped the car in a small lay-by, switched off the engine and allowed his body to relax into the plush seat as he folded his arms across his chest, waiting.

'Why have we stopped?'

'There's your *ladies' room*.' He nodded at a nearby copse of trees and bushes.

'Are you joking? I'm not going in the bushes like an animal.'

'Then hold it.' He started the engine.

Barbie crossed her arms and huffed.

There was silence in the car for all of ten seconds before she flung the door open and got out, muttering some incoherent words. His lips curled into another smirk. He wasn't worried about her running off; her bag was still in the car, and they were miles away from the nearest town. He watched her with amused interest as she picked her way delicately over the gravel and inched herself into the undergrowth.

Oh, this was going to be fun to watch.

Chapter Twenty

ASHLEIGH
2 July 2022 – 09:10 a.m.

I have never felt so humiliated in my entire life. I cannot believe I'm being forced to urinate in a bush on the side of the road like a common woodland creature.

Oh no … What if there are bears in these woods?

Wait … Bears don't roam around freely in this country, do they? What am I thinking? Hungry wolves are a strong possibility though or maybe really big squirrels, which are basically rats with cuter outfits.

My mind is all over the place, quite possibly because I'm dehydrated and starving. I can't think straight. The Twix had curbed my hunger for about ten minutes. I'd had a major sugar high and then crashed like a nose-diving plane not long afterwards. I need more food soon otherwise my stomach is going to start gorging on itself. I miss my protein, high-fibre smoothies with added vitamins and minerals. I also miss pizza.

As I pick my way over the gravel, I do my best not to wince at every sound coming from the trees in front of me, or every time a stone digs into the soles of my feet. My poor beauty therapist who does my pedicures is going to have a heart attack when she sees the state of them. She'll probably have to cancel all her other appointments for the rest of the day so she can sort them out and get them looking their best again. There's a blister forming on my left heel and numerous cuts on the other, not to mention my nail varnish has lost its shine and is chipping in the corners.

Once I'm far enough into the woods I glance back at the car, satisfied that Curtis can't see me. I could make a run for it, just take off in the opposite direction and never look back, but then what would be the point in that? I still don't have my bag and it is what I came all this way for and why I'm putting my life on the line. Plus, it would be a silly idea to run away right now because I have no idea where I am and there *could* actually be bears, wolves, or gigantic squirrels in these woods who might fancy chasing a scared woman through the trees.

I drag my knickers down my thighs, grimacing at the fact I've been wearing them for over twenty-four hours, and perform an awkward squat, feeling momentarily elated as I urinate on the ground for the very first time in my life.

But wait? Now what?

I don't have any toilet paper to wipe …

Well … here goes nothing.

I perform a funny little shake, but I still get a drip or two on my legs. I roll my eyes as I slide my knickers back up my thighs, wondering how much longer I'll have to wear them. I need to get my bag back. I need clean underwear. Yes, I keep clean underwear in my bag, ever since an ill-fated incident in a nightclub where … actually, I'd rather not talk about it. I still get nightmares about it.

That's when I hear a crack in the trees behind me. I spin around, heart thumping, as I scan the area, my eyes on high alert for anything out of the ordinary, like a vicious grizzly bear rearing up on its hind legs, a killer wolf with rabies, or a humongous squirrel with blood dripping from its mouth. It may be warm outside, but the growing cloud cover has darkened the sky, which means the woods look shadowy and spooky and have scary-looking shapes peering out from behind the trees that may or not be a crazed maniac waiting to pounce.

'Hello?' I call out, squinting my eyes, as if that will help them magically see better.

Another cracking sound.

I take a step back, stepping on a twig.

I scream and trip over my own legs, landing in the puddle of my urine. If there was ever a time to start swearing, I'd say this was a pretty good moment.

The sound of footsteps makes me look up. Curtis is standing over me, a smug and arrogant grin across his stupid face. His jaw is clenched, as if he's fighting the urge to burst out laughing.

'Did you break a fingernail or something?'

'No. I thought I saw something in the trees.'

'It's probably a squirrel. Watch out, cos they can bite.'

'Are there actually killer squirrels out there?'

Curtis looks at me blankly. 'Are you insane?' he asks.

'No ... I ... never mind, doesn't matter. Will you help me up, please?'

Curtis reaches out his hand, grabs my arm and hauls me to my feet with ease. He sniffs the air and grimaces. 'What's that smell?'

'I … I …' *Oh God*. I've never been so embarrassed.

'Did you piss yourself?' I shudder at the word. 'What … I can't even say *piss*?'

'I fell over and landed … in the wet spot.'

Curtis stares at me for five long seconds, his face deadpan, and then bursts into hysterical laughter. He laughs so hard that he has to bend over and lean on his knees to try and catch his breath. I bite my lip as I feel it start to wobble. But I can't help it … I laugh too. It bursts out of me before I can stop it and, before I know it, I'm also bent over double, clutching my sides.

It feels good to laugh. If I don't, I fear I might cry instead.

I manage to stand up straight and gingerly step over the gravel and twigs back towards the car. Curtis is still chuckling to himself. I stop walking when I realise he isn't following me.

'What?' He's stopped laughing now, staring into the woods. 'Did you see something too?'

'Like you said, probably just a killer squirrel,' he replies.

'That's comforting.'

I reluctantly get back into the car and remain quiet as we pull out onto the road. I lean against the headrest and close my eyes, feeling the rhythmic motion of the car as it lulls me into a relaxed state.

My eyelids flutter open. My neck is leaning at an awkward angle and, as I straighten it, a sharp pain shoots through my muscles. I wince and sit up straighter.

'Ah, she lives.'

'Huh?'

'You've been asleep for almost six hours, Barbie.'

'What?'

'It's three in the afternoon.'

I stare blankly ahead and blink several times, attempting to kick-start my brain into gear. Then it all comes rushing back to me.

Ah yes, I'm in a car with a strange man who stole my bag. Delightful.

'What's that smell?'

'I'm pretty sure that's you.'

'Urrgg, I feel disgusting.'

'Well, you look pretty disgusting too.'

'Like you're one to talk.'

'Is that any way to speak to someone who bought you a whole bag of food and drink?'

I open my mouth, on autopilot to argue back, but then his words click into place. 'Y-You have food? Real food and ... and water?'

Curtis grins as he reaches down between my legs into the passenger foot well. He expertly keeps his eyes on the road and one hand on the wheel as he hands me a TESCO carrier bag. My eyes are immediately drawn to the sandwich and bottle of water, which I open and down in one go.

'You're welcome.'

I gulp the last drop and sheepishly look at him. 'Sorry ... Thank you ...' Curtis nods and focusses his attention back on the road. I tear into the sandwich, not even caring what the filling is (it's cheese and ham; not my all-time favourite, but I'm not complaining). 'Where are we?'

'Scotland.'

I choke on a bite of sandwich. 'Scotland! Whereabouts in Scotland?'

'We passed Edinburgh about half an hour ago.'

I chew my food, gulping it down as fast as possible and speak with my mouth full. 'Why are we in Scotland?'

'Didn't your mother ever teach you not to talk with your mouth full? An upper-class British girl should know better.'

I swallow. 'I'm hungry.'

'No shit.'

I shudder as I wipe my mouth. 'Can I check my phone quickly?' I ask, sounding hopeful. 'Just to make sure no one is freaking out about me being away.'

'Nice try. No.'

'Please?'

'No, but I'll check it for you.'

I sigh forcefully, digging into the bag to see what other surprises await. 'Fine.' I find a packet of crisps. Yes! Cheese and onion flavour; again, not my favourite, but I'm beyond grateful.

Curtis leans over and plunges his hand down between my legs again and under the car seat. I gasp, taken aback by his abruptness, squeezing my thighs together. He grins as he pulls out my bag.

'Relax, Barbie. You're not my type.'

'What? Blonde and beautiful?'

'Fake.'

'As if the trailer trash you probably grew up around is any better,' I snap.

Curtis stares at me. 'It's better than a spoilt bitch who has never worked a hard day in her life and has everything handed to her on a diamond-encrusted platter, and who feels the need to fake everything about herself just to get more followers on fucking Instagram or TikTok.'

My body involuntarily shudders at his language, but my skin flushes with anger. 'How dare you! Is that what you think I'm like?'

'Prove me wrong. I dare you.'

'I shouldn't have to justify my existence to a low-life, poor, scruffy-looking loser who has to steal women's bags just to get by. You're pathetic and a criminal and you deserve to be in jail for the rest of your life and, when I eventually get my bag back, that's exactly where you'll be going.' I tear open the bag of crisps and start munching as I stare out the window, my face burning.

There's a long silence as he scrolls through my phone.

'You don't have any messages,' he replies, eventually.

'What?'

'No one has messaged you.'

'No one?'

'No.'

'No one at all?'

'You do understand English, right?'

I attempt to snatch the phone out of his hand, but he's too quick and pulls it away at the last second. 'I don't believe you.'

'Well, there's a shock. Fine, don't believe me? Here ... see for yourself, but don't be calling the cops or I'll knock you out.' He passes me the phone, which I grab as if it's my only lifeline.

The moment my fingers touch the familiar oblong object they begin scrolling and tapping away as if they've never been apart. My eyes absorb the information on the screen, instantly scanning all the messaging apps and social media inboxes. There are the usual comments on pictures and reels I've posted, and the odd message regarding what I'm wearing or whatever, but no messages whatsoever from people wondering where I am or if I'm okay.

No WhatsApp messages.

No text messages.

No missed calls.

Nothing.

That's really ... odd.

Maybe Curtis deleted them all before he handed me the phone. But unless he has the quickest fingers known to man there is no way he could have done it without me seeing. I lower the phone to my lap, the once-tight grip fading, and stare blankly out of the window again. The screen gently dies in my hand.

'Why does no one care that I'm missing?' I ask.

Curtis shrugs. 'Does anyone even *know* you're missing? You told someone that you were leaving, right?'

'Not really, no. I met Mrs Brown in the hallway, but she didn't even know I'd been in a car accident at the time. I don't understand ... No one cares where I am? No one at all?' I sit and ponder for a while as I try and wrap my head around the fact no one in my life cares I've been missing for over twenty-four hours. No one has noticed I haven't posted on social media. I *always* post on social media, almost every hour of my life is on there, recorded and documented for the world to see, yet there's no one out there who cares enough to send me a message asking if I'm okay ... or just to check in.

I hand Curtis my phone and he looks at me with a frown, as if he doesn't understand what I'm doing. 'I don't want it,' I say, a solemn tone to my voice. And I mean it too. The idea of looking at my phone now makes my stomach flip, and not in a good way.

'Okay, look ... I understand you're going through some sort of weird crisis right now, but there's no need to freak out, okay? I'm sure, come tomorrow morning, there will be a news report regarding your disappearance, and they'll have the cops out searching for you with dogs and helicopters and offer a million-pound reward for your safe return.'

'Do you really think so?' Curtis rolls his eyes at me. 'Right ... you were being sarcastic.'

'Try not to freak out about something so trivial.'

'Trivial? You think my life is trivial? You have no idea who I am, not really. I'm an important businesswoman, model and social media icon. I earn millions from endorsements. I get hundreds of offers for huge modelling contracts every year. Everyone wants to be me. Everyone wants to be my friend.'

'And yet, no one has messaged you in more than twenty-four hours. Let me take a wild guess here ... *you're* always the one who calls *them*? Maybe you should wake up, Barbie, and re-evaluate your life choices. Answer me this right now without thinking ... Who's your best friend in the whole wide world?'

My mouth opens, but no words come out.

The truth is ... he's right. He's right about all of it. I have no *real* friends. Only people who want something from me, who use me to get themselves noticed, who rely on me to promote their products. I don't have a girlfriend I can call to gossip with. No one invites me out for drinks on a Friday night. I'm always the one calling them and inviting myself along. The thing is ... I know all this already. It's not new information, but this is the first time I'm seeing things from a different angle; a different perspective. And I don't like what I'm seeing.

I've always assumed that everyone loves me. They always smile at me and seem happy to talk to me. I have an army of business associates who are always wanting my advice about what to do, yet they haven't bothered to check in with me, even after I missed that meeting. What about my agent? Why has she not called to confirm our plans for tomorrow? I'm sure I had a few more meetings lined up. Nothing makes sense and, for the first time in my life, I feel utterly and completely alone.

'I don't even know what I'm supposed to do anymore.' I let the words hang in the air for a while as I watch the world pass me by. In that moment I notice the beauty of the real world, outside of a phone screen.

Wow … Scotland is breathtaking.

The wide-open spaces, the greenery, the mountains. It's all so spectacular and I find my frown slowly turning into a smile as my eyes absorb the magnificence all around me. In this moment, I find my mind clearing of all negative thoughts, of all worries and stress.

Is it time to leave the old Ashleigh in the past?

Am I missing something here?

How to Commit the Perfect Murder
Step Five

Don't Trust Anyone

This one is a no-brainer. All you need to do is answer this one simple question: do you trust anyone enough to tell them that you're going to kill someone? If the answer is no (and it most definitely *will* be) then that's all you need to know. Be honest with yourself. Would you really trust your best friend or your partner to not turn you in to the police for plotting to murder someone?

No. Exactly.

The bottom line is that you can't trust anyone in this day and age. Everyone is out for themselves in one way or another, which means you have to be too, if you want to succeed. Yes, make friends if you absolutely must, blend in and all that crap, but don't trust anyone. The moment you do, you've failed.

Think about it this way: only you know your plan inside and out. If you attempt to bring someone else in on it, then it's twice as likely fail and the more people you trust and invite into your secret circle the more chances there are of failing.

Once you get this into your head, it's plain sailing. It's you and you alone who will accomplish your plan. No one else.

After you've completed your plan, then maybe you can branch out and start trusting people, but never share your plan with anyone. *Anyone*. Got it? It's your burden to carry and you really don't want someone knowing all your dirty secrets.

Trust me.

Chapter Twenty-One

HANNAH
7 July 2022 – 02:30 a.m.

My head is pounding so hard I can barely keep my eyes open as we continue to drive along the country roads. From what I can decipher, due to the dual-language road signs, we are somewhere in Wales. My stomach churns uncomfortably at every bend and my vision blurs. I try to fight against the urge to vomit, but it overwhelms me, and eventually, I shout at Bryan to stop the car.

I barely make it out the door before my stomach releases its contents, but I clearly haven't eaten for a while because only bile comes up. I hear a car door open and shut and then Bryan comes and stands beside me. He holds out a bottle of water. Once I stop retching, I take it and sip.

'Thanks,' I say.

'I think you might have a serious concussion.'

'Gee … you think?'

'Let me take a look at your head.' He leans over to touch me, but I dodge out of reach. 'Han, I'm trying to help you. I just want to check the stitches.'

'I don't need your help, and who stitched me up?'

'I beg to differ, and it was me.'

'You? Are you a doctor?'

'Do I look like a doctor to you?'

I sigh, frustration as clear as day across my face. 'Look, I'm just trying to figure all this out. How would you feel

149

if you woke up in a weird, fake hospital and some stranger grabbed you and forced you to go with them? I keep having random flashes of memory, but none of them make any sense.'

'Tell me. What are you remembering?'

I take another sip of water, swirl it around my mouth and then spit it out. 'I remember I was attacked by a man, and we fell, but everything is jumbled. I think there was a lot of blood. Also ... who's Ashleigh Carmichael?'

Bryan tilts his head sideways. 'Wait ... you don't remember her either?'

'No, I told you, I barely remember anything, but her name is familiar, and her blonde hair keeps appearing in my mind. Who is she?'

'She's ... She's no one you need to worry about right now.'

'Why not?'

'Because she no longer exists.'

I gasp. 'Oh my God, did you kill her?'

'What? No! I didn't fucking kill her. Why are you so quick to jump to the worst possible conclusion about me? I'm the good guy, okay?'

'And what ... Curtis Redding is the bad guy?'

'Something like that.'

'So where is Curtis now?'

Bryan glances back at the car. I follow his eye line, not liking where this is going. 'He's tied up in the boot.'

Chapter Twenty-Two

3 July 2022 – 03:31 a.m.

Despite Barbie's constant complaining at the fact she smelled bad and needed a five-hour long shower, he'd refused to book them into a hotel for the night. It was too risky, and he needed to save money. Instead, he parked the car somewhere in the Cairngorms National Park and told her to shut up and go to sleep. And he was surprised when she had done so without too much resistance. She must have been exhausted because her body relaxed against the door and her mouth parted within minutes. As soon as she started snoring gently, he placed another jacket under her head, so she didn't have a sore neck when she woke up again. A dribble of drool hung from the side of her mouth, and he smirked at how cute she looked.

Hours later, he woke with a start. His first thought was that Barbie had fled while he'd been dreaming, but, after seeing her still slumped in the passenger seat beside him, the moonlight highlighting her face and snoring softly, he relaxed.

But what had woken him?

He sat up straighter, rubbing the back of his neck and then his eyes. He squinted into the inky night. Thanks to the lack of light pollution in this rural landscape, it was difficult to make out any sort of shape, apart from the tall trees nearby.

The silence was ... too quiet.

The hairs on the back of his neck raised and goosebumps danced across his skin under his shirt. There was someone or something out there, but who or what? Barbie's ridiculous assumption of giant killer squirrels entered his mind, and he couldn't help but smile. As far as he could tell when he'd parked up, they hadn't been near a farm or a local village; he'd made sure of it. The only life forms for miles were sheep and the odd free-roaming wild pony.

Convinced that Barbie was sound asleep, he reached behind his seat and pulled out a claw hammer, a weapon he'd hidden there earlier. Then he opened the car door as quietly as he could, leaving it ajar so as not to disturb her slumber, and crept over the gravel, which, despite his efforts, still made a louder crunching sound than he would've liked.

Yes … There …

A humanoid shadow up ahead.

Hammer raised, he crept closer to the looming silhouette. His heart thudded hard in his chest, causing his breathing to become laboured and erratic. He dared not make a sound, so he held his breath as he approached.

But it was nothing; a trick of the moonlight – just a scarily shaped tree trunk and branches.

A snap of a twig sounded up ahead. It was unmistakable … Someone had stepped on it and broken it.

He froze, his eyes focussed like laser beams, willing them to find the cause of the noise. But there was nothing but the light summer breeze rustling through the trees, which still looked eerily like long limbs.

He shuddered, turning back towards the car. That's when he saw a dark shape hunched low, approaching the rear of it. He sprang into action, his skin coming alive with more goosebumps as he crept closer. His immediate response was to defend his car and, more importantly, the sleeping, vulnerable woman inside.

It was definitely a man.

It was *him*.

And he was attempting to pry open the boot of the car.

He performed a wide circle to avoid the intruder's line of sight and snuck up behind him, but the crunch of gravel underfoot let him down again and gave away his position. The intruder spun around, a look of sheer horror on his face as his mouth dropped open. He tackled the solid lump against the car, pinning his body against it. He tried to ignore the scratches that would no doubt appear on the paintwork due to the manoeuvre as he grabbed the man's light jacket and held him tight, raising the hammer above his head, ready at any second to deal the fatal blow.

'What the fuck are you doing here?' he spat. 'How did you find me?'

'That's not really the right question you should be asking, is it?' answered the intruder, who was holding his hands up. He didn't look afraid, despite holding a defensive position.

'Give me one good reason why I shouldn't split open your skull right now.'

The man dropped his hands to his side, his body language shifting to one of strength and determination. He puffed his chest out, aggression emanating from every movement.

He stood his ground, the hammer still raised in his right hand, his other clenched at his side.

'It's over,' said the man. 'You've lost.'

He shook his head. 'It's not over till I say it's over.' He raised the hammer a few inches higher and then smashed it across the intruder's face.

Chapter Twenty-Three

ASHLEIGH
3 July 2022 – 03:45 a.m.

I jolt awake from sleep just as the scary man in my dream is about to catch me. I'm quite glad a random noise wakes me before I'm killed. I don't like being killed in my dreams. It's always very disconcerting.

What's that noise?

It sounds like it's coming from the back of the car.

I lift my head off the jacket that's tucked under it (Curtis must have put it there once I'd fallen asleep) and wipe the drool from my otherwise dry lips. The darkness is so thick I can barely see anything, even with the moonlight above, but there's certainly a rustling noise coming from nearby.

That's when the clouds part and the light from the moon briefly illuminates Curtis, who's creeping around near the trees.

What's he doing? And what's he holding?

There's that sound again; a sort of scuffling noise.

I turn and crane my neck towards the rear of the car and see a man hunched over it. I let out a short gasp and cover my mouth to stop from screaming. I don't recognise him. It's not Curtis. Is the man trying to break into the boot?

I remain quiet as I watch Curtis perform a wide circle around the area and then disappear. Has he just left me alone with this strange man to be stabbed to death? Oh no ...

'What the fuck are you doing here?' Curtis says. 'How did you find me?'

'That's not really the right question you should be asking, is it?' comes a new male voice I don't recognise. I can barely see either of them because I'm looking at them through the car interior, but it looks as if Curtis is holding an object in his right hand above his head.

'Give me one good reason why I shouldn't split open your skull right now.'

I hold my breath, too afraid to even move.

'It's over,' says the strange man. The tone of his voice tells me he isn't afraid. 'You've lost.'

'It's not over till I say it's over.'

Curtis raises his arm higher and then there's a horrible crack as he hits the man across the head. I open my mouth to scream, but no sound escapes; nothing. Not even a whimper. I turn away and close my eyes, humming my favourite tune in my head, hoping it will distract me from the terror, but it doesn't.

There's a loud thud and then silence.

I keep my eyes closed as footsteps approach. The passenger side door is wrenched open and that's when I let out the blood-curdling scream that's been stuck in my throat for the past minute. I do that thing all women do in old-school horror movies; I cover my face with my hands and scream through my fingers, then attempt to scurry backwards away from my attacker. I get myself wedged against the centre column in my haste and my dress rides up my thighs and starts gathering around my waist, my pink knickers on show.

'Stop screaming!' shouts Curtis.

But, of course, I don't stop.

I've just witnessed a murder.

I somehow manage to get into the driving seat and scrabble around for the door handle, but the door is already open, so I fall through it and onto the gravel in a heap, my hair sticking to my face. The stones scratch my bare skin as I crawl forwards, attempting to get my legs to work so I can stand and run away, but they have turned to jelly in the past two minutes. My head is spinning so fast I don't even know which way to turn.

Fast footsteps approach.

He's after me; I know he is.

Curtis grabs my flailing limbs and pins me down on the ground. 'Stop fucking screaming ... please!' he pants just as I manage to kick him in the face with my left foot. And it really hurts. Who knew kicking someone with bare feet hurt so much?

He grunts, steps back slightly, but then regains his composure and continues to hold me down on the ground. 'I'm not going to hurt you. Just stop and listen to me. Give me a chance to explain.'

I make a weird whimpering noise, which sounds vaguely like a dying cat. I bite my bottom lip to stop it from quivering and I'm pretty sure a trickle of urine escapes from my bladder. *So much for those pelvic floor exercises I do daily.*

'Please don't hurt me,' I beg.

'I'm not going to hurt you. If I wanted to hurt you I'd have done so hours ago. Just calm down and listen to me, will ya? It's not what you think.'

'Really? So, you didn't just kill someone by bashing their head in?'

Curtis doesn't answer. We stare at each other for several seconds and then I scream again, as loud as I can, but my voice starts cracking and then I start to cry.

'Stop. Please ... just stop. Just listen.' Curtis lets go of my wrists. I rub them instinctively. I'm pretty sure I'll bruise because I tend to bruise like a peach. That time when my ex-boyfriend beat me up, I was black and blue for weeks. It took a mountain of make-up to cover. Luckily, no one seemed to notice ... either that or they didn't care.

I wedge my back against the side of the car and rest my head against it as I continue to weep softly. Snot and tears stream from my nose and eyes and mix together on my chin. I've got nothing to use as a wipe except for the sleeve of the jacket I'm wearing. I don't care if I've ruined it.

Curtis, seemingly convinced I won't start running or screaming again, collapses to the ground and kneels in front of me. 'Yes ... I attacked that guy. But, if I hadn't, you'd probably be dead right now. Also ... he's not dead. I didn't kill him.'

'H-He's not dead?'

'No. I just knocked him out. He'll have a mighty headache when he wakes up.'

'Who is he?'

Curtis's eyes flick towards the back of the car where the collapsed body is laying. 'He ... His name is Curtis Redding.'

Alarm bells start ringing in my head. Did I hear him correctly or is my brain so overwhelmed right now that I'm hearing things?

'B-But ... that's your name. You told me *your* name was Curtis Redding.'

He shakes his head. 'No ... I lied. My name's Bryan Matthews.'

Chapter Twenty-Four

CURTIS
One day earlier

Bryan fucking Matthews. He'd showed up, dragged Curtis out of the car, knocked him unconscious, driven him to the middle of nowhere and dumped him in a stinking alley. He'd also taken what little money he had and his phone. If Curtis hadn't already been planning to, he'd have wanted to track him down and kill him.

This was not part of the plan, but when had that ever stopped him before? He knew he needed to act fast if he was going to catch Bryan before he moved on again. And, thanks to tipping him off about Blondie, he could almost guarantee that he'd wait around to see if she turned up with the money. Not even Bryan Matthews could resist a hundred grand.

Getting back to Skegness had been difficult, but not impossible. Due to a possible cracked rib and broken nose, he had almost passed out while hobbling along the road in the middle of the night. Luckily, a kind man in a van had stopped and offered him a lift, but even so, Curtis barely made it to the meeting point at the beach resort by eight in the morning. He thanked the man, who also gave him some loose change for food, and hid behind the toilet block, ensuring he had an ample view of the car park.

Luckily, Bryan hadn't searched his pockets that well and had missed the small tracking device he'd kept hidden. Even if he did lose Bryan again, he could find him with it, but he was curious as to whether Blondie would show up or not. She didn't. That was a shame, as he'd been looking forwards to that encounter.

He watched as Bryan drove out of the car park. Curtis checked to ensure the tracking device was working. The green flashing light on the gadget blinked several times, but it was useless without a phone app to go with it. He needed a new phone and a set of wheels.

It was time to adapt and overcome.

Chapter Twenty-Five

August 2005

The problem with me was that I clearly had issues. Not like, deep-rooted, psychological issues, but issues in general. I mean, technically, I probably *did* have psychological issues, but they weren't the problem. No, the problem was everyone else.

Like ... I had an issue with people being rude to other people for no reason.

I had an issue with my dad constantly being away and having to look after myself or being stuck with my uncle and forced to do whatever he wanted to do.

I had an issue with the guy at the checkout counter who wouldn't let me buy my groceries because I was a few quid short.

I had issues with everything and everyone and sometimes I wished things would just go my way for once, so I wouldn't have to feel this pent-up anger all the time.

It didn't help that Bryan Matthews still walked around with a smug grin on his face, acting as if he owned the entire world and everyone in it. How did a person get like that? Were they born that way or were they raised to believe the sun shone out their butt hole?

One day, I was going to kill him. I've mentioned that many times.

I was fifteen now and, over the years, I thought the urge to kill him might fade, like my urge to kiss a girl so I could know what it was like, but it didn't fade. And yes, I did kiss a girl and it was okay, but now she wouldn't look me in the eye, so I suppose that ship had sailed.

In fact, the urge to kill Bryan Matthews grew stronger every day. It started as a small flicker of a flame and then fuel kept being added. Fuel like Bryan being a dickhead. I was beginning to think one day I'd snap and go on a murder rampage like those terrorists did in America who run into schools and shoot everyone. Except, of course, I'd never do that because they almost always ended up dead and I had no intention of cutting my own life short just to end his. Oh no, when he died, I would continue to live a perfect and happy life because it would no longer have him in it.

I watched him a lot. He didn't know I watched him, obviously. I kept to the shadows and hid behind bushes. Once, I had to leap into a bush, so he and his cronies didn't see me coming and it just so happened the bush was full of brambles, and I scratched myself to pieces. But if they'd caught me spying on them then it could have been a lot worse. I had to pick my battles sometimes.

Oh, I almost forgot … Bryan got himself a new girlfriend. She turned sixteen about a week ago and now she thought she was some sort of queen, and he was her king. I didn't even know her name, but she was the sister of one of his cronies. She was constantly at his side, holding his hand or hanging on his every word, laughing at his stupid jokes even though they weren't remotely funny. Why did girls do that? It was so sad; pathetic really. I really wanted to warn her what a terrible human being he was, but I was certain she'd find that out on her own one day. Poor girl. Live and learn.

It was the summer holidays now, so you'd think I'd get a break from him, but no. Everywhere I wanted to go to read my book, he usually turned up.

The park. He was there.

The quiet bench by the river. He was there.

Honestly, I was beginning to think maybe he was following me around too. Maybe he was as obsessed with me as I was with him. No, I wasn't obsessed, not really. I was just … okay, maybe I was a little obsessed … obsessed with killing him.

I started working out a few weeks ago and could already feel my strength increasing. I also started kick-boxing lessons and could easily defend myself against his attacks, but I didn't. I allowed him to think he had the upper hand; that I was weak and easy to abuse.

And then one day … one day he'd find out exactly how dangerous I was.

But then something happened. Something bad. *The incident,* as I liked to call it, happened and the urge to kill Bryan erupted into a huge fireball. *The incident* would always and forever be ingrained in my mind and there was nothing I could do about it because I was following the plan, and the plan was to wait and bide my time.

The incident would never be spoken about. Not until the opportune moment. But the fire was now well and truly lit. In fact, it was the size of a bonfire on steroids.

Bryan Matthews was on the countdown to his death.

Dear Diary

Date: 23 August 2005

Dear Diary,

Today my dad found me crying at the bottom of the garden. Something happened and I can't talk to anyone about it and it's eating me up inside. I can't even write it down. Bryan told me that if I ever spoke a word of what happened, he'd kill me … and I believed him.

I never let my dad see me cry. I'm fifteen for fuck's sake. I shouldn't cry at silly things. I tried to do it in secret like most kids my age do, but he saw me. He didn't shout at me like he usually did. He just stared at me for a few seconds and then walked away. Later, he pretended like he hadn't seen me at all. I think I'd have preferred it if he'd shouted at me because, as I watched him walk away, I realised that not even my dad cared about me. I was alone … completely alone.

Date: 25 August 2005

Dear Diary,

Today was amazing! I punched someone in the face, and it felt so good to cause someone else pain for a change. After *the incident* I needed to let out my frustration and anger because crying about it wasn't helping, so I marched up to a kid and punched them clear in the face. Bryan clapped and cheered, and I felt good about myself. What was the harm in that? It did make them cry a bit, but they were too chicken to say anything about it so what did it matter? Anyway, it felt damn good to punch someone. I feel like I have a taste for blood and pain now ...

Date: 27 August 2005

Dear Diary,

Okay, I feel pretty bad about what happened. My sister didn't think it was funny, but who the hell cares what she thinks? She's so up her own butt. She thinks she's so amazing and pretty and she hangs around with Bryan way too much, which means he comes over to the house a lot, but it's never to see me. It's always to see her. I don't like it.

Date: 28 August 2005

Dear Diary,

I wish I was dead.

How to Commit the Perfect Murder
Step Six

Play to Your Strengths

This step of the plan depends entirely on several things: i.e., your *actual* strengths. Now, I don't know what your strengths are so this is somewhat difficult to explain, but I'll do my best.

It could be that you're an expert marksman or a long-distance runner or – I don't know – a fucking trapeze artist. The point I'm trying to make here is that you have to use your strengths to your advantage, whatever they may be.

Ah, but what if you don't have a strength? Rubbish. Everyone has a strength. Just like everyone has a weakness. Find yours. Use it in any way you can to build on your plan, to make it stronger, to ensure it won't fail.

Also, it doesn't hurt to have some strength. By which I mean, physically. Physical strength is useful too, especially if you find yourself in a particularly nasty situation, so go to the gym, lift some weights, take self-defence classes. Hell, do yoga if that's what you're in to, but build on your physical and mental strength.

Because one day, both will come in handy.

Trust me.

Chapter Twenty-Six

HANNAH
7 July 2022 – 02:40 a.m.

'What do you mean, he's in the boot?' I try hard not to allow my voice to wobble, but it appears I barely have control over my voice box because the last two words of that sentence come out garbled and squeaky.

'I mean exactly that ... He's *in* the boot of the car.'

'What's he doing in there?'

'Oh, you know, having a nap, chilling out, reading a book ...' Bryan rolls his eyes, and it makes me want to slap him across the face and watch his cheek turn blood red.

'Okay, fine ... let me rephrase. What are you going to do with him? If he's the bad guy, then why haven't you taken him to the police station?'

'It's not that simple.'

'Of course it isn't. Look ... my head is pounding so hard I feel like it might explode at any minute. Can you please just take me to a real hospital and explain to me why I was in a fake hospital in the first place?'

'It wasn't a fake hospital. It's just an abandoned building that had a small nurse's office-type room. I thought it best you recovered there until you woke up. You were safe. I stitched you up.'

'Why not take me to a *real* hospital?' Bryan goes to open his mouth, but I put my hand up, silencing him. 'Wait ... let me guess. *It's not that simple.*'

'You got it.'

I close my eyes for several seconds, hoping the brief break will dissipate the tension in my skull. It does not. 'What do we do now?' I ask in a much calmer tone, even though on the inside I'm anything but calm.

'Now you need to fucking listen to me and do what I say.'

'I don't see why I should as you're not exactly filling me with warm, fuzzy feelings of comfort.'

Bryan drags his fingers down his face. 'Fuck me, I wish your memory would come back already. This is fucking exhausting. This was never supposed to happen.'

'Well, gee, I'm sorry my brain injury is causing you so much grievance. Maybe if you'd just tell me the truth, I'd be able to remember more.'

'All I can tell you is that we need to get rid of Curtis Redding for good. He can't stay where he is for much longer.'

I glance at the car, imagining a man tied up inside the boot. 'Right ... and why is that again?'

'Because he's dead and stinking up the inside of my car. And, in this heat, he'll start to get ripe real soon.'

Chapter Twenty-Seven

3 July 2022 – 03:50 a.m.

Blood pumped around his body so hard he could practically hear it as he stared at the woman on the ground in front of him, cowering and trembling like a wounded dog. This wasn't how it was supposed to happen. He hadn't meant to let his real name slip, but, then again, she hadn't meant to see him attack the *real* Curtis Redding. She wasn't even supposed to be here, for fuck's sake. Her being here had jeopardised everything and she'd put her own life in danger for a fucking bag. It was ridiculous and he wished he could just make her go away once and for all, but damn it if he wasn't beginning to like her.

How had Curtis found him? He'd dumped him over fifty miles away and he'd been unconscious and bleeding heavily from his broken nose. When Barbie asked his name, he'd used Curtis's as a ploy; a quick, on-the-spot decision, that had been paying off until the real Curtis had shown up.

Bryan had been trying to hide for years. His name wasn't registered on any local government list, not anymore anyway. His last known address was his father's house, but it had been years since he'd lived there. He drove around the country, worked for cash from time to time, and used the money his father had left him to keep himself afloat. But the money had to run out sometime and stealing Curtis's identity and the possibility of receiving a hundred grand from Barbie had been too enticing to ignore. But it hadn't worked out like he'd planned and now he was stuffed.

At least he had his car back; the car he'd built and restored with his father. He'd always been a huge fan of American muscle cars, especially having watched the TV show *Supernatural* over the years. His idea of heaven was driving around in a muscle car, living life on the road and that's what he'd been trying to do until Curtis had stolen the car a while back (hence why the engine was making weird noises now, because clearly he didn't know how to treat this car like the lady she was), but they were in the middle of nowhere, so how had he found them? The only explanation was that there was a tracker hidden in the car somewhere. Bryan should have known Curtis would have thought of everything. He always did and always seemed to be two steps ahead of him.

'What do you mean your name is Bryan Matthews? You said your name was Curtis Redding.' Barbie's high-pitched voice jolted him back to reality.

'I lied.'

'B-But ... I don't understand,' she whimpered.

Bryan sighed as he pointed to the body slumped on the ground, blood oozing from his broken nose. That nose would probably never heal right after being broken so many times. 'That sorry-excuse-for-a-man is Curtis Redding. I don't expect you to understand, but I do expect you to listen to me. Right now, you must do exactly what I tell you or you'll end up hurt, or worse ... dead.'

'Are you going to kill me?'

'No.'

'How am I supposed to trust you!' She buried her face in her hands and sobbed like a little girl. She looked in such a pathetic state, covered in dried mud, dried urine and fresh tears. She was also starting to smell slightly ripe. It was time he did something to help her and gain her trust. They were both in need of a shower and a set of clean clothes, especially now he was covered in splatters of blood.

Bryan sat down next to Barbie and leaned his head against the car, breathing softly. 'I'll be honest with you ... You can't trust me. Not really. There's nothing I can say to make you trust me, but you're in on this now whether you like it or not, so you have to do as I say so I can get us both out of this.'

'Out of what? In on what? What are you talking about?' Now she glared at him; angry tears filled her eyes.

'Are you sure you want to know all the details?'

Barbie stared at him dead in the eyes for several seconds without blinking. Her drastic change in demeanour surprised and terrified him at the same time. 'Yes. Tell me.'

'How do I know I can trust *you*? How do I know you won't attempt to escape and go running to the cops the first chance you get, huh?'

'I won't, I promise.'

Bryan grinned. 'You're gonna have to do better than that, Barbie.'

'I'll make a deal with you,' she said as she straightened up. 'You can have everything in my bag apart from one thing. Do whatever you want with it. Sell it. Bin it. I don't care, but I only want one thing from the bag. Then, when I eventually get home, I'll give you as much money as you want. Name the price. It's all yours.'

Bryan pursed his lips and rubbed his chin stubble as he stared into the darkness ahead. He felt her eyes boring a hole into the side of his head, but he continued to face forwards for several minutes, making her wait. 'Deal, but what's in that bag that's so important to you?'

'Why do you want to know so badly?'

'I want to know what means more to you than your phone and all your expensive possessions.'

Barbie scrambled to her feet, opened the car door and rooted around under the driver's seat, eventually pulling out her bag. She grabbed every item and tossed them like discarded tissues on the ground in front of her. Then she unzipped a small compartment inside and pulled out a notebook and held it up.

'I just want this,' she said, throwing the bag into the dirt. The pink exterior was dirty within seconds. He stared at the discarded bag and then slowly turned his head to look at the notebook.

'What's that?'

'A notebook.'

'I can fucking see that. What's in it?'

Barbie shuddered as she clutched the notebook to her chest as if it were a shield made of solid metal. 'It's my diary from when I was a child.'

Bryan scoffed. 'Why would you want to keep that?'

'You asked what I wanted from my bag. This is it.'

Barbie and Bryan locked eyes, neither one wanting to show weakness or to back down, but he had no choice. They had to try and trust each other, or they'd land up in jail or dead.

'Fine,' he said with a sigh. 'Keep your bloody diary. Just listen to me carefully and you have to promise that whatever I tell you to do, you'll do it. No questions asked. Deal?' Barbie nodded slowly. 'Say it.'

'Fine. Deal.'

'Good. First things first. No running off to tell the cops. No phone calls. No contact with anyone apart from myself. Got it?' She nodded. Bryan relaxed his shoulders. He was aware they had been tight with tension during the last few minutes and, now the adrenaline was wearing off, his head was a little clearer. He knew what he had to do. 'Good. Now, second ... Help me get Curtis into the boot.'

Barbie screwed up her nose. 'Do I have to? He's covered in blood and this dress is *Dior*.'

'Am I supposed to know what that means?'

'It means it cost £2,000.'

'I don't give a shit. Besides, it's already covered in dirt and your own piss.'

Another shudder, but she didn't argue any further.

Bryan walked over to her discarded bag and phone. He raised his foot and then stamped onto the phone screen, cracking it into the gravel. He heard her gasp behind him. He ignored her as he grabbed all the items and tossed the lot into the nearby trees.

Now they needed to disappear.

Chapter Twenty-Eight

ASHLEIGH
3 July 2022 – 04:00 a.m.

As I watch Curtis – I mean Bryan – smash my phone into the ground, I'm stunned to realise I don't care. I mean ... okay, I care a little (there are a lot of cute photos of me on there), but I'm not completely hysterical like I thought I'd be. If someone had done that to my phone two days ago, I would have had a nervous breakdown (I'm being totally serious by the way).

But it's been a strange couple of days to say the least. One minute, I've been terrified and the next, completely elated. It feels as if I'm riding a rollercoaster of emotions and I'm not even due on my period for another week. And, after realising that no one is looking for me or cares that I'm missing, I've almost lost touch with the person I was before all this happened. Isn't that strange? Less than forty-eight hours ago I was lying in a bubble bath filming a TikTok video for my fans, talking about the latest LUSH bath bomb and how it smelled like summer rain (it didn't; it smelled like wet socks, but if I'd told my followers that then I doubt LUSH would invite me to take part in their next campaign). I got over two hundred thousand views within an hour of posting that reel. It's kind of sad to think that was my last post before I disappeared. I bet it'll go viral when the media find out what's happened to me. Maybe LUSH should thank me ...

And now I'm here, having agreed to basically run away with a man whose name wasn't what I thought it was. It's amazing how quickly one's life can change and how quickly one can realise how little materialistic things matter … like bath bombs.

I'm convinced that my disappearance will be noticed eventually. How can it not be? Even random nobodies get reported missing on the news. It happens every day. And I'm certainly not a random nobody. I'm an important *somebody* and someone, somewhere, at some point, will think, 'Hey, where's Ashleigh Carmichael?' And then the media will get involved and my face will be plastered on every news channel in the UK, and I'll become even more famous than I already am. Just imagine the job prospects that will come from this once I'm found safe and well …

If I'm found safe and well.

Oh no … What if I'm *never* found and I end up being murdered by this Bryan Matthews person and tossed in a ditch?

To be fair, I do prefer the name Bryan Matthews to Curtis Redding. It's a much nicer sounding name, don't you think? Surely a man named Bryan Matthews wouldn't kill a helpless woman. Curtis Redding on the other hand … Well, the man on the ground looks dodgy to me, but, then again, even the most normal looking person can end up being a raging psychopath. Just watch any Netflix serial killer documentary; it's always the quiet and weird ones. Like Joe Goldberg in *You*.

As I cautiously approach Curtis (the real Curtis) my body shudders against the cold and shock. The dim light from the car interior is casting strange shadows across his face. His eyes are closed, and his hair is a dirty blonde colour, all matted and full of dust and twigs. This man certainly does not take care of himself.

I glance at Bryan as he moves the sleeping body into an outstretched position on the ground. He's rummaging through the man's pockets. All Curtis has on him is a phone and a weird, black dongle that's flashing. Bryan studies it for a second before tossing it into the boot. Every fibre of my being is screaming at me to run away from this situation, that something is dangerously wrong, but what choice do I have? I don't have any choice but to play along and see how things pan out.

'Grab his legs and I'll grab his head,' says Curtis – I mean Bryan. It's going to take me a while to adjust to the new name.

I moan as I grab his boots and lift, but unfortunately, the yoga and body combat classes I take regularly aren't enough for me to be able to lift half a grown man, even the lighter end. I barely lift his legs off the ground before I drop them, panting heavily.

'Put some fucking effort into it.'

'Don't rush me!' I shout.

Bryan (yes! I got it right) rolls his eyes at me. It's starting to get light now, so I can just about make him out. I shuffle position several times, squat down, grab both of Curtis's ankles and lift again. I don't know how I manage it, but somehow, I summon super strength to lift his bottom half as high as the boot of the car, then Curtis (damn it! *Bryan* ...) gives him a swift kick and he rolls the rest of the way inside, landing with a hollow thud that makes my skin crawl.

Bryan kicks loose gravel over the spots of blood on the ground until it's barely noticeable while I catch my breath. That's when I peer inside the boot and catch a glimpse of a large black bag, nestled against Curtis's feet.

I throw a quick glance over my shoulder at Bryan to ensure his back is turned and then duck my head inside the boot, holding my breath as I do so I don't catch a waft of blood and body odour. Blood is still dripping from Curtis's broken nose and soaking his chequered shirt.

I unzip the bag and jump backwards as I spy the contents, banging my head on the open boot. Bryan looks up from kicking gravel.

'What happened?'

'Just hit my head,' I say as I rub it.

He frowns at me and continues with his gravel kicking.

I hold my breath once more and duck down, peeling back the top of the bag. Now I know what's inside, I don't react in shock, as before. Inside are several knives of varying lengths, handcuffs, medical equipment such as scalpels and such, some sort of blow torch and various saws and hammers. I zip the bag shut and straighten my back as I stare at the man in front of me.

A million questions race around my mind, all of them at super-fast speed.

Who is this man? Am I going to die? Is he some sort of serial killer? Why did Curtis Redding attack him? What did Curtis know that Bryan didn't want to get out? Am I in danger? Why is he so afraid of letting me go?

For a crazy moment, I think about grabbing one of the weapons from the bag and using it against Bryan, but the reality of the situation stops me. There's no way I'd be able to overpower him. Even Curtis hadn't been able to do it, so what chance do I have?

'Hey, Barbie … Get in.' Bryan points at the car.

'Where are we going?'

'Someplace where we can shower and change so we don't look like horror movie survivors.'

'And then what?'

'Then we get rid of him.'

'How?'

'Must you always ask so many questions?'

'Must you always be so vague about everything?'

'Do you trust me or not?'

'Of course I don't trust you. I may be blonde, but I'm not stupid, despite what you may think.'

'Speaking of the blonde … you should maybe think about dying your hair and taking those stupid extensions out.'

'Absolutely not. This hair costs me nearly a grand a month to maintain.'

Bryan raises his eyebrows at me. 'Wow, you *are* high maintenance.'

'I have to be. It's my job.'

'What if you didn't have that job? Who would you be if you didn't have to be high maintenance?'

I purse my lips and stare at him. No one's ever asked me that before. I've always been told I have to look and act a certain way, and I've always gone along with it because I've never had to be anyone else. His question throws me, and I spend the entirety of the drive to the nearest supermarket contemplating it.

Chapter Twenty-Nine

BRYAN
3 July 2022 – 08:00 a.m.

The four-hour car ride to the supermarket was spent in relative silence. They'd had to drive a long way to find civilisation and, even when they did enter the small Scottish towns, there was a lack of large shops. Bryan kept driving until he found a suitable location near John o'Groats, the furthest point north in the country. He'd always wanted to visit but never imagined it would be under these circumstances.

There hadn't been a sound from the boot of the car. For all Bryan knew, Curtis had died during transit, but that was a problem for later. It was risky driving around with a man bundled in the boot, but he didn't have any other choice. Curtis was too much of a loose wire; he was unpredictable and that made him dangerous. Bryan had always known the type of man he was, but the dynamic between them had shifted over the years.

Barbie spent the entire drive staring out of the window, barely blinking. She appeared to be in some sort of trance, or maybe she was in a state of shock. Bryan concentrated on the road and when he pulled up in a parking space at the shop, he turned to her, nudging her shoulder.

'You coming in with me?' She shook her head slowly in response. 'You want anything?'

'More water … and clean clothes.'

Bryan nodded. 'Can I have my jacket back?' he asked, nodding at her. 'To cover the blood stains,' he added. Barbie shrugged out of his leather jacket without a word and handed it to him, then crossed her arms over her chest. 'Be as quick as I can. Don't run off. I'm trusting you.'

She merely screwed her nose up and turned her face away.

Bryan hurried around the shop, grabbing everything he could off the shelves that they needed; water, food, clean clothes, a pair of trainers for Barbie (he guessed her size as a 5), hair dye, bleach and a few cleaning products. He paid using cash and then jogged back to the car where she was waiting for him, leaning against the side of it, looking like a run-down hooker in her sparkly dress covered in dirt.

'It smells in the car,' she said by way of an explanation.

Bryan opened the door and threw the bag of items onto the back seat, keeping back a bottle of water. 'He's probably shit himself back there.'

'Sounds like you have a lot of experience with transporting people in the boot of your car.'

Bryan chuckled. 'Some.'

'Way to make a girl feel better.'

Bryan chucked the water bottle at her. Barbie wasn't prepared and missed catching it by several inches. The bottle clattered to the floor and rolled underneath the car. Bryan squeezed the bridge of his nose between two fingers and inhaled deeply.

'Fuck my life,' he muttered before bending down to retrieve the bottle.

'Next time warn me before you throw something at my head!'

'I didn't throw it at your head. Maybe you should learn to fucking catch.'

'Stop swearing at me.'

Bryan thrust the bottle into her hands. Barbie frantically opened the cap and downed half the water within seconds.

'Careful or you'll—' She started choking and spat water all down her front. '—Choke.'

When she stopped coughing, she got back into the car and slammed the door, leaned over to the back seat and grabbed the bag. She pulled out a sandwich.

'Ham and cheese again?'

'If you wanted a different sandwich then you should have placed your order.'

She tore into the wrapping anyway. It was like watching a wild animal rip into a carcass. Then she pulled out the box of hair dye.

'Really? Caramel brown? Do you realise how badly that will clash with my skin complexion?' Bryan gave her the side eyes. 'Right ... stupid question. Of course you don't, because you're a man and men are useless with that sort of thing. Except for my make-up artist, Carl. He always knows exactly what colours work for me.'

Bryan muttered a few swear words, started the car and pulled out into traffic. 'We'll stop at a hotel quickly to shower and change and then get back on the road to get rid of … well, you know … *him*.'

Barbie nodded with a mouth full of food. 'Where are we going and how are we going to get rid of him?'

'The less you know the better.'

'Just a rough direction of travel will be great.'

'Well, since we can't go any further north, we'll go east.'

'Huh? Where are we?'

'Right at the top of the UK.'

'Remind me again why we're just driving around the UK randomly?'

'Harder to track.'

'I wish I hadn't asked.'

An hour later, they arrived at a cheap hotel along the top of the mainland. The receptionist had given them raised eyebrows but didn't question why they only wanted the room for a couple of hours. They had to pay for the entire night anyway.

Barbie had been in the bathroom for almost an hour. How long did it take to have a shower for fuck's sake? He was glad he'd gone first and made her wait as he'd only taken ten minutes from start to finish to get the blood and dirt out of his hair and skin. All their clothes would be bundled in a black bag and destroyed later. He'd dressed himself in the simple grey tracksuit bottoms and black t-shirt he'd bought. Luckily, his leather jacket was salvageable.

After quickly checking on Curtis, who was still out for the count and looking a little worse for wear, Bryan sat on the edge of the double bed, refusing to relax. He had the television on low just for some background noise. His bicep muscles flexed as he ran his fingers through his damp hair. He stared at the bathroom door, picturing her naked behind it. He stirred and promptly looked away towards the screen where a news presenter was delivering some breaking news.

'A thirty-year-old actress and model and sole heir to the Carmichael Foundation was reported missing in the early hours of this morning. Ashleigh Carmichael was last seen at her residence in Kensington at around half past three in the afternoon on Friday the 1st of July by her housekeeper. She was then reported missing by her business associate, Sawyer Croft, when he turned up at her house for a scheduled meeting this morning to find she wasn't there. Sources say she was involved in a traffic accident early on the morning of the 1st of July and was treated at Chelsea and Westminster Hospital. The CCTV around her home is being checked now to see whether she left of her own accord.

'The model and actress is perhaps best known for her social media presence, often posting several times a day to her millions of followers, but all of her accounts have been deleted. We are not sure whether she did this herself or someone else who has access to her accounts deleted them. More on this story as it develops ...'

This wasn't good. Now the whole country would be on the lookout for her, but what the hell was the deal with the deleted social media accounts? She certainly hadn't deleted them, so who would do such a thing?

Sawyer Croft ...

There was a name he hadn't heard in a while.

His stomach twisted in an uncomfortable knot as he remembered what he'd done to the man all those years ago. The fact that Barbie was here was no coincidence. Something didn't add up and he'd be damned if he was going to let her escape any time soon.

Bryan sighed as he switched off the screen, plunging the room into silence. The shower had stopped running. He couldn't even hear movement from behind the bathroom door.

He remembered there was a small window in the bathroom, which led out onto the street.

Surely not?

'Shit!' He bolted upright and lunged towards the bathroom door.

Chapter Thirty

ASHLEIGH
3 July 2022 – 10:00 a.m.

The mirror's foggy thanks to the ridiculously hot shower I've just stepped out from. The running, clean water had felt like an absolute dream, despite the water pressure being non-existent. I can't even begin to explain how relieved I feel to be clean again, to have the lingering smell of sweat, dirt and my own urine finally gone. Upon inspection, my body is covered in small bruises and scrapes, but otherwise in decent condition, although it had taken several rounds of shampooing to remove the dried seagull faeces from my hair.

Speaking of my hair.

Now comes the hard part.

I stare at the box of dye on the side and then up at my long, wet locks. I have been blonde my entire adult life. In fact, I went blonde the day after my father died. People thought it was strange that I went to a salon and got it done so soon after such a tragic accident. They thought I didn't care about his death. They were wrong. Of course I cared. Getting my hair done was my way of distracting myself from the tragedy and it was also the start of the new me; the one who had to put on a show and become the boss and a super career woman. People always think they know me and my intentions, but they don't … except for Bryan Matthews. He seems to know a great deal about me and I'm not sure I like that. But I bet he doesn't know everything …

My extensions are practically coming out by themselves now, so I carefully start to pull them away from my natural hair. I know I shouldn't do it as it's likely to damage my hair follicles, but other than taking a pair of scissors to them I don't have any other way of removing them. It stings my scalp and I pull out a lot of hair in the process, but, one by one, I remove the extensions until only a short bob remains. My natural hair only comes to just above my shoulders.

Then I begin to apply the hair dye.

Urrgg, this colour is positively hideous.

Now I'm saying goodbye to my blonde hair I feel as if I'm becoming a different person, like I have a new identity. Who is this woman with caramel brown, short hair staring back at me in the mirror? I hardly recognise myself without a phone in my hand too. I still get an itchy feeling in my fingers from time to time. They're still longing to hold it, to type away and check how many likes I have on my recent post, but to be perfectly honest ... I feel ... free.

I feel ... alive.

Once I've applied the dye, I wait the recommended amount of time, then rinse my hair under the shower, which has now turned cold and pad back out to the mirror. I put my hand over the red notebook on the side. I brought it into the bathroom with me because I didn't trust Bryan not to look at it. Wouldn't want that now, would I?

I squeal and jump away from the door as it bursts open. Bryan barges in, not caring that he's just broken the lock on the door. I'm still dripping wet and standing in a towel, which is barely big enough to cover my modesty. His eyes flick over my body.

'Can I help you?' I ask politely.

'I thought—'

'What? You thought I might have tried to escape out of the window? I know I'm small, but I'm not *that* small.'

Bryan's eyes dart to the tiny, fogged-up window, the notebook and then back to me. A smile spreads across his face. 'I like the new hair. Much better.'

'I'm so glad I finally have your approval. I can now die a happy woman.'

'The sarcasm needs work though.' I open my mouth to say something sarcastic back, but the words get stuck. I can't think of a good enough comeback quick enough. 'Anyway, thought you'd want to know that your dream has come true. You've made the national news. You were reported missing early this morning and someone's deleted all your social media accounts. Congratulations.'

My mouth falls open. 'What!'

'I'll admit the deleted accounts is weird. Who else has access to them?'

'My manager. My agent. My assistant.'

'Right. So basically everyone.'

'What does this mean?'

Bryan shrugs. 'It means you've disappeared, and people are looking for you and if they find you then they find me, so you and I have to keep on the move. You have five minutes.'

'B-But I still need to dry my hair. If I let it dry naturally then it goes all frizzy and I look as if I've stuck my finger in an electrical socket.'

'I don't give a fuck if you end up looking like a fucking sheepdog at Crufts, just be ready to leave in five minutes. Nice tits by the way.'

I shudder, clutching the towel tighter across my chest as he slams the door behind him. This man is the most infuriating person I've ever met with his stupid wavy hair, haunting green eyes and muscles that ripple when he ... No, stop!

Get a grip, Ashleigh.

I towel-dry my hair as quickly as possible and put on the most hideous pair of trousers I've ever seen in my life. Bryan forgot to buy me a bra (or did he?), so when I put the grey t-shirt on my nipples are clearly on show. I check out my shapeless frame in the mirror. I've scrubbed what was left of my make-up off, my hair is short and dark, my tan is patchy, and you can't see that I even have a female body. I look like an average, boring thirty-year-old. Even if someone who knew the old Ashleigh Carmichael laid eyes on me, I doubt they'd recognise me.

I'm a whole new woman ... and here's the weird thing.

I think I like it.

Dear Diary

Date: 4 February 2006

Dear Diary,

I can't believe what I'm writing right now. The words don't even make sense. Nothing makes sense anymore. BRYAN MATTHEWS IS MOVING AWAY. Yes, that's right. He's leaving me and moving away. I feel like I'm about to lose a limb, a piece of my heart. He can't leave me! I don't even know if there's an emotion to describe what I'm feeling ... except all I want to do is curl up into a ball and die so I don't have to feel this pain anymore.

Date: 7 February 2006

Dear Diary,

I've been miserable for days. Bryan hasn't said exactly why he's moving away, but I think it has something to do with his parents. I haven't seen them around lately. Actually, that's not true. I saw his dad the other day in town, but I haven't seen Bryan's mum in a long time. Bryan keeps saying that his parents want a fresh start, whatever the hell that means, but how am I supposed to continue living without Bryan around? My sister is obviously deliriously upset, and I think it's only a matter of time before Bryan ends it with her.

Date: 10 February 2006

Dear Diary,

I was right. Bryan has broken up with my sister two days before the Valentine's Day school dance and now it's too late for her to get a date. Even I think that's a bit mean, but I don't say anything to him. Instead, my sister is screaming at me for no reason and telling me what a dick Bryan is and that I shouldn't be his friend anymore. But she doesn't understand. I can't not be his friend, otherwise my life would have no meaning. She'll get over it.

Date: 14 February 2006

Dear Diary,

Bryan came to my house today. He told me some stuff that I can't repeat, not even here. I'm not sure why he decided to spill his guts to me, but now I'm left with a difficult decision. Should I tell someone what he did or keep it a secret?

Chapter Thirty-One

February 2006

The news that Bryan Matthews was leaving spread around the school like wildfire caught in a strong wind. I wasn't sure where it originated, but by the end of the day the entire school knew, and so did the two schools down the road.

It made me sick, watching as everyone cooed over Bryan and showered him with sympathy and pats on the back. They said stuff like, 'We'll miss you, man,' 'I hope you keep in touch,' and 'We love you, Bryan.'

WHY!

Why did everyone love him when all he did was bully them and steal their lunches? Yes, even at sixteen years old, Bryan still stole lunches from the smaller kids. He didn't even eat them. He just threw them in the bin. Did everyone have some sort of Stockholm Syndrome?

Clearly, he was lapping it up, loving all the extra attention. As if he didn't have a big enough head already. There was even a giant card which said, 'We'll Miss You!' going around the school and everyone wrote long essays about how much they loved him. Even some of the teachers wrote in it.

Really! They loved him. Why!

Two days later, Bryan Matthews dumped his girlfriend, which wouldn't have been that bad had it not been only two days before the Valentine's Day school dance. I had never seen a girl's face so red before; it turned beetroot. She stormed off, crying her eyes out.

An hour after that, every girl in school (even the ones who already had dates) were lining up to talk to him, hoping they'd be the one he chose to take to the dance instead. In the end, he chose two girls to take (because clearly, one wasn't enough); a blonde stick-thin creature and a girl whose boobs had grown at least two cup sizes in a week (yeah, right).

I, on the other hand, had no date.

Not that I cared ...

I didn't want to go to the stupid dance anyway.

A month later and Bryan was gone. At first, I felt relieved and free and pretty damn happy, but spending time at school without my arch enemy around seemed pointless. What was the point in even going to school anymore? His group of cronies moped around, and their bullying started to get worse. They continued to pick on smaller kids who had no way of defending themselves, but without Bryan there to control them, they often took things too far. There was no direction. The fat ginger kid, who'd started to slim down last year, began to take over and ordered the group around, attempting to take Bryan's place.

It didn't work ... because no one could take Bryan's place and I think he knew that.

I was at a loss because I had no way of watching Bryan and I started to wonder if perhaps my plan of killing him one day would fade, but then I'd remember *the incident* and my hatred came flooding back.

No, Bryan Matthews had to die. There was no doubt about that. I just needed to come up with a new plan. Adapt and overcome was one of my steps, after all. And the ability to adapt and overcome appeared soon after.

A new social media platform called Facebook launched last month. It was open to anyone over the age of thirteen with a valid email address, so I signed up on a whim, secretly hoping that Bryan Matthews had joined too. He had; of course he had, because Facebook was merely a new way of keeping in touch with his friends to show how popular he was. He already had nearly one thousand friends, although I highly doubted that most of those people even liked him. They were just nosey and wanted to know what he was up to ... like me.

His profile was open so that anyone could see his pictures. Therefore, there was no need to send him a friend request, but I did anyway because I was curious if he'd accept it. He did; of course he did, because he was the type of person who wanted as many friends as possible. He didn't care who they were. I doubted he'd even looked at my name and profile when he clicked the accept button. He wouldn't have recognised me anyway because I used a fake picture. I didn't want any photo of me online ... not yet.

Anyway, Bryan Matthews appeared to be living life to the fullest now that he'd moved away. His dad had bought him a custom motorbike for his seventeenth birthday. He had a new girlfriend, who looked every bit like a stuck-up bitch.

Rather than my obsession to kill him fading the longer he was away from me, it grew. In fact, I wanted to end his life so badly that it was all I could think about. My grades started dropping again. I stopped reading books. And, instead, I began plotting everything down in a small diary. Every insignificant detail went in there, every small snippet of information about him that I either already knew or learned about him through Facebook. This new era of social media was a huge stepping stone for me. It made my life a lot easier. Obviously, I'd prefer it if he were closer to me, but I'd visit him in due time. He wouldn't get away with the things he'd done to me. I wouldn't let him.

One day he would pay.

One day he would suffer.

One day I would track him down and I would kill him.

How to Commit the Perfect Murder
Step Seven

Make Them Trust You

This one is a bit of a strange one, I'll admit. Why would you want to make your target trust you? How is that even possible? Well, if you've made it this far then you should already be adequately set up for this step. No, it won't be easy, but getting to know your target inside and out means you'll have a better chance of catching them off-guard at the perfect moment.

A word of warning: don't rush this bit.

It takes time to build trust; sometimes it takes years. If that's how long it takes then suck it up and do it. Trust takes time to build, but only seconds to destroy, so you need to be careful how you approach this step.

One thing I would suggest is to play to your strengths (remember step six) and trust your judgement (that should totally be a new step).

Stay strong.

Keep your head up and your eyes open.

Listen and learn.

It will come in handy one day.

Trust me.

Chapter Thirty-Two

HANNAH
7 July 2022 – 03:00 a.m.

The blood drains from my face and seems to pool in my feet. My body sways to the side before I know what's happening. Bryan lunges forwards and grabs me before I face-plant the ground.

'H-He's dead?'

'Yep. Pretty fucking dead.'

'How did he die?' As soon as the words leave my mouth, I know the answer.

Bryan killed him.

'You killed him, Han.'

Wait … that wasn't the answer I was expecting.

'I killed him?'

Bryan looks at me as if I've spoken a foreign language. 'Yeah, but don't beat yourself up about it. It was an accident. He attacked you and he deserved it.'

I stare at Bryan, my mouth hanging open like a fish.

I've killed a man.

I've killed someone and now I'm supposed to help this stranger dispose of the body. What is going on here? Am I in some sort of prank show for television? Any second now someone is going to jump out of the bushes and shout, 'Haha! Got you!'

I wish my memories would come flooding back because then at least I'd be able to piece together all the

199

details and know what the hell is going on. The few snippets of memory I do have fit together like pieces of a hundred different jigsaw puzzles.

'Look, if it makes you feel any better, I whacked him over the head first, so he was already in a bad way. He was probably going to die eventually. I mean, I should have killed him years ago when I had the chance, then none of this would've happened.'

I narrow my eyes at Bryan. 'That does *not* make me feel any better.'

Bryan shrugs. 'I did say "if it helps".'

'How did it happen?' I whisper, as if saying it too loud will alert the whole world.

'Maybe I shouldn't tell you right this minute. You're clearly in shock. I don't want to send you over the edge.'

I nod, for once agreeing with him. It is probably best I don't know. 'What are we going to do with the body?' A sentence I never thought I'd utter.

'The same thing you do with every dead body ... bury it.'

'Where?'

'I spied a graveyard on the outskirts of town. There was a freshly dug grave waiting for a coffin. We're going to bury him at the bottom and then they'll put the coffin on top when it's time for the funeral. It's the perfect way to dispose of a body where it'll never be found.'

That is quite an ingenious solution. 'Why do I get the feeling you've done this before?'

Bryan shrugs. 'I haven't, I just read a lot.'

'I highly doubt that.'

'Are you coming with me or not? If you say no, I'm going to have to tie you up in the boot with Curtis and, trust me, you don't want that. You're coming with me one way or another.'

'Fine. I'll come with you, but first I want you to tell me more about Ashleigh Carmichael.'

'Why?'

'I want to make sure she's okay.'

'Look ... if you must know ... she's dead too.'

His words knock the breath straight out of my lungs. 'What! Don't tell me I killed her as well?'

Bryan bites his bottom lip and gives me a look with his eyes that tells me everything I need to know. I make a gargling sound, clutching my throat as I sink to the ground, my legs finally giving up on me. 'Oh God ...'

Bryan places a hand on my back. The warmth from his palm seeps through my clothes and into my skin. It's a comfortable sensation, but nothing can stop the cold sweats that ripple through my body. Who am I? How have I killed two people and not remembered a thing? Maybe that is why I can't remember — I've purposefully blacked the memories out. It can happen.

'Here ...' Bryan hands me a mobile phone, which shows a frozen video from a BBC news website. I take it and clutch it in my trembling hands as I watch and listen.

'Ashleigh Carmichael has been confirmed dead. Her body was found at the bottom of a ravine in Wales two days ago. She was reported missing eight days ago by her business associate, Sawyer Croft. Her body was recovered, and Mr Croft confirmed her identity, despite the fact her body was badly decomposed and unrecognisable. Ashleigh Carmichael was the sole heir to the Carmichael Foundation, and it looks as if her entire fortune and estate, including the business, will be transferred to Sawyer Croft, her trusted friend and colleague. More on this story during the news at six ...'

The video cuts out.

I lower the phone as the screen dies and hand it back to Bryan. 'I need to know what happened, Bryan. You need to tell me how I killed her.'

'You didn't kill her, Hannah.'

I frown. 'B-But you said—'

'I didn't say anything. Look, maybe you'll regain your memories in time, but for now I need to keep you safe.'

I nod and swallow the solid lump in my throat. 'Okay,' I say with a whisper. 'Okay ... let's go and bury Curtis Redding.'

Chapter Thirty-Three

BRYAN
3 July 2022 – 15:05 p.m.

He knew he'd taken things too far. He'd basically kidnapped this woman and was now holding her hostage, but as he glanced at her out of the corner of his left eye while keeping his right focussed on the winding road, he realised she was here of her own free will. She was the one who'd traipsed across the country for three hours in search of some guy who'd stolen her bag. She was the one who'd refused to leave because she wanted to stay with her precious bag, and now she was willingly coming along on a road trip with him, clutching an old diary, having discarded her bag and personal belongings. She didn't look anything like the woman he'd first met. In fact, her whole demeanour had changed, not merely her outward appearance. She looked better with darker, shorter hair. Her fake tan was fading, now covering her skin in mottled orange patches, but she didn't seem to care. For the past several hours, she'd either been sleeping or staring out of the windscreen, her eyes wide with wonder as the countryside whizzed past.

She was a fascinating creature; unlike any woman he'd ever met. Ever since sixth-form, or even before that, he'd been a natural with the ladies. They'd flocked to him like wild geese due to his rugged good looks and muscular body, which he barely had to work for. He did like to use a gym, but ever since leaving his past behind and travelling across the country, he barely had the time to work out.

He missed having a steady job, a regular income. Years ago, he'd worked as a mechanic for his father's business. He knew a lot about cars and how they worked. His father had taught him everything. Learning about engines had captivated his attention as a teenager when his dad had moved them across the country from his childhood home near Milton Keynes to a more rural setting outside of Nottingham. He'd been sad to leave his cohort of friends, but as a child, he'd been troubled. He never liked to talk about his childhood in Milton Keynes because he was ashamed. He used to terrorise other kids, pick on boys smaller than him and would enjoy it; that was the worst part, but the move away had changed him, turned him into a better young man and set him on a different path in life. Well ... until that night when—

Bryan shook his head to dispel the demons. It wasn't worth dwelling on the past. He was different now, a better man. Okay, so he wasn't the definition of a perfect gentleman, still rugged and rough around the edges. He swore too much and slept around, but at least he didn't go out of his way to hurt people ... That was, until Curtis Redding had shown up a year ago—

'Hello ... earth to Bryan!'

Bryan shook his head, dispersing the memory of that fateful day when Curtis had turned up on his doorstep. He turned to look at Barbie who was frowning. 'What?'

'You've been quiet for the past hour, and I was starting to get worried,' she replied.

'I'm fine.'

'Sure ... and while I'm so relieved that you're *fine*, you may want to know that the body in the boot seems to have woken up.'

Bryan checked the rear-view mirror instinctively, even though there was no way of seeing into the boot from his angle. Then he heard it.

Banging.

Thud ... Thud ... Thud ...

'Shit,' he muttered.

Without another word, he pulled the car over, skidding the tyres slightly on the loose gravel. He grabbed the hammer from under his seat, kicked open the car door and marched around to the boot. Seconds later, Barbie joined him.

'No ... Stand back, Barbie. You don't know this guy like I do. He's dangerous.'

'Says the guy holding a claw hammer.'

'It's for self-defence.'

'Sure it is.'

'Look, will you just do what you're fucking told and stand over there.' He pointed a straight arm at a spot several feet away from the car. Barbie, after she stopped shivering from his bad language, dipped her chin to her chest and went and stood where she'd been told, looking like a pathetic puppy who'd just been told off for peeing on the floor.

Bryan inhaled deeply and then opened the boot.

A booted foot swung out and almost caught him full in the face. It was followed by another boot, which he also barely managed to dodge. Bryan didn't give Curtis another chance to fight back. He whacked the hammer into his right leg. Curtis screamed through his duct-taped mouth, his eyes wide and dilated. Bryan heard Barbie yelp behind him.

'Are you going to try and attack me again or do you want me to break your other leg?'

Curtis stopped screaming and shook his head. Bryan couldn't be sure that he'd broken bone, but it would've fucking hurt none the less.

'Good.' Bryan took a deep breath. 'Now … I don't want to have to kill you, but to be honest, I don't know how else to stop you. I've tried talking to you. I've tried reasoning with you. I'm not the same guy I was in school, okay?'

'Y-You've known him since school?' Barbie had taken a step forwards and was now standing next to Bryan, peering at the beaten and bloody man cowering in the boot, his mouth and hands surrounded by thick duct-tape.

'Unfortunately … yes.'

'Why does he want to kill you?'

'Maybe you should ask him that. We were best friends at school. I even dated his sister for a while.'

'What happened?'

'It's a long story.' Barbie rolled her eyes at him. Bryan sighed, his head shaking slowly. 'I tormented a lot of kids back then.' This received an eyebrow raise from Barbie. 'Hey, I'm not proud of it, okay? But I changed when I was around seventeen. I didn't beat kids up anymore. I just never expected … him. He was obsessed with me from the start, always wanted to be part of the gang. And now he wants to kill me. I think he's mentally deranged or something.'

Bryan and Barbie stared at the man in the boot whose eyes were widening as he glared back at Barbie. Maybe he recognised her or was wondering what the hell she was doing with Bryan. Curtis shook his head violently from side to side and more pained sounds emerged through his taped mouth.

'He's trying to say something,' said Barbie as she went to move towards him.

'Don't!' Bryan slapped her arm away and stepped in front of her. 'Don't touch him. I can't even begin to explain how dangerous this man is. Given half a chance, he'll attack you and use you to try and get away. He wants to kill me and, since you're with me, I expect he'll try and kill you too.'

'But we can't just leave him like this. He needs to eat and drink. This is torture.'

'He … is … trying … to … kill … us. Why are you not listening to me? What else do I have to say to make you realise he's a dangerous man who needs to be locked up?'

Barbie threw her hands up in the air. 'Let's take him to a police station then.'

'And say what, that we've had him tied up in the boot for the past day?'

'Tell them he's been trying to kill you.'

'I've tried. They won't believe me.'

'Why not?'

'Because no one fucking believes me! Everything he does is calculated and planned out down to the smallest of things. Everything bad he does, he makes it look as if I've done it. He's been framing me for the past year, making me make fucking mistakes, say the wrong fucking thing, do the wrong fucking thing and now he's pushed me too fucking far.'

Barbie clutched her throat as if she was being strangled and shuddered violently as she lurched to the side of the car, expelling her lunch all over the ground.

Bryan grimaced. 'What the ...'

Chapter Thirty-Four

ASHLEIGH
3 July 2022 – 15:30 p.m.

My body can't take it any longer. I fight with all my strength against the force erupting from my stomach, but I'm too weak and the vomit splashes down onto the gravel at my feet. I lean one hand on the car to steady myself as the world spins, but my knees give out and I sink to the ground. I hear a crunch of gravel behind me and then a rough hand grabs at my hair, pulling it out of my face as I finish vomiting. I'm panting like a dog, my body shaking so violently I can barely catch my breath.

I start counting backwards from ten, slowly and cautiously, breathing in and out at a steady pace, waiting for my body to respond to my command. What seems like hours later, I raise my head to look at Bryan, who's barely said a word other than 'just breathe' to me since the vomiting started.

'I-I'm sorry,' I manage.

He hands me a bottle of water, which he fished from the car a few moments ago. 'No, *I'm* sorry. I had no idea just how bad your reaction to swearing was. I thought you were just being difficult.'

I sip the luke-warm water and grimace. 'I haven't had a reaction that bad for a while, but you swore a lot, and I couldn't control myself.'

'What the hell—I mean, what *on earth* happened to make you react so badly to swear words? And yes, I genuinely want to know this time.'

I sigh loudly. 'Why on earth do you think I'd tell you?'

'Because you find me easy to talk to?'

'Hardly.'

'Because I'm charming and handsome and a good listener?'

'Might I remind you that you have a man tied up in your car boot right now?'

'Are you going to hold that against me forever?'

'I might.'

Bryan rolls his eyes as he straightens up. He takes both his hands and runs them through his hair, those biceps flexing perfectly again. His brows are furrowed in a very manly sort of way, and he stares into the distance with a hazy look in his eyes.

'Fine. I'll tell you,' I say as I rise to my unsteady feet. I step around the pile of vomit and join him, standing close to his left side. 'But let's keep driving.'

Bryan doesn't look at me as he asks, 'So you're with me on the whole Curtis-trying-to-kill-me thing?'

'I won't lie ... I'm a bit confused by it all. Maybe I can talk to him and try and understand his side of the story. Maybe I can help you both get over ... whatever this is between you.'

Bryan scoffs. 'We're way beyond help, Barbie. It's too late for that now.'

'I think you should come up with a new nickname for me.'

'That's very true. You no longer look like a Barbie. Fine ... Ash—'

'That makes me sound like a tree.'

'Fine, I promise I'll work on the nickname. Now let's get the f—*fudge* out of here.'

I grin at his feeble attempt to cover up a swear word. 'What are we going to do about Curtis? He's not going to stay quiet during the drive, is he?'

'He will if he knows what's good for him. If not, then I have some drugs hidden away in the car that will do the job.'

'Drugs?'

Bryan glances sideways at me without moving his head. 'Drugs,' he repeats.

'Do I even want to know why you're smuggling drugs in your car?'

'Probably not, but it's good sh—*stuff.*'

I bet it is.

The landscape around here is breathtaking. I still can't get my head around how much wide-open space there is. There's barely a house for miles, and the roads are so windy and narrow that whenever we meet another car coming in the opposite direction, we have to pull over to let them pass. I haven't seen a set of traffic lights for over a day. I have no idea where we are, but we're somewhere still in Scotland, on the outer edges in the rugged mountains. I never knew the sky was so blue. I never knew there were so many trees and so much grass and so many birds flying around. I've lived in cities my whole life. The countryside has always been one of those alien things I know nothing about and have only really seen in movies, but this ... this is something else.

Now that I no longer look like the old Ashleigh Carmichael, it feels as if my whole persona is changing too. I don't have my phone anymore. The old Ashleigh would have been checking it every minute to see if there was any signal, but right now it's the furthest thing from my mind.

Bryan has the radio on, but it keeps cutting out. I think maybe he's hoping to catch a news update about my disappearance. Maybe he's worried about the whole thing. I'm not. I'm quite glad people now know I'm missing, but I don't care how they're feeling about it.

I don't know how this is all going to work out. I don't know why Curtis is trying to kill Bryan, but what I do know is that Bryan Matthews is innocent. And I need to help him ...

He has a bead of sweat that's been gradually falling down the side of his face for the past several minutes and he hasn't noticed. I want to lean across and mop it away because it's really bugging me—

'Why are you staring at me like that?'

'Like what?' I say, a little too quickly.

'Like you want to eat me or something.'

'Ha! Don't flatter yourself.' My face burns.

'You *don't* want to eat me?'

'I haven't decided yet.'

'Then what were you thinking about?'

'Are you genuinely wanting to know or just trying to get in my pants again?'

'Ha! Don't flatter yourself. And when have I ever tried to get in your pants?'

'You *don't* want to get in my pants?'

Bryan slides his gaze over to me and my whole body goes cold, like someone has just walked over my grave. I've always found that a strange phrase to use, but in this case, it's spot on. 'I haven't decided yet,' he says in a low, gravelly voice.

'Liar,' I say with a smile.

Something's changed between us. It's like, for the first time since we've been on this rollercoaster journey, we're bonding and enjoying each other's company. I can't talk for him but being with him is soothing and, dare I say it, fun.

There's a beat of silence and then Bryan says, 'So ... are you going to tell me why you shake and vomit when you hear swear words? I must admit I've never come across anyone who does such a thing. It's weird.'

I sigh, having secretly been hoping he'd have forgotten about it. No such luck.

'My father used to swear a lot, like every other word was usually a swear word. So, when I was a little girl, I assumed that swearing was part of a person's normal speech. The first time I swore in front of my father he slapped me across the face. I was only three and I'd only been copying what he said. But he continued to use those bad words in front of me. I didn't swear for a while, but one day I

accidentally swore in front of him again and he ... well, he ...'
I'm trying to force the words out, but they're getting stuck at
the back of my throat like a tickly cough. My mouth turns so
dry that I have to lick my lips and move my tongue around to
get the saliva flowing again.

Bryan turns his head to me. 'You don't have to say it.
I think I get it.'

I shake my head. 'No ... I *should* say it ... H-He ...
grabbed me so hard that he broke my arm and then locked
me in the basement for nearly two days. When he finally let
me out, he took me to the hospital where I received medical
treatment. My arm was badly infected, and I was delirious
with pain and fever. All these years later, I still don't have
complete function in it, but no one knows about it. I haven't
said a swear word since. Whenever I hear one, I'm taken back
to the basement and the pain and the terror I felt. It all comes
rushing back in one big swoop.'

'How old were you when he broke your arm?'

'Nine.'

'Shi—*wow*.' Bryan shoots me a quick apologetic look,
but I return it with a small smile, appreciating his attempt to
shield me. 'I'm sorry,' he says.

I shrug my shoulders. 'I've seen a few therapists
about it, but to be honest I get the feeling they aren't really
bothered about helping me because it's not something that
needs to be fixed for me to live a normal life. But it does affect
my whole life. I'm just getting better at hiding it.'

'What about films with swear words in?'

214

I shake my head. 'I basically look like I'm shivering with cold all the way through. If it gets too bad, then I have to switch it off. There's a lot of good films I haven't seen or have only seen part of the way through. I once got invited to a movie premiere and had to walk out halfway through, which was embarrassing.'

'Yeesh.'

'But you know, in a weird way, I feel better after telling you about it. I've never told anyone before, other than a therapist who's paid to listen.'

'No one?'

'No.'

'Friends?'

'I have none. You told me that.'

Bryan rolls his eyes. 'Yeah, but I wasn't being serious. A woman like you ... you must have loads of friends.'

Tears well in my eyes and I blink them away, turning my head slightly to avoid Bryan noticing, but I think he does anyway.

'Okay,' says Bryan after a few seconds of uncomfortable silence, 'this is what I'm going to do. I'm going to be your makeshift therapist and I suggest we try the gradual exposure approach.'

'My real therapist tried that. Didn't work.'

'Ah, but I'm no normal therapist,' he responds with a wink that sets my soul alight. Butterflies start dancing around inside me and my breath escapes out through my mouth. I quickly gulp in air and nod to show him I'm prepared.

He over exaggerates clearing his throat. '*Hell.*' His voice is low, a mere whisper.

I stare at him for several moments before I realise what he's just said. 'Is that it?'

'Yes. *Hell.*'

'Say it again?'

'Hell.'

Nothing.

'I'd say that's progress,' he says with a satisfied nod. 'I mean, technically *hell* isn't a swear word because it's a word that explains the underworld and where Satan lives, but hey … it's progress.'

I grin from ear to ear. 'I can't believe something as simple as telling a complete stranger about the abuse I suffered as a child was enough to fix me!'

'Calm down, Barbie. You're not cured yet … See … *Fuck.*' I shudder and retch in response, my body responding before I even take in the words. 'Small steps, Barbie. Small steps.'

'I thought you were going to come up with a new nickname for me.'

'I'm still working on it.'

It starts raining as we turn right off the main road (I say *main road*, but what I mean is a road that doesn't have grass growing in the middle of it). The heavens open and the torrential downpour makes it impossible to see more than two feet in front of the car, but Bryan keeps inching forwards, as small drips of water leak through the cracks in the doors and windows. I keep quiet, not wanting to point out that most cars shouldn't leak, as we rumble over potholes and my head slams against the roof. The clouds are so thick with rain that it's almost dark, even though it's not even six yet. We haven't seen another car for miles. Where even *are* we?

Bryan eventually rolls the car to a stop, his hands gripping the steering wheel so tight his knuckles have turned white.

'Where are we?' I ask.

'No idea and that's the beauty of it.'

'Okay ... follow-up question. What are we doing here?'

'Giving Curtis Redding an ultimatum.'

'Which is?'

'You'll see.'

My mind drifts to some dark thoughts.

Is Bryan going to threaten to kill Curtis if he doesn't back off? Are we going to have to bury a body? How many people have buried bodies out here?

It's the perfect place to get away with murder when you think about it. There are no CCTV cameras, no eyewitnesses ... Nothing. Perfect. A small jolt of joy erupts in my chest. What is going on with me? Why am I happy we're possibly about to bury a body and get away with it?

Bryan lifts his collar up around his neck, which seems like a pointless gesture considering the weather outside. He clears his throat. 'Right ... I'll grab Curtis. You grab a shovel.'

Wait ... what!

'Um ... come again?'

Bryan looks at me. 'For self-defence in case he attacks you.'

'Can't I have a hammer instead?'

'No.'

'Why not?'

'Because I don't trust you with a hammer.'

'But you trust me with a shovel?'

We hold eye contact for a few seconds. Even in the dim light I can see large shadows under his eyes, like he hasn't slept in a week. His skin is in desperate need of moisture and a chemical peel and he's well overdue for a shave, but ... it suits him. In fact, it makes him look rather dashing.

Bryan sighs heavily and gets out of the car without another word, dispelling my weird daydream. The fact I am crushing on my captive is not lost on me. I'm aware it's sick and disturbing but being with him is filling me with adrenaline and I've never felt so alive, not in my whole life.

It's raining so hard the ground has turned to mush, and Bryan's already drenched by the time he reaches the boot. I sigh as I lever myself out and squeal as the rain soaks me instantly. By the time I've reached the back of the car, I resemble a drowned rat.

Bryan chucks a shovel at me, which I accidentally drop so I bend down to retrieve it, my hands slipping due to the water. A loud clap of thunder echoes around us, followed five seconds later by a crash of lightning, which illuminates the contents of the boot. I jump in fright as a pale face stares up at me, his eyes wide open in shock, blood matted in his beard. I shudder as Bryan hauls him out and lifts him onto his shoulders, as if he weighs nothing (so if he can lift him easily why did he get me to help lift him into the boot the other day?). Curtis grunts, but doesn't attempt to fight back, possibly because he's weak and disorientated.

I could go to prison for this, for aiding and abetting a … a … kidnapper? Is that what Bryan is? What does that make Curtis? He's the bad guy … and Bryan is the good guy. I must remember that. If I did go to prison, then what? I don't know how long I'd be locked away for, but it would be a long time I expect. I don't think I'd do very well in prison. I'd likely be picked on due to my naturally good looks, but they would fade eventually, wouldn't they? I'd turn into one of those haggard and violent female prisoners who never wear make-up and who work out all day. I'd get mega fit … and maybe—

'Earth to Barbie! You coming or what?'

I shudder ever so slightly at his tone of voice and that's when I realise he's already taken off without me. I follow him as quickly as I can, considering my shoes keep slipping on the mud with every step I take. Bryan is ploughing ahead through the wind and the rain. I can barely make him out. I assume we aren't using torches for a reason. Even in the middle of nowhere they may be seen for miles.

Bryan storms ahead, keeping a steady gait for what seems like miles, but is probably only a few hundred metres. He stops and chucks Curtis on the ground with a loud thud. I glance around, unable to get my bearings. We seem to be between some hills, in a valley of some sort. Water is gushing down from the slopes, filling the area with mud.

We stare at each other, both of us drenched to the skin, rain running down our faces in rivers. Through the torrential rain I see him grin at me. I'm not sure what he's thinking, but I don't smile back.

Chapter Thirty-Five

BRYAN
3 July 2022 – 19:05 p.m.

Barbie looked nervous. He could tell by the way she wasn't returning his smile. He didn't blame her. They'd become closer recently, or so he'd thought. She wasn't annoying and inconvenient like she once was (maybe a little annoying). He hoped she trusted him, but he didn't even trust himself. How was he supposed to get out of this without doing something serious, something that would destroy not only his life, but her life as well? Because what he was about to do was extremely serious and, once he'd done it, there was no going back. Curtis had to be stopped. There was no other way around it.

He looked down at Curtis rolling around on the sodden ground, unable to get a grip on the slippery mud. His hands were tied behind his back and duct tape still covered his mouth, but due to the rain it was beginning to come loose at the corners. Bryan grabbed hold of his soaking jacket, holding him still, and ripped the tape off in one swift movement. Curtis barely flinched even though it must have hurt as the tape tore open a prominent cut on his lips. The blood mixed with the rain, diluting it as it ran in rivers down his chin.

'Now … I think it's time we had a little chat, don't you think?' asked Bryan.

Curtis's eyes bore into Bryan, never blinking. 'Perfect location for a *chat*,' he said with a hint of a snarl. 'What do you wanna talk about, huh?'

'How about you tell me what it's going to take for you to stop hunting me like an animal?'

Curtis grinned, his teeth stained red with blood. The darkness was closing in now, but no one seemed to notice. 'Never. I'll never stop.'

'Why? Just tell me why you're doing this?'

Curtis laughed. 'Like you don't know—'

'I don't fucking know!' Bryan lunged at Curtis and grabbed his jacket again, his whole body shaking. 'I never did anything to you, you fucking prick.'

'You killed my sister!' Curtis's shout echoed through the surrounding trees. Time appeared to stand still for a moment. Everything and everyone froze in place, apart from the rain, which continued its relentless tirade.

Barbie stepped forwards, breaking the frozen moment. 'What do you mean?' Her voice had developed a stronger tone recently, even Bryan had noticed. She was becoming a stronger, more independent version of herself. He liked it.

Curtis ground his teeth together and then spat a mouthful of blood onto the ground. 'You're pathetic. What are *you* even doing with him? Yeah, I know who you are, but I bet you don't remember me, do you?'

Bryan glanced at Barbie through the rain. She shrugged her shoulders, eyes wide. 'Don't look at me. I've no idea who he is!'

'No, of course you wouldn't, cos you're a little princess now. All thanks to Daddy's untimely death. Such a shame.'

Barbie's chin rose a fraction of an inch. 'You knew my father?'

'No, not personally, but I know *of* him.'

'And what is it you think you know?'

Curtis nodded towards Bryan as he spoke. 'Ask him.'

Bryan lunged forwards and punched Curtis directly in the nose, sending him splashing backwards into a large puddle of mud. Curtis laughed; a sickening laugh that made Bryan's stomach clench. The man was a psychopath; even pain didn't affect him.

'What's he talking about?' asked Barbie.

'I have no idea. He's trying to twist and manipulate us. Turn us against each other. Don't listen to him. This is what he does. He's a pro.' Bryan took a step towards Barbie. 'I promise you; I have no idea who your father is.'

'What about what he said about you killing his sister? Didn't you say you dated her once?'

Bryan nodded. 'Yes, I dated her and broke her heart apparently, but I didn't kill her. Like I said, Curtis and I were friends and yes, he was a bit weird, but I never bullied him or anything. He was part of my gang.'

'Your gang?' Barbie smirked. 'Like the T Birds?'

'Like the what?'

'Oh wow … Have you never watched *Grease*?'

'What the fuck are you on about?'

Barbie shuddered as she shook her head. 'Never mind. So, you broke his sister's heart and then what happened?'

'Then I moved away and never saw him again until … well, until about a year ago. I told you, I'm not proud of breaking his sister's heart, but for him to come after me all these years later is ridiculous. I never killed your sister,' he reiterated, turning to watch as Curtis righted himself on the ground.

Curtis spat again and focussed on Bryan. 'You don't even remember her fucking name, do you?'

Bryan froze. He didn't, it was true. Had she meant so little to him that he couldn't even remember her name all these years later? He remembered her as an attractive girl, a little clingy perhaps, a bit shallow, but then most teenage girls were like that back then. Hell, they were worse now that social media had taken off.

'Her name was Mia!' screamed Curtis. 'Do yourself a favour, Blondie, and get as far away from this prick as possible and do it fast.'

'I don't believe a word you're saying.'

Bryan felt a flutter in his stomach. She believed him. That's all that mattered. He wasn't alone in this anymore.

'No? Then you'll be the second stupid woman who hasn't listened to me.'

'The second?'

Those flutters turned to knots and nausea rose from within. He stepped forwards, ready to strike Curtis across the head.

'There's a lot you don't know about Bryan Matthews,' continued Curtis.

'Like what?'

Don't say it ...

Curtis grinned. 'Hannah ... Hannah Baker.'

FUCK!

Dear Diary

Date: 27 September 2007

Dear Diary,

Bryan has a new girlfriend called Hannah Baker. She's pale, has dark hair and is quite plain looking. Why does he prefer her to my sister? I don't get it. I miss Bryan every day but thank goodness for Facebook because it means I can watch him without him even knowing. I haven't become a stalker, I promise. I just want answers and I want to know what he's up to. I wonder if he misses me as much as I miss him. Once I'm old enough to leave home I'm going to move closer to him. I only have to wait a few more months until I'm 18.

Date: 1 October 2007

Dear Diary,

Mia is acting weird. She never speaks to me anymore. Shouldn't you want to speak to your twin brother? Why is everyone shutting me out? I feel so lonely. All the kids who were once in Bryan's group have dispersed. I tried to keep us all together, but we eventually all went our separate ways and they all made new friends. Except for me ... I have no one. Not even my fucking sister wants to be my friend.

Date: 5 October 2007

Dear Diary,

Okay, something is definitely wrong with Mia. She came home drunk the other night and I think she's been smoking weed. I had to help her up the front steps of the house and cover for her too. She's never done anything like this before. What's going on? She says she's met someone. She just blurted it out while she was laying on her bed and staring at the ceiling. Then she started talking … and she told me stuff … stuff no brother would ever want to hear coming from his sister's mouth.

Date: 6 October 2007

Dear Diary,

Once Mia passed out on her bed, I went straight to my room and I'm writing all this down now while I remember it. She's seeing an older guy. She didn't say his name. He lives in London. Apparently, when she was supposed to be on a college trip she was actually at his house. And she had sex with him. I feel sick. Who is this older guy and why can't he have sex with women his own age and not my two-minutes-younger sister? For once I'm not thinking about Bryan Matthews ...

Chapter Thirty-Six

HANNAH
7 July 2022 – 03:30 a.m.

It's a short drive to the graveyard, but neither of us says a word. I keep sneaking glances at Bryan as he drives in the moonlight; his eyes are dark, serious and sinister. His body language suggests he is exhausted; his shoulders are slumped forwards and he is making no effort to stop himself from yawning. He has a few cuts and bruises across his face and a nasty-looking head wound, like my own. He looks like hell, like he's been there and back again quite recently. After checking the reflection in the car mirror, I surmise that I don't look any better. In fact, I look a lot worse.

Dark circles surround my eyes. One of them has received a knock or a punch recently as there is a purple bruise around the socket, turning green at the edges where it's starting to heal. My dark hair is knotted, limp and greasy, and my skin is as pale as the ghosts that possibly haunt this graveyard.

I get out of the car and shut the door quietly while I watch Bryan check out the grave we are standing next to. It has been freshly dug; a blue tarp is draped across the large mound of dirt that has been removed from the hole. A rich, earthy scent drifts up my nostrils as I breathe in the cool air. It's a clear night, just about light enough to move around without needing a torch.

'This will do,' says Bryan, opening the boot. He chucks a shovel at me, which I catch expertly with one hand. It seems my reflexes are returning.

Bryan hoists the body onto his shoulders. I've never seen a dead body before. At least, I assume I haven't. I still can't remember clearly, but the face of the dead man does look familiar. His hair is shaggy, and blood has dried around his nose and mouth, making him look as if he's taken a mouthful of bloody flesh. The thought makes me cringe as I envisage him as a vampire sucking blood from a victim. There's also a rather deep slash across his throat, which makes me gulp and clutch my own.

Did I slice his throat open?

'How long has he been … you know … dead?'

Bryan stops at the edge of the hole and looks down into it. 'A day.' He then drops the body into the abyss below and it lands with a sickening, hollow thud.

'I was unconscious for a day?'

'Give or take, yeah.'

'Give or take, what … a day, a week?'

'An hour or so.'

I purse my lips together, somewhat not convinced by his answer. I most definitely don't trust this man, but I am in somewhat of a predicament, since I'm the one who's killed the man who is now lying contorted at the bottom of someone else's grave. Plus, there's the whole thing about Ashleigh Carmichael that I need to figure out.

'We need to cover him up, so it looks as if the bottom of the hole is flat,' says Bryan. I nod and stick my shovel into the nearby pile of dirt. 'But don't make it look like we've taken dirt from the pile, otherwise people will get suspicious.'

I frown. 'Right … so … how are we supposed to do that? I'm not exactly an expert at burying bodies.'

'Neither am I.'

'You could have fooled me.'

Bryan wordlessly returns to the car for a second shovel and joins me back at the hole. We begin to dig and throw dirt into the grave in silence, but then the questions in my head get so loud that I have to let them escape.

'Tell me more about Curtis. Why did he attack me? If you tell me, I'm more likely to start remembering the details.' It probably isn't true, but I need to get him to start talking somehow. I'm quietly surprised when Bryan starts. He seems almost relaxed as he speaks and digs at the same time.

'Curtis has been stalking me for years. I didn't even know he was doing it until about a year ago, but apparently, he's been obsessed with me since childhood. We went to the same school when we were kids, but I moved away when I was a teenager. We were friends once and I dated his sister for a while, but he wanted to kill me.'

I stop digging, leaning against the shovel as I catch my breath. My hands are already sweaty, and dizziness is blurring my vision. 'Bloody hell,' I say. 'He actually wanted to kill you?'

'Oh yeah. He's a total lunatic. He even accused me of killing his sister.'

'The girl you dated.'

'Right.'

'What was her name?'

'Mia. Apparently, she jumped out of a ten-storey building just before she turned eighteen.'

'She killed herself?'

'Yeah, but Curtis never believed it. He kept going on about the Carmichael Foundation and how they covered up her murder.'

My ears seem to perk up as a new memory forms. 'The Carmichael Foundation? As in Ashleigh Carmichael? The woman who was found at the bottom of a ravine a few days ago?'

'Yeah.'

'So how does she fit into all of this? In fact, how do *I* fit into all of this?'

Bryan chucks a shovel of dirt into the hole. 'Still no memory, huh?'

'No.'

'That's convenient.'

'Excuse me? You think I've lost my memory *on purpose*?'

'I didn't say that.'

'No, but you insinuated it.'

'All I'm saying is ...' Bryan rests both hands on top of the handle of the shovel. 'I'm just going along with the plan. You losing your memory is unfortunate, but it doesn't change anything. We made a plan together and I'm trying to get us to stick to it. I will tell you what happened to Ashleigh

Carmichael once we've dealt with this issue.' He gestures to the hole and continues. 'Deal?'

I lower my eyes to the ground and twist my heel into the dirt. 'Fine. Deal.'

I guess my curiosity can wait a little longer.

How to Commit the Perfect Murder
Step Eight

Never Hesitate at the Final Hurdle

Okay, buckle up because this is when shit starts to get serious. This is the time when those nerves will kick in, your brain will start to throw all sorts of doubts your way and you'll consider backing out of the whole thing.

Don't you fucking dare! Not when you're so close to the end.

This is the moment that will define you, that will separate you from those who aren't serious about ending someone's life. Don't be one of those people. Never hesitate. Just keep moving forwards. Even if your plan goes wrong or you have to make shit up on the spot.

Just do it. Get on with it.

You've made it this far. You've done all the steps I've taught you so now is not the time to doubt yourself or hesitate.

You've been in it for the long haul, possibly for years.

You've adapted and overcome every situation you've come across.

You've sorted out your priorities.

You've blended in and become part of the crowd (or not).

You've ensured you haven't put your trust in anyone.

You've played to your strengths.

And you've made them trust you.

Now it's the final hurdle and you're coming up to the home straight.

Keep going. You've got this.

Trust me.

Chapter Thirty-Seven

October 2007

Every waking moment I thought of Bryan Matthews. He was more than an obsession now. He was … my *everything*. And he needed to die. I'd spent the past seven years developing into a headstrong teenager. Gone was the timid bookworm. I was now a black belt in karate. I spent a few evenings a week developing my boxing skills and working out in the gym lifting weights. When I started, I was feeble and skinny, but now my adult body was taking shape. Strong and lean and ready … ready for the moment I knew would arrive one day.

One more year …

One more year and then I would be a legal adult and could leave home to pursue Bryan Matthews. My father had other ideas. Now I was almost an adult, he wanted to send me away to a private university to study law, then eventually work for him. That was never going to happen, but I couldn't tell him about my plan to kill a man. He didn't know the real me and I was beginning to think he never would. Maybe I needed to rethink things. Maybe I needed to get rid of the people standing in my way first.

There were several, but my father was certainly top of the list. It wasn't that he was a bad man who deserved to die, but he'd never shown me any sort of love or attention, so why should I continue to allow him to control my life? He was no father to me.

It hadn't been in the original plan – to kill my father – but what choice did I have? I couldn't allow him to send me away from my overall goal. But killing two people (or possibly more) made things complicated. How would I accomplish it? What would happen when he died? His death would raise a lot of suspicion and, while I was underage, his estate and business would bypass me and go to his business partner. Perhaps I could change that …

There was a lot to consider.

While I pondered the future, I sat at my desk and scrolled through Bryan's latest updates on Facebook; something I did at least five times a day.

Bryan Matthews is … helping my dad in the garage.

Bryan Matthews is … hanging out with the coolest girlfriend ever. Love you, Han.

Bryan Matthews is … thinking.

Bryan Matthews is … glad to have moved away from MK. Best thing I ever did.

Bryan Matthews is … missing his old friends.

And that was just one day.

Fucking hell, this guy was still full of himself, and this stupid social media profile was helping him gain sympathisers and more friends than he ever needed. Little did he know that there was little old me, nestled in his extensive friends list, plotting his demise and using every tool I had in my arsenal to do it.

I always envisioned I'd never deviate from the plan, but I had to adapt and overcome and take care of a few issues. It was time to have a chat with my father.

Chapter Thirty-Eight

ASHLEIGH
3 July – 19:30 p.m.

The name rings a bell in my head, but it doesn't register. As I stare at the two men in front of me, I realise I'm in way over my head. Like … I don't even know where to begin or how to answer. My body freezes as I wait for one of them to expand, but they don't. I want to scream, 'So who is Hannah Baker!' but they just continue to glare at each other through the pouring rain, which hasn't shown any hint of slowing down in the past few minutes.

Bryan's fists are clenched at his sides and Curtis is grinning like a mad man, which is strange, considering he's the one tied up on the ground and covered in mud. He really must be crazy. He certainly doesn't look sane.

The vein in Bryan's forehead looks ready to pop. I don't think I've ever seen such an angry man, not even when— *Nope, not the time, Ashleigh.*

'Is someone going to elaborate on who Hannah Baker is?' I finally shout. A rumble of thunder answers my question.

'Hannah Baker is – *was* – my girlfriend back when I was in my late teens and early twenties,' answers Bryan solemnly. The way he says her name tells me it causes him pain to do so.

'Why do I get the feeling you guys didn't just *break up*?'

Bryan huffs and turns to me. 'Because we didn't break up. She died.' His eyes are dark, and I can't be sure if he's crying or if it's merely the rain running down his cheeks. His face is bright red; even in the darkness I can see it. Bryan turns to Curtis and takes a deep breath, as if what he's about to say is causing him actual distress. 'You had no right to bring her up.'

'She was my girlfriend first.'

Bryan laughs out loud, which surprises me considering he was practically in tears moments before. 'You are deluded! You never dated Hannah! You're just some crazy psychopath who makes all this shit up in your head until eventually you believe your own lies. You've just been pretending to be me.'

'That's not true.'

'You never even *met* Hannah.'

Curtis grins. 'Oh, I think I did. You have quite the ex-girlfriend history, don't you? Both of them relate to me in some way, but both are dead because of you. Now do you understand why I told you to get away from this man, Blondie? You're not safe with him.'

Bryan grinds his teeth. 'I didn't kill either of them' – there's a very long pregnant pause when it feels as if all of us are holding our breaths – 'on purpose,' finishes Bryan.

I can't help it; I gasp loudly.

Bryan turns to me again. 'I promise you, I don't know what happened with Mia. I can't hold myself accountable for her death, but Hannah ... Hannah's death *was* an accident. I promise you. I didn't mean to ... I was drunk and ... and someone was following me. I was driving and I shouldn't have been. I was on my way home but was too focussed on the damn headlights in my rear-view mirror. I took my eyes off the road for a second. I didn't know she was walking over to see me in the middle of the night. I hit her ... and she ... she was dead instantly.'

A rumble of thunder shakes the ground.

'That's not the whole story though, is it?' asks Curtis, changing his kneeling position ever so slightly.

My stomach drops and nausea bubbles up from inside. I can't believe what I'm hearing. I hold my breath as Bryan begins talking again.

'No ... I left her there. I was so drunk. I saw what I'd done and ... and I left her on the side of the road.'

Another gasp escapes before I can control it. 'You what!' I clap my hand across my mouth, but it's too late. My tone is full of accusation.

'I regret it every day,' he adds. 'And I've been running ever since, staying on the road, keeping out of trouble. It was classed as a hit and run, and they eventually arrested someone over it.'

I narrow my eyes. 'Who?'

'Does it matter?'

'Yes, it does.'

Bryan swallows and pauses before saying in a low tone, 'Sawyer Croft.'

Yet another gasp escapes and, this time, I stumble and have to use the shovel I'm holding to stop myself from slipping in the mud. 'What the ... My father's business partner? *My* business partner?'

Bryan winces at the tone of my voice. 'I guess he never told you why he went to prison for five years?'

'It was years ago. I didn't think anything of it. My father told me it was to do with fraud, but then he died and when Sawyer came back to the company, he never spoke of it again. It was sort of brushed under the rug. Nothing was mentioned in the news or anything.'

'Funny that,' Curtis interjects with a snort.

Bryan spins around and grabs his jacket again. 'Give me one good reason why I shouldn't kill you right fucking now?'

'I can't. I mean, you've proved you can get away with murder already, so there's no reason to suggest you couldn't do it again.'

Bryan grits his teeth; his arm with the shovel raises above his head. 'I didn't ... murder ... Hannah. I ... it was an accident.'

'And yet you ran away like a coward because you couldn't face up to what you'd done, just like you did with Mia.'

'I didn't kill Mia. You've got it wrong. I don't know why she killed herself, but it had nothing to do with me.'

'Maybe ... or maybe I'm focussing on the wrong person here ...' His eyes drift over to me, and I shudder as I stare into them. It's like he has no soul, no humanity, like he's not even a real person. His eyes are black, and they make my insides want to shrivel up. Maybe Bryan is right; maybe Curtis is a psychopath who makes stuff up and twists the truth until he believes it. Has he been making everything up this whole time?

'Why are you looking at me, you crazy freak?' I ask.

'Your father, Sawyer Croft, Mia, Hannah Baker, Bryan Matthews, me, you … We're all linked and you're too stupid to even see it.'

I shake my head, unable and unwilling to accept any of this is happening. How has this situation turned into a murder enquiry? How did I even get into this ridiculous situation in the first place? How did I … wait …

Click.

'It was you,' I say, taking a small step towards Curtis. Bryan has now let him crumple into a wet, muddy heap on the ground. 'You started all of this, didn't you? You're the one who originally left me that note, aren't you?' I turn to Bryan. 'The reason you lied to me and told me your name was Curtis was to try and cover up the fact you'd just stolen his identity. The note … it was left by Curtis to draw me out. It was him I crashed into, not you.'

Bryan nods ever so slightly. 'I tracked him down and took my car back. He told me you'd be on your way to see him and about the money and your bag, so I played along, hoping I'd get some money out of you, but things have changed since then as you well know.'

'So, you lied to me and tricked me.'

Bryan has the decency to look sorry for himself. 'I'm sorry. I needed the money and thought I'd have a bit of fun, but I don't care about that now. I think I—' He stops and looks away from me. 'It doesn't matter what I think I feel. The bottom line is that I lied to you, and you have every right to hate me for it. I wish I could take it back, but now all I care about is keeping you safe.'

Curtis laughs out loud, breaking the tension. 'This is what he does! He's lying to you even now. This man deserves to die for what he's done and the sooner you get that into your thick skull the sooner we'll all be free of him.'

I round on Curtis, seething. Yet another man who's trying to control me. I've had enough. I'm taking a stand. I believe Bryan, not Curtis.

'So, what ... you're upset he broke your sister's heart a decade ago? Big deal. He bullied a few kids back in the day. He accidentally killed someone. We've all made mistakes in the past. We've all done things we're not proud of, but at least Bryan has the decency to change and try and make amends, whereas you ... you're still stuck in the past and think it's justification to hunt someone like an animal and murder them. You're weak and pathetic and I don't care what happens to you.' I finish my speech, attempting to hide the trembling in my hands by clutching the shovel tighter.

Curtis doesn't respond. He merely kneels there, in the mud, staring at me, as if he's trying to figure me out or read my mind. It makes me feel vulnerable and naked and I voluntarily take a step backwards towards Bryan.

We stand next to each other, looking down at the man on the ground. I don't know what Bryan's thinking, but I'm pretty sure it's along the same lines as me.

We must kill him if we want to survive.

I look at Bryan and he looks at me and we nod in unison, like we have a mutual understanding. I don't know how, and I don't know why, but over the course of the past few days I've become the Bonnie to his Clyde (except without the bank robbery bit). The woman I was three days ago is unrecognisable to the woman I am today ... and I'm never going back.

'It's going to be tricky,' says Bryan. 'You'll have to stick with me, and you probably won't ever be able to go home again.'

I nod. 'I've come too far to turn back now. I need to see this through, no matter what happens. I'll change my name if I have to.'

Bryan sighs. 'I hate to do this to you, Barbie. I won't stop you if you decide to bail out now. Everything we've been through, just forget it. The money, everything. The slate's wiped clean, but if you decide to come with me then we're in this together. No matter what happens.'

I'm filled with such exhilaration that I can barely take a breath. This is it. I'm really doing this. I'm jumping in with both feet.

'Let's do it.'

Bryan's lips twitch into a smile.

Chapter Thirty-Nine

BRYAN
3 July – 19:45 p.m.

Something had changed in Barbie. Had he really done this to her? He'd never expected any of this to happen. She was never supposed to have gotten involved in his mess, let alone change her whole identity and life to suit him. And he'd meant what he said, that if she wanted to bail out now, he wouldn't blame her, but here she was, standing over a man they were about to kill ... in order to save himself. Maybe Curtis was right. He really was a coward and now he was allowing his mistake to corrupt another innocent woman ...

Barbie cleared her throat. 'So ... how do we do this then?'

Bryan shook his head, his head dipped low against the rain. He could barely see through the streams of water running down his face. 'Barbie ... I can't ... I can't let you do this for me.'

Her whole demeanour changed. She stood up straighter as if she was offended. 'W-What? But I just agreed to—'

'Curtis is right. I'm a coward. I made a mistake, and I ran away. I'm not a murderer and neither are you. I won't make the same mistake again. We have to let him go.'

Barbie dropped the shovel, disappointment clear in her eyes. 'I can't believe you! You can't let him get away with this. He'll kill you. He'll come after you. He'll come after *us*. We're not safe if he's still alive. You get that, right?'

Bryan took a deep breath and held it for several seconds while he studied his enemy, still hunched on the ground, quietly listening, awaiting his fate, but he didn't look remotely afraid. In fact, he seemed to be enjoying the drama unfolding in front of him.

'Curtis ... I'm sorry for everything I've done to you. I'm sorry Mia killed herself. Truly. But this must end sometime.'

'It will end when you are dead and cold in the ground.' The reply was instantaneous and filled with hatred.

Bryan closed his eyes. 'I'm going to let you go. I can't do this anymore. I can't run any longer.' He knelt in front of Curtis and reached for his tied wrists.

'You let me go and you're a dead man. Don't think this changes anything between us,' snarled Curtis.

Bryan didn't respond as he began to loosen the bindings around Curtis's wrists.

'You're making a mistake, Bryan,' said Barbie. 'This is a mistake.'

He managed to pull the duct tape loose and then stood up. Curtis rubbed his sore wrists but remained kneeling.

'Run,' said Curtis in a deep, throaty voice. 'I'll give you a five-minute head start.'

Bryan laughed. 'We're about to leave you in the middle of bloody nowhere and drive away in a car.'

'Ten minutes then.'

Bryan rolled his eyes and turned to walk away, placing a hand on Barbie's shoulder. 'Come on, let's leave him.' But Barbie refused to move. She stood rooted to the spot, every muscle in her body tensed. He squeezed her shoulder gently. 'Barbie ... it's over. Please ... I'll hand myself in. We don't have to do this.'

Barbie turned and stared at him and let out a long breath. 'Okay. You're right. I don't know what came over me. Just know I'll do whatever I can to help you. I'll use all my connections to get you the best lawyer.'

Bryan nodded his thanks and they turned and walked back towards the car.

'I'll be seeing you both very soon!' shouted Curtis.

Neither of them turned or stopped walking.

Chapter Forty

ASHLEIGH
4 July – 07:05 a.m.

I wake up to the smell of coffee. Not the yummy, freshly brewed, expensive type I'm accustomed to, but the cheap, hotel type that's instant and doesn't dissolve properly. Trust me, I can tell the difference merely by smell. I have a heightened olfactory sense. My eyes blink open and I see a mug, that was probably once white but now a faded cream, sitting next to me on a bedside table.

'Morning,' says a rough voice from behind me.

I twist erratically towards the sound and let out a small yelp as I see Bryan lying next to me on the bed, one arm tucked behind his head and the other holding a remote control. He's topless and the sight takes my breath away. You could grate cheese on his abs and his pecs ... Oh boy, I'm in trouble.

'Hi,' I say stupidly. Why won't my brain catch up with this situation? All I can think about is dragging my tongue across his chest. Where am I? Why am I here? Why is Bryan lying topless in bed beside me?

'Hope you like shit coffee.'

I flinch slightly as I sit up. My hair is damp and—

'Ahhh!' I clutch the duvet against my chest as I realise I'm also topless. I quickly check and ... yep, I'm completely naked. 'Why am I naked?' I gasp.

'Your clothes are hanging up to dry. We were both drenched by the time we got here last night.' I open my mouth to ask the next obvious question that's dancing on my lips, but Bryan gets there first. 'Relax. We didn't have sex.'

I'm not sure if I'm relieved or disappointed. Then again, if we did have sex and I don't remember it then surely it couldn't have been that good. But, luckily, we didn't, so ...

Bryan smiles, which lights up his whole face. There's even a cheeky sparkle in his eyes. 'We can change that if you like.'

I don't respond because I'm focussing too hard on not pouncing on him like a dog in heat. Once my heart stops hammering, I risk reaching over and picking up the dingy coffee mug. I take a sip and grimace, but then take another sip. My eyes flick over the television screen.

The news is on and Bryan, having seemingly just read my thoughts, says, 'Nothing on your supposed disappearance yet, but I've only just put it on. I can turn it off if you like.'

'No, that's okay. I'd like to keep myself updated on what's happening.'

'Look, about last night. Things got a bit crazy. That's what Curtis tends to do. He makes people crazy, and he spreads lies to cause chaos and mistrust. He always has. I'm just glad I got you out of there safely.'

'I would have done it, you know.'

'I know ... and that's what's scaring me. I don't want to turn you into a murderer. We need to sort this out together. I'm going to go to the police once I figure out a few things.'

'What things?'

'Like … who really killed Mia. Maybe if we find out the truth about her death then we can tell Curtis and it might make him, I don't know … move on from his vendetta against me.'

I nod, taking another sip. 'That's a good idea. I think I need to speak to Sawyer.'

'He's in charge of your father's business now, right? Now that you've disappeared, and all your social media pages have gone. Do you think he's the one who deleted them?'

'I'm not sure, but it's suspicious, like he's trying to get rid of me or is happy that I'm gone.'

'So … that's the plan then? Find and speak to Sawyer and find out the truth about what happened to Mia so we can hopefully get Curtis off our backs.'

'I guess so. It's a good a place as any to start, but what are we going to do about Curtis in the meantime? He found us before so it's highly likely he'll find us again. We have a crazy murderer after us.'

'You let me worry about him, but I suggest we get rid of the car. It breaks my heart, but I think he's tracking it somehow.'

'I have to ask … Who does the car *actually* belong to?'

'Me. It's my car. I bought it and restored it with my dad years ago. We had it shipped over from America. You've seen *Supernatural*, right?'

I stare at him as if he's asked me the stupidest question in the world. 'Of course I've seen it. Jensen Ackles is a god.'

Bryan rolls his eyes. 'Right. Whatever. Anyway, I always wanted an Impala after seeing that show, so me and my dad bought one. But Curtis stole it a while back and I've been trying to get it back ever since.'

'There's no love lost between you two, is there?'

'We've had a complicated relationship over the years.'

'Do you think he made you accidentally kill Hannah?'

'Possibly, but I have no proof. But the truth of the matter is that I was driving while drunk and I hit her, so it was my fault.'

'But you said there were blinding headlights behind you, and someone was following you. Maybe it was him. Maybe he wanted you to lose control and do something bad.'

Bryan stares at me for several seconds. 'Thank you.'

'For what?'

'For believing in me even though you have every reason not to.'

I shrug, placing the now almost empty coffee mug back on the bedside table. I can't bring myself to swallow the last dregs of un-dissolved coffee granules. 'What can I say? Maybe you've grown on me.'

'You've grown on me too, you know.'

'You don't think I'm a spoilt, fake ... B word?'

Bryan smiles. 'No. Do you still think I'm a low-life, poor, scruffy-looking loser?'

I laugh out loud. 'You're still a bit scruffy looking.' We lock eyes for a moment, and I feel goosebumps all over my body and a familiar tingle ... *down there.*

Oh jeez ...

Before I get the chance to chicken out and register what's happening, Bryan kisses me. He tastes like cheap coffee (and I'm sure I do too), but I don't care. His hair smells freshly washed with a hint of mango (must be the shampoo they have here). My body tenses, as if unsure if this is a good thing or a bad thing. He pulls away, clearly sensing my unease.

'Sorry ... I just ... I've wanted to do that for a while.'

Now his lips aren't on mine I feel an overwhelming sense of loss. I need them back. I need his tongue in my mouth and his hands all over me. I grab him round the back of the neck with both hands, allowing the duvet to drop, revealing my breasts.

We lock lips again and he climbs on top of me.

This is perfect.

Chapter Forty-One

HANNAH
7 July – 03:30 a.m.

We cover Curtis with the last of the dirt and stand next to the grave, side by side. It looks perfectly ordinary, exactly how it had looked when we first arrived, but only we know the truth. Only we know that, when this grave comes to be filled with a coffin, there will be another dead soul underneath, hidden for eternity. I don't know why, but I feel … strangely okay with it.

Bryan holds out his hand and I stare at it, wondering if he means for me to place the shovel in it for him to carry it back to the car or whether he means for me to hold his hand. I go for the former and he seems satisfied with that choice.

We walk back to the car in silence, and I watch him while he chucks the shovels in the boot and slams it shut.

'Now what?'

Bryan looks at me. 'Now I tell you what happened to Ashleigh Carmichael.'

I hold my breath and count to ten, but he still hasn't said anything. I frown. 'What?' I ask.

'You need help.'

I narrow my eyes. 'O … kay?'

'You're sick.'

'Excuse me?'

'I think you're broken.'

253

'Will you stop fucking talking in riddles and just tell me in plain English?'

Bryan raises his eyebrows at my tone of voice. It almost looks like he flinched when I swore. He takes a deep breath and lets it out slowly as he runs both his hands through his hair. 'You *are* Ashleigh Carmichael.'

I blink several times as the sounds of the words fade in my ears. They make no sense. Yes, I heard them, but the words ... they ... they can't be true.

'I-I don't understand. You said my name was Hannah.'

'Yes, because that's what we agreed on. It's what *you* agreed on. When we found out that someone had killed off Ashleigh Carmichael, we decided to change your name. Not officially of course, but that was the plan eventually. We changed it so you could run away with me, and we could be together, but—'

'But what?'

'But things went wrong. Badly wrong.'

'How so?'

'Curtis came after us and we— Shit!' Blue lights wail in the distance. 'We have to go. Now!' Bryan grabs my arm and pushes me towards the passenger side door. He sprints around to the driver's side, yanks the door open and has the car running before I even know what's happening.

'Hannah! Get in the fucking car!'

I jump in and slam the door. Bryan puts his foot down and the car skids on the loose gravel. The sirens fade as we speed along the road to an unknown location. My heart hammers so hard in my chest I'm having a hard time catching my breath, like I've sprinted 400 metres round a track.

'Are you okay?' he asks me, placing his free hand on my knee. I don't mean to, but I flinch at his touch, which prompts him to swiftly remove his hand as if he's burned me.

'Sorry ... I forgot. You don't remember me.'

'Why can't I remember anything? The truth.'

'I don't know for sure, but I think you've suffered some sort of mental breakdown. I know you got hit on the head, but I don't think that's the reason you can't remember anything.'

I shake my head. 'That's absurd!'

'Really? Because you're practically a different person than Ashleigh Carmichael was. You swear, for a start. Plus ... I think what happened to you pushed you over the edge.'

'Why? What did happen to me?'

'It's a long story.'

'Tell me.'

Bryan nods. 'It all started when we went to see Sawyer Croft ...'

Chapter Forty-Two

November 2008

The new plan worked as it should have done. Granted, it wasn't my first choice, but I was happy with the result. Bryan Matthews was living his life to the fullest, blissfully happy and enjoying his pretty and perfect girlfriend. It made me sick to see him like that, but I had to be patient. One day he'd suffer for his crimes. One day he'd pay the ultimate price.

But for that to happen I had to step away from his spotlight. I had to let him live his life without me watching him every second of the day. I knew where to find him. I'd be back for him later down the line. I had a plan for him in a couple of years' time, so until then I'd have to wait and sort out the mess that was happening in my own life.

My father (God rest his soul) was dead.

To be perfectly honest, I didn't miss him one little bit because he was barely around anyway, so him being dead made no difference. My uncle, on the other hand ... Well, he was a different story. He was constantly hovering over me, demanding that I hand over the reins to him. But he eventually agreed to be my business partner and, luckily, he began to pay less and less attention to me.

There wasn't a lot left to do except let the years drift by ... until the time came.

Bryan Matthews was going to wish he was dead.

And then he would be.

Dear Diary

Date: 7 July 2008

Dear Diary,

Time seems to have moved on quickly. I haven't written in my diary for a long time. Not since ... not since ... Mia died. Even writing her name is painful. I feel as if I've lost a piece of my soul. So much has happened yet I can't bring myself to write about any of it. I don't think I want to keep writing in a diary anymore because it reminds me of everything that's going wrong in my life. It's all his fault ... Bryan Matthews ...

Date: 8 July 2008

Dear Diary,

Bryan Matthews started all of this. If he'd never broken up with Mia, then she never would have had her heart broken and run into the arms of a stranger. I found out his name. Sawyer Croft, some businessman from London. He works for the Carmichael Foundation, whatever the hell that is. The owner of the company has recently died in a car crash, so I saw on the news.

Date: 15 July 2008

Dear Diary,

My life is falling apart. I need Bryan Matthews to understand the pain he's caused me and is causing me daily. Nothing can bring Mia back, but taking out the people responsible is a good start. First, I'm going to make sure that Bryan Matthews knows what it's like to lose someone he loves in the most horrific way. Then I'm going to frame Sawyer Croft and have him sent to jail. I could kill him, but he's untouchable. It would be too risky.

I know I've always had the urge to kill people, but it always seemed to go away. But now that Mia is gone, I have nothing left to live for. I used to worship Bryan Matthews, but it's funny how time has a way of changing your perspective on things and on people. I realise now how evil he truly is, and he deserves to pay for what he's done ... and especially for what he did to that poor girl. Plus, he's the reason my sister is dead.

Date: 16 July 2008

Dear Diary,

I can't quite believe I'm doing this. I don't think I should write in my diary anymore. It's too risky. What if someone found it and read it? So ... I guess this is my last entry. I'm not sure what I'll do with all my old diaries. Maybe burn them. Maybe keep them. All I know for sure is that one day, I'm going to kill Bryan Matthews.

Chapter Forty-Three

ASHLEIGH
4 July 2022 – 11:00 a.m.

We're on the road again.

A few hours ago, we dumped the Impala in an abandoned field and covered it with branches to shield it from view. Bryan was practically in tears when we turned to leave. 'It's only a car,' I told him, and he shot me a look that made me want to shrivel up into a ball. Okay, got it. Never question a man's love for his car.

We then walked to a nearby town where Bryan acquired a new set of wheels. Take that however you like (we stole it, okay?), and he told me that we'd have to keep changing cars every few days to avoid being detected because once a car was reported stolen then the police could track it down.

Anyway, we're on the road again in a blue Ford Mondeo (there was a time, not too long ago, when you wouldn't catch me dead in a common car like this) and, I don't know about Bryan, but I'm grinning like an idiot, still high from my multiple orgasms earlier this morning. We keep sneaking glances at each other like we're immature teenagers, but it doesn't feel awkward. He holds my hand during the long stretches of road. I'm so giddy with excitement and happiness that I almost miss the news bulletin that comes on the radio.

'Good morning. This is the eleven o'clock news with Mary Clark. More information has been revealed with regards to the disappearance of Ashleigh Carmichael, the multi-million-pound heiress who went missing four days ago. Two policemen in Skegness have come forwards with details and have said they were approached by Miss Carmichael on the first of July at approximately six forty-five in the evening.

'PC Stevens said she seemed quite distressed and wasn't wearing any shoes. She asked for money to buy food and said her bag and phone had been stolen in London after being involved in a car accident. PC Stevens offered to take down her details, but she declined and then drove away. The London Met, however, have not been informed of any car accident involving Miss Carmichael. It is highly likely that she has run away, as she was in possession of her car at the last known sighting. More information on this story as it develops ...'

I reach over and switch the radio off. 'That's rubbish. Those policemen didn't want to help me. Why wasn't the car accident reported? I mean ... obviously Curtis wouldn't have reported it, but surely the hospital made some sort of record of me being there.'

Bryan bites his bottom lip, which makes him look incredibly sexy. He catches me watching him. 'I know that look.'

'What look?'

'That you-want-to-eat-me look.'

'I might get car sick if I do that right now.'

'Ha ha. Now, can you stop picturing me naked and focus. Clearly, something dodgy is going on here. Someone is covering up the fact you've disappeared.'

'Sawyer.'

'Good job we're on our way to see him then.'

'But we've been friends and colleagues for years. He was best friends with my father. He looked after me when I was a little girl. I called him Uncle Croft. Why would he do this to me?'

'That's what we'll find out.'

'He'll be surprised to see me.'

'I bet. I expect he's hoping you're dead.'

'Yeah, well, I'm about to disappoint him.' I nestle my bum into the soft car seat. My clothes are still ever so slightly damp from the downpour yesterday, but I'm warm and comfortable, adequately hydrated, full of delicious food from the breakfast bar at the hotel (I went for a full English because ... well, why not?) and 100 per cent sexually satisfied after over an hour of rambunctious and totally hot sex.

Life is good.

I don't even remember the last time I thought about my phone or social media or how many likes I've received on my latest reel. That part of my life is a distant memory and one I'm happy to leave behind and never think about again. I want to be with Bryan and, despite him wanting to turn himself in and admit what he did all those years ago, I've decided I'm not going to let him throw his life away because of one mistake. I want to be with him, and I want to sort this out together, get to the bottom of why someone is trying to destroy my life and get rid of Curtis somehow too. That's not too much to ask, is it?

It doesn't make sense that Sawyer would be out to get me, but it can't be a coincidence that he was the guy who got sent to jail for Bryan's mistake. Everything seems to be linked and I'm determined to get to the bottom of it.

We're heading back to London, the city I used to call my home, but now it feels like an alien environment. The thought of all the tall buildings and traffic sets my teeth on edge and makes me feel claustrophobic, and I haven't even got there yet. It will most likely take us all day to arrive, but that's okay because the more distance we put between us and Curtis, the better. He's probably tracked down the Impala by now (if it was indeed fitted with a tracker). He seems like a smart man (if a little crazy), so I expect he'll put two and two together and realise we're heading to see Sawyer to get some answers. It wouldn't surprise me if he's on his way to London now too.

It feels strange and somewhat surreal to know that we're being hunted by a deranged lunatic who wants to kill us (or wants to kill Bryan at least, as I don't think he has anything against me, but what do I know?). How long will it take before he finds us? We're on borrowed time and the quicker we can get answers the better.

It's nearly nine in the evening by the time we enter the city. I use Bryan's phone to look up Sawyer on social media to see if there are any clues as to his whereabouts. From the looks of his Instagram stories, he's at a bar called *iBar* having a few drinks with work colleagues (aka *my* colleagues). I can't just waltz in there and announce myself and cause a scene. I need to get him alone and my best bet is to wait until he returns home and meet him there. Luckily, I know the security code and where his spare set of emergency keys are hidden.

Bryan and I let ourselves in to his lavish London townhouse. It's not as big or as expensive as mine, but it does have a wine cellar. Everything in his house is pristine and all one colour palette – silver and black. It's basically the biggest, most ridiculously over-the-top bachelor pad you can imagine, complete with a huge fur rug in front of a silver-gilded fireplace. I mean, it's a little too much for my taste, but each to their own.

Bryan spies the extensive bar and creeps over to investigate. He pours himself a top shelf gin and gulps it back. 'Damn, that's good shit ... sorry ... stuff.'

I smile but am pleasantly surprised to find I don't flinch at the bad word. Could it be I'm changing for the better? That I'm putting all my childhood demons behind me? A small glimmer of hope blooms inside my cold heart.

'I'll have one of those,' I say, nodding as he refills his glass. He pours one out for me, and we clink and drink in unison. 'Cheers.'

'When do you expect him home?'

'Work drinks usually continue long into the night, but since it's a Monday I doubt it'll be a long one.'

'What's the plan? He's not going to be happy to find that we broke in.'

'We didn't break in. I have a key. I used to use it all the time when—' I stop myself and gulp back my drink, thankful for its welcoming burning sensation down my throat. I've said too much and now my cheeks are blazing and Bryan can tell I'm hiding something.

'When what?' Bryan stops drinking and lowers his glass, his gaze burning a hole right through me. I attempt to avoid his eye contact, but it's useless.

I look up at him. 'Sawyer and I ... we used to ... you know—'

'Fuck?'

I shudder. 'Must you use such a vulgar word? But yes, okay, we used to ... have sex.'

Bryan grimaces. 'How old is he?'

'Why does it matter?'

'Because you said he was friends with your father so that must mean he's not your own age. Plus, you said you used to call him Uncle Croft, which is just plain wrong on so many levels.'

I can't hide my red face, which clearly tells Bryan all he needs to know. His eyes grow darker, more focussed, like there's a fire burning somewhere inside him. He's angry. I don't blame him. I'm angry at myself for letting it go on for as long as it did.

Here's the truth ...

The truth is that Sawyer took advantage of me when I was younger, and I let him. I'm not saying it was a good decision on my part, but I was young and naive, and he was an older man and he paid me more attention than my own father. I was fifteen the first time it happened. He asked me to come over late at night and I didn't think anything of it, so I escaped from my house and made my way over here and let myself in with the hidden spare key. Then he got me drunk and told me it would be our own little secret. It happened a lot after that, at least once a week. He would have his way with me and then I'd leave. It may have been our own secret arrangement, but I got nothing out of it (so I realised years later when I'd grown up a bit). It wasn't enjoyable for me, but I couldn't say no or he'd—

'Tell me everything,' interrupts Bryan.

'I'd rather not. Let's just say that him going to prison was the best thing that could have happened because it put an end to it. We didn't continue once he got out.'

'Did your father ever find out?'

'If he did then he never said so.'

'Fucking prick.'

'Look, you can't bring it up when we see him. It has nothing to do with anything.'

'The hell it does!'

'If you start shouting at him then you'll jeopardise this whole thing. Just promise me you'll let me handle it and talk to him. When he arrives you need to stay hidden because if he finds out that you're the guy who killed Hannah Baker then I can't guarantee you'll leave here alive. And I need you to stay alive, Bryan. Please.'

Bryan's body language reminds me of a coiled cobra ready to strike. I've never seen him so angry and fired up. It must mean he really likes me though, right? But there's nothing he can do about what happened and there's no need to bring it up with Sawyer when he gets here. I hope he realises that there's more at stake than my own tortured innocence.

An hour passes and I can feel the beginnings of nervous butterflies fluttering in my stomach. I'm shivering, but it's not cold. Maybe I'm in shock, I don't know. This all feels wrong, but I'm in too deep to turn back now. We need answers and speaking to Sawyer is the only way to get them.

A scraping noise pierces the darkness and silence. I take a sharp inhale and hold my breath, too scared to breathe in case Sawyer hears me. Bryan is hiding somewhere. I have to trust him not to blow his cover. I'm hiding just down the hallway out of sight.

The lights flick on as heavy footsteps echo on the tiled floor of the entrance hall. I press myself flatter against the wall even though I can't hide myself any better. I hear a deep male voice muttering, possibly wondering why the alarm hasn't gone off, despite having obviously set it before he left.

I chance a peek around the corner and into the brightly lit hallway. Sawyer is stumbling against the wall, kicking his highly polished black shoes off. He's clearly drunk, which could work to my advantage. I watch as he digs his phone out of his pocket, checks it and then throws it on the side table where it skids across the shiny metal surface and clatters to the floor. He picks it up with a sigh. To be honest, I was half expecting him to have brought a woman home with him. It's how his usual work nights out end, but he's alone ... and he looks bad. Not unattractive, as he's always been a handsome, well-groomed man, but the shadows under his eyes are darker than usual, his hair slightly dishevelled, compared to his normal perfectly quaffed style. I'm almost certain he dyes his hair black, as I once noticed a few flecks of grey around his ears and temples.

He reminds me of my father. They were both hard-working, dedicated businessmen who never let family or distractions get in their way. I guess you could say I am like my father too ... or at least I was.

It's now or never ...

I step out from my hiding place, adjusting my baggy t-shirt. I know I look a state and I'm not expecting him to even recognise me at first.

'Hello, Sawyer,' I say.

Sawyer jumps and loses his balance on the tiled floor. He grabs the nearest solid object to him, which happens to be the side table and stumbles into it. He clutches his heart. 'What the fuck! Who the fuck ... how did you ... who the hell are you?'

I flinch at every swear word, but hold my ground, stepping towards him with my hand outstretched. 'Sawyer. It's me. Don't freak out.'

'Who the fuck— Wait ... Ashleigh?' He laughs to himself.

I nod and stop, watching as he stands up straight and squints at me, as if he can't quite understand what he's seeing. He must think his eyes are deceiving him.

'Ashleigh? Oh fuck, it *is* you. What the hell happened to you? You look … well, I'm sorry, love, but you look like shit. Your hair! Your clothes! Sorry … what am I saying? It's good to see you, love.' He regains his composure, even though I see a red flush across his cheeks, and totters towards me on wobbly legs, his arms open wide. He wraps them around me but doesn't squeeze me into a hug. He doesn't even try and grope my butt like he normally does.

Something's wrong. Something's … *off*.

'What in God's name are you doing dressed like a homeless person? Where have you been?'

Sawyer lets go of me, pushing me away from his body as if he's offended by my presence.

I don't smell that bad.

'It's a long story,' I say, following him into the large lounge area. He makes a B-line straight for the bar and pours himself a double whiskey. I see him clock the two used gin glasses, but he doesn't mention them.

'Well hell, love. I've got time. We've had the police and everyone looking for you.'

'Really? Because according to the news it seems like everyone is convinced I ran away and there is no search anymore.'

Sawyer scoffs behind his glass. 'Yeah, cos we didn't want the media to blow up over it. I handled it.'

'Right.' *What a load of rubbish.* He's lying. 'Well, I'm back.'

'That's great!' He grins, but it doesn't reach his eyes. They remain focussed on me, like he's trying to stare right through me, trying to read my mind.

'Actually Sawyer, I'm not back. I've only come here to ask you some questions.' I can feel my nerves attempting to overpower me.

'Questions? What do you mean? What questions?'

'About Curtis Redding.'

'Who?' He makes a good show of acting nonchalant, but I notice the slight tremble in the hand that's holding the whiskey glass. He places the glass down on the bar to hide the tremble and turns his back to me. 'I've never heard of a Curtis Redding.'

'How about Mia Redding?'

This time the reaction is more prominent and there's nothing he can do to hide it. He stumbles against the bar, grasping the edge for support. I see his fingers clutch the edge, his knuckles turning white from the exertion.

'Ashleigh ... what have you got yourself involved in?' His tone is low, slow and to the point, completely different to the tone of a few minutes ago. He appears to have sobered up miraculously quickly.

'I think that's the question I should be asking you, Sawyer.'

He turns around on the spot and leans against the bar, still clasping his hands around the edge of it. He locks eyes with me. 'Who else is here?'

'No one.'

'You never were very good at lying.'

'Neither were you.'

'I should call the police. You broke into my home.'

'And tell them what ... that I let myself in using the same key I used when I visited you in the middle of the night as a fifteen-year-old?'

Sawyer blinks several times and clenches his teeth. 'Are you blackmailing me?'

'I'd never dream of doing such a thing. I just want answers and then I'll be on my way.'

Sawyer turns on the spot again and begins to make himself another drink. He's taking his time on purpose, probably enjoying making me squirm. I don't want to be here. I don't feel safe, but knowing Bryan is nearby is enough to keep me calm and focussed on what I need to do.

He turns around, a fresh drink in his hand. 'Mia Redding jumped to her death fourteen years ago from my office window. I was nowhere around at the time. It was a tragic loss of life. Obviously, we managed to keep it out of the papers or your father's business would have suffered.'

'How did she get into your office in the first place?'

'Probably the same way you got into my house. She had a key.'

'You were sleeping with her.'

Sawyer's silence confirms my statement. He takes a sip, holds the whiskey in his mouth a few seconds then swallows. He's cool and calm whereas I'm fighting back the urge to hyperventilate at any moment. 'She wanted to frame me.'

'Wait ... you think she jumped on purpose and didn't actually want to kill herself?'

'I think she was told to jump.'

'By who?' A beat of silence passes. I already know the answer. 'Her brother,' I whisper. Sawyer nods and drinks again. 'But why would Curtis want his sister dead? He loved her.'

Sawyer shrugs. 'How the hell should I know what goes through the mind of a crazy lunatic?'

'How do you know Curtis?' I ask.

Sawyer sighs. 'I don't. I've never even met him. But what I do know is, he's dangerous. He was the one who got me locked up. Your father, luckily, was able to keep everything under the rug.'

'He said you went to jail for fraud.'

Sawyer chuckles as he drains the rest of the glass. It's now empty. 'Yeah, well ... I've probably been guilty of that at some point too.'

'I have it on good authority that you went to jail because you killed a girl in a hit and run.'

Sawyer's fingers clench the glass so tight I fear it might explode into a million pieces. 'Says who? Wait ... don't tell me ...' He laughs. 'I think it's time we had a chat now ... *Bryan Matthews* ...'

Chapter Forty-Four

BRYAN
4 July 2022 – 22:36 p.m.

Bryan sucked in a breath as he heard his name leave Sawyer's lips. It sounded like a threat, a taunt, a dare. It was time he faced up to his demons. He owed it to Ashleigh, to Hannah, to himself. While he'd listened to Ashleigh and Sawyer talking, the tight knot in his chest had coiled tighter and tighter, practically suffocating him. Now he could barely breathe. The tension and adrenaline that flowed through his body was all that was keeping him upright, otherwise he would have gladly collapsed onto the ground to relieve the pressure. But this was no time to hide or act weak. Ashleigh needed him.

Bryan walked into the room, his head held high, his fists clenched, ready for anything. He locked eyes with Sawyer, ignoring Ashleigh completely.

'You.' The single word from Sawyer dripped with rage. 'How dare you step foot in my house.'

'I came for Ashleigh.'

'Ah, I see she's got her claws into you as well then.'

Bryan ignored his pathetic attempt to bait him. 'I want to make amends.'

Sawyer's eyebrows shot upwards. 'It's a little late for that now, don't you think?'

'You're not completely innocent in all of this, Sawyer. I think you were there when Mia died. We need to know the truth.'

Sawyer's lips curled into an evil snarl. 'Maybe so, but I certainly had nothing to do with Hannah's death.'

'No, that was all me.' There was no point in denying it anymore.

'Damn, I wish I'd been recording that. I've waited years for you to come forwards and confess. I was locked up for five years and framed because you were too chicken shit to confess. Tell me … why now?'

'Curtis Redding is after me.'

Sawyer laughed. 'Now, there's a new twist to the story.'

'He's crazy. He's been trying to kill me for years.'

'Hmm, I wonder why. It's not like you don't deserve it for what you've done.'

Bryan clenched his fists even tighter as he took two steps forwards. 'I'll admit I've made some mistakes, but I don't deserve to die. He needs to be stopped so he can't hurt anyone else. If you're right and he did convince Mia to jump to her death to frame you then there's nothing he won't do. He's a master at manipulation.'

Sawyer's eyes flicked towards Ashleigh, who was standing next to the ornate fireplace, using it as a support. 'Sounds like someone else I know.'

Bryan took another step, this time in between Sawyer and Ashleigh. 'Don't bring her into this.' His sense of protection towards Ashleigh was like a fire in his belly. He knew he'd rather die than let anything happen to her. Was this … *love*? Had he fallen in love with her? It was the only logical explanation for all of this.

'Why not? She's why we're all here in this mess in the first place. She may look cute and innocent – although right now she looks less *cute* and more *homeless* – but the point is that Ashleigh Carmichael is a conniving, ruthless bitch who'll stop at nothing to get what she wants. At fifteen years old she seduced me and then threatened to tell her father that I'd raped her. Oh, you know she killed her father too, right?'

Bryan opened his mouth to answer back, but the words got lost. He risked a glance towards Ashleigh, who was visibly trembling.

'How dare you!' she shrieked, her face flaming red. 'You're a liar, Sawyer. You're the one who killed my father because you thought his will still left everything to you, his best friend. You knew that, when I turned eighteen, I had a say in his business so you killed him before I turned eighteen so you could take control. It didn't work out that way though, did it? My father changed his will a few weeks before my birthday so I'd inherit everything and left you nothing.'

Sawyer narrowed his dark eyes. 'Yes, he did … and I wonder why he did that, hmm?'

Bryan watched as Ashleigh's face turned from red to white. Her jaw was clenched so tight he could see the muscles in her face twitching under the pressure. She was ready to attack him. He had to intervene before anything happened that she'd later regret.

'Stop. Just stop. This isn't about Ashleigh and her father's business. Sawyer, we came here for answers. Did you or did you not have anything to do with Mia's death?'

Sawyer sighed as his shoulders visibly relaxed. 'No, I had nothing to do with her death. It's true we slept together for a while, but she became clingy and far too high maintenance so I told her to leave me alone, that it was over between us, but she wouldn't take no for an answer.'

'Then what happened?' asked Ashleigh.

Sawyer's eyes flicked over to her and then straight back to Bryan. 'Then I left her in my office while I went to get her a drink of water because she had become hysterical, and when I came back, she'd ... she'd jumped.'

Bryan looked over to Ashleigh, who shrugged her shoulders. 'We need proof,' she said. 'Otherwise, Curtis won't believe us.'

Sawyer laughed. 'What? You think I have hidden cameras in my office or something?'

'Wouldn't be the first time,' muttered Ashleigh.

Sawyer laughed again, a deep throaty laugh that echoed around the spacious room. 'Even if I did have proof, I'd never help you or your toy boy. You can both go to hell. I'm calling the police right now.'

Bryan saw red. A switch flicked on somewhere inside and he knew he had to put a stop to this.

It all happened so fast.

The first thing he realised was Ashleigh was lunging towards Sawyer at the same time he was. He couldn't risk her being hurt, so he shoved her aside and she went tumbling into the safety of the nearest armchair. Bryan continued his charge towards Sawyer. He rugby-tackled him around the waist. Sawyer let out a grunt as Bryan collided with him, the air rushing from his lungs. Bryan grabbed for Sawyer's mobile, which went skidding across the floor and underneath the bar, out of reach.

Bryan landed a blow to Sawyer's face, right across the jaw. The snap of teeth crushing together echoed through the room.

Sawyer let out an almighty yell as he attempted to fight back, but Bryan was strong and managed to wrestle him into submission. He dragged Sawyer to his feet and pinned him against the bar, grabbing his crisp white shirt in his fists.

'You listen here. You're not doing yourself any favours, you fucking dick. Now help us, or I'm going to report you for having sex with underage girls.'

Sawyer bared his red-stained teeth in a nauseating grin. 'You don't have any proof. Besides, you should have heard her beg for it. At age fifteen she screamed my name and begged me to fuck her harder, to make her bleed, to—'

A loud burst of fury escaped from Bryan's mouth as he grabbed the nearest object on the bar and smashed it across Sawyer's face. It was one of the empty glasses. The glass disintegrated against his face, embedding itself into skin and hair. Blood dripped down Sawyer's white shirt and onto the floor.

Ashleigh screamed.

Bryan snapped his head around to make sure she wasn't in agony. That was all the distraction Sawyer needed.

He grabbed an almost full whiskey bottle from the bar and cracked it against Bryan's skull. It was heavier than the glass and it did the trick.

Bryan stumbled backwards, clutching his head, but the blood oozing from his head wound was making him lose consciousness. He staggered to one knee, on the cusp of collapse. He looked down at his hands, drenched in blood. Ashleigh rushed to his side and tried her best to keep him upright, but Bryan slumped sideways and landed with a thud.

Sawyer panted as he loomed over them. He spat a shard of glass onto the floor beside Ashleigh. 'This is all your fault, bitch.'

'Sawyer, whatever this is ... stop it. This ends now.'

'The hell it does. You've taken everything from me. You and your fucking trained dog have destroyed my life and now I want to play a game of my own.'

'A-A game?'

'It's called hide-and-seek. You remember how to play, don't you?'

Bryan groaned as he rolled onto his side. The last words he heard out of Sawyer's mouth were, 'You've got ten seconds, Ashleigh ... and then I'm coming for you whether you're ready or not.'

And he faded into darkness.

How to Commit the Perfect Murder
Step Nine

The Big Reveal

This is where the fun begins. The big reveal is my favourite part of the whole plan, and it should be yours too because, at the end of the day, it's where everything comes together, and your target will learn the truth about you.

I can't tell you how arousing it is to see the look in their eyes as they realise what you've done to them. It's pure magic. It's better than sex. It's better than anything you'll ever experience and it's well worth the wait.

The big reveal has to be right. Again, you can't rush it. You must allow things to play out. You must adapt and overcome any barriers, just like you've done from the start. It's a work of art to behold. And, as the realisation dawns on their pathetic face, you can revel in the fact that you've won, and your plan is nearly at an end.

Remember one thing: savour every fucking moment because, before you know it, it'll be over. You want to remember this big reveal for as long as you live.

Trust me.

Chapter Forty-Five

ASHLEIGH
4 July 2022 – 23:02 p.m.

The unmistakable prickle of fear shoots adrenaline through my body as I force my legs to work. I must leave Bryan on the floor. I don't have a choice because I know exactly what will happen when Sawyer *finds* me. Before I was fifteen, before I started sleeping with him, we'd play hide-and-seek around his house when he looked after me. It wasn't very often, as usually it was Mrs Brown who took care of me, but when she couldn't, she'd drop me off at Uncle Sawyer's house.

And I never liked those days.

When he found me, he'd touch me in places that no child should ever be touched. He told me it was my reward, which I always found strange. Why would I get a reward for being found? Surely it was his reward for finding me. I knew something wasn't quite right, and I'm not sure why I didn't tell anyone. I did tell Mrs Brown once, but she laughed at me and said what a crazy little imagination I had.

But I'm a grown woman now and I thought that Sawyer's 'strange tendencies' had vanished as he'd matured too. Clearly not. He's still a vile and sick paedophile. Who knows how many young girls he's lured back here over the years. I should have done something about him sooner. Well, now's my chance.

I scrabble on hands and knees across the slippery tiled floor and out into the hallway. My feet keep slipping on the tiles. It reminds me of my first time on a pair of ice skates. Luckily, I know every nook and cranny in this house, having spent hours attempting to hide myself. But he knows all my hiding places too.

I run straight to the front door, but it's locked. As a child, I'd thought it a brilliant idea to not be able to open the door from the inside unless you had a special key. Now I know better. He traps his victims inside his cage and plays with them.

I turn, my eyes darting from side to side, desperate to spy a means of escape or something to defend myself. But there's nothing. My hands are wet with Bryan's blood. He's in a bad way. I need to get help and fast …

'Ready or not, here I come!'

I sprint across the hallway and into the nearby study. I know there are some valuable collectables in here that I can possibly use as a weapon. I'd always admired Sawyer's antique sword collection. I used to stand and stare at them in awe as they glistened under the soft lighting, but never fully appreciated them … until now.

I yank one from its plinth. It's heavier than I anticipate. The tip drops to the floor and embeds itself into the stained floorboards. I grasp the handle as tight as I can and pull it out. I'm not quite sure what I'm doing. I've never picked up a sword in my life. But it's my only defence now.

'Come out, come out, wherever you are.'

Sawyer steps into the room, his whole body blocking the doorframe. 'Well, I must say I'm disappointed. You were much better at hiding when you were little.'

'You're a sick freak!'

Sawyer laughs as he holds up a pair of metal handcuffs. 'Remember these?'

I shudder and fight the urge to vomit. 'Sawyer, stop this now. Don't make me hurt you.'

'Oh please, you couldn't hurt a fly, Ashleigh. Look at yourself. Just look at the state of you. What the hell happened to you?'

'Something I wished had happened a long time ago.'

'Just drop the sword and come here like a good little girl. I won't make it hurt this time. I promise.'

My grasp tightens. 'Why have you deleted all my social media profiles?'

Sawyer's head lifts a fraction of an inch. 'You don't know?'

'Know what?'

'You're dead, Ashleigh Carmichael. Your bruised and battered body was found at the bottom of a steep ravine in Wales. I confirmed your identity myself.'

My jaw drops open. 'I'm dead! You killed me!'

'I'll admit I could have handled it better. Maybe made it less … messy. That poor, innocent girl, but hey … She's just collateral.'

'You did all this just so you could inherit my dad's business?'

'Clever, huh?'

'But why? It's only a business. You're rich and powerful as it is. Why do you need more?'

Sawyer sighs, as if I'm physically boring him. 'Oh, Ashleigh ... one always needs *more*.' He takes a step forwards, the handcuffs raised. 'Now ... come to Daddy.'

I retch and step backwards. I lift the sword tip off the floor. The weight makes my arms shake even more than they already were, but I hold the sword in front of me, a pointy barrier between him and me. I pray that my limited strength is enough to get me out of this situation. My mind flitters to Bryan, bleeding on the floor in the other room. He doesn't have much time left.

Sawyer lunges at me. I swing the sword, but the unbalanced weight causes me to lose my footing. I stumble sideways, attempting to right myself, but Sawyer has the upper hand, despite having several whiskeys in him. He always did take on a demon persona when he was drunk or high. He grabs my arm, twisting it into an unnatural position behind my back. I scream as pain radiates through my arm. The sword clatters to the floor and he kicks it away.

Sawyer holds me down with one hand and with the other he slaps one of the cuffs on me. Then he attaches the other side of the cuff to his own wrist.

I gasp and pull at the restraint. 'What on earth are you doing!'

'We're in this together now, love. You're not going anywhere.'

I stare down at our wrists cuffed together, my left and his right. The man must have lost his mind. What is he thinking cuffing us together like this?

The questions start buzzing around my head as he drags me out of the study and into the hallway. The cold metal digs painfully into my wrist, but he doesn't seem to care. I attempt to dig my heels into the floor, but his strength wins. I'm like a puppet on a string.

'Where are you taking me? What are you doing? Where's the key?' The questions spill out of me. I'm desperate for answers. I catch sight of Bryan still slumped on the floor; the pool of blood around his head has grown since I left him. I don't even know if he's alive.

Sawyer stops and faces me. He holds up a tiny metal key in his free hand, grins and then places it into his mouth and swallows it. My mouth drops open. My brain can't even comprehend what's just happened.

This is a bad dream.

No, it's a nightmare.

Sawyer starts dragging me again, but I fight back. I'm not the scared little girl I used to be. I'm not just going to lie down and take it from him anymore. I hit and punch and kick, but my attempts are futile. I feel like I'm on the way to my death, like if I don't do something right this second, I'm going to die.

Come on, Ashleigh. Do something!

'Come on, love. It'll be fun, I promise.'

I see red and snap. The vile words erupt from my mouth like lava.

'Get off me you fucking dick!' I push against him, but he's like an immovable boulder. The fact I've said my first swear words in two decades barely even registers in my mind. It's a shame Bryan isn't around to hear them because he'd have been proud of me. I hear them, I say them, and they don't fill me with dread or fear. They don't cause me to dry heave or tremble. They fill me with an anger, a strength, a determination I never knew I had.

The anger welling up inside me is taking over.

I'm so *fucking* angry that this man is taking everything from me, that he groped me as a child, raped me as a teenager and controlled me as a woman. And killed an innocent woman too.

And he's still doing it.

No more ...

No *fucking* more ...

The moment arrives.

We pass by an open door, which I know leads down to the wine cellar. I'm so disorientated and determined to get away my brain doesn't even comprehend the danger of what I'm about to do.

I use every ounce of strength and shove my body weight against Sawyer and through the open door. There's a moment when time freezes as he helplessly dangles on the edge of the doorway, at the top of the wooden stairs, and then he falls in slow motion ... and I tumble down with him.

I allow my body to go as floppy as possible and close my eyes, waiting for the inevitable pain.

I hear a crack, several thuds, a scream (I think that's me).

Then everything goes silent ... and dark.

Chapter Forty-Five

ASHLEIGH
5 July 2022 – 02:32 p.m.

My tender eyelids flutter open like the wings of a newly hatched butterfly, but all I see is inky darkness; the type of darkness that swallows you whole, disorientating you so much you don't know which way is up and which way is down.

I don't know where I am.

I don't know how I got here (wherever here is).

And I don't know why my head is pounding like a steel drum.

It's strangely warm, but not a comforting warmth one gets from a log fire or a snugly duvet on a winter's night. It is a familiar warmth though; one that sets my heart racing and my teeth on edge. I've been here before and I think I've been here for some time because my body is trembling uncontrollably and my shoulder—

A scream escapes my lips and disappears into the darkness, then bounces off a nearby wall. The echo that hurtles back sends shivers down my spine. I think my left shoulder is dislocated. My whole arm is numb, hanging lifelessly by my side. It may as well belong to someone else.

My shaky fingers grope around in the dark, desperate to find something, *anything*, to reassure me that I'm safe and secure, but I already know by the way my heart's racing and the terror is creeping over my body like a spider I'm far from safe.

My memory is foggy at first, but, after a few seconds, I remember why I'm here and everything that's happened over the past few days. Memory after memory pops into my head, playing out like broken snippets of a movie.

I remember everything …

Oh God … that means …

There's a strange smell wafting through the air; damp and something else – something earthy. My nostrils scrunch up and I can almost taste the aroma in my mouth; putrid and vile. I lick my lips, trying but failing to moisten the cracked, delicate skin. After running my tongue over my front top teeth, I realise it's likely I haven't brushed recently due to the thick film of plaque that's formed on them.

There's also blood in my mouth.

My head still pounds relentlessly. It's not a sharp or agonising pain, but a dull throbbing ache that's enough to cause discomfort and unease. I'm lying awkwardly on my back, so I slowly raise my body into a seated position and attempt to adjust my injured arm, but I can't … because it won't move.

Pop …

Another memory.

They start flooding my mind in nauseating waves.

With my right hand, I feel around in the dark again, prodding my left arm in a desperate attempt to wake it up. That's when I touch the cool, solid metal encased around my wrist.

Handcuffs.

Pop ...

Another memory.

I gently pull on the cuff. There's a slight give, but no noisy sound to suggest I'm cuffed to anything metal or solid. But I'm attached to something ...

The cuff is tight and digging into my soft flesh. Blindly, I feel along the metal chain that links one cuff to the other and when I get to the end let out another loud scream.

There's a hand at the end that isn't mine.

'Hello?' I whisper, unable to control the trembling in my voice.

There's no response, so I summon up the courage and fumble around in the dark, feeling for the strange hand again.

I shudder when I touch cold, clammy skin.

The hand is bigger than mine, thicker; male.

I reach the other cuff and realise it's attached securely to the other person's wrist.

I call out again, but there's no reply.

I know the answer before I even check the pulse in his wrist.

I'm handcuffed to a dead man.

Sawyer is dead.

The scream that escapes my lips is more animalistic than human.

I've killed him.

I didn't think ...

I didn't expect him to—

How else were you going to get out of this mess, Ashleigh?

I scream again, but by the time the sound fades it's more of a whimper. The light from the hallway at the top of the wine cellar stairs is taunting me. Freedom is within my grasp. Just fifteen wooden steps away. Help is within reach. But I'm shackled to a dead man and Bryan is slowing dying upstairs.

There's enough light to illuminate my immediate surroundings, but not much further than a few feet. Expensive wine racks, dozens of them, line up along the edges of the room. I know this cellar well; too well, having spent many an hour down here drinking with Sawyer and ... Well, it's where he brought me sometimes.

There's a secret doorway behind one of the wine racks that leads to a small room with a cot bed and nothing else. I don't know if it's still there. It wouldn't surprise me if it was. A shiver runs up my spine at the thought of someone else, another innocent girl, being trapped down here, but I can't hear any banging that indicates he has a prisoner. It's not like he kept me in there by myself. I used to hide in there sometimes, but he was always with me in that little room. It was our little secret.

I stare down at the dead man on the floor next to me. His neck is twisted at an unnatural angle, his eyes glazed over, but still open. To be honest he always looked as if he was dead inside whenever I looked into his eyes, so they don't look too different now. A small dribble of blood is trickling out of his mouth.

I bite my bottom lip and tug at the cuffs again, but all I do is yank his arm slightly. He's a heavy man; well-built and muscular. There's no way I can drag him up these stairs.

'Bryan!' I call out a few times, my voice quivering with sobs.

That's when I realise no one is coming to rescue me. I have to get myself out of this mess. No shining knight is going to waltz over and save me.

My head throbs in time to my heartbeat. There's sticky blood matted in my hair. I'm not sure how long I was unconscious for after Sawyer and I tumbled down the stairs. But I'm weak and can feel the darkness threatening to creep closer every second. I must fight to stay awake or it's all over.

'Bryan.' My voice is a mere whisper now. I can barely see through the haze of tears and the looming threat of blacking out.

I inhale as deep as possible, hold it for five seconds and let it out. I'm trying to remember my yoga training (not that my instructor ever told me that *this* was the type of situation in which to use yoga breathing techniques, but it can't hurt to try). Once my brain receives some much-needed oxygen, my head begins to feel clearer and the small cellar around me stops spinning at lightning speed.

The first thing I need to do is get myself unshackled from Sawyer. Having not seen too many horror movies, I'm not altogether sure if there's an official technique involved in getting oneself out of handcuffs having been attached to a dead body ... other than the obvious, which doesn't bare thinking about. The only idea I have is to list my options and see which is the best. At least that way I can make a rational decision.

Number one: cut open Sawyer's stomach and retrieve the key.

Number two: cut off his hand, leaving me still wearing the cuffs, but only on one hand.

Number three: cut off my hand ...

Number four: break Sawyer's fingers and wrist and try and squeeze his hand through the cuffs – but his hands are twice the size of mine.

Number five: break my own fingers and wrist and try and squeeze my hand through the cuffs.

None of these options seem appealing. In fact, all of them require either a great deal of pain or a sharp instrument of some kind, which I don't even have.

Or there's number six: drag Sawyer upstairs and call for help using his mobile phone, which is under the bar.

Or number seven: wait for Bryan to wake up and help me.

Bryan may be dead already, so I can't depend on him right now, but number six sounds the least painful and messy out of all of them.

I'm going with number six. It can't hurt to try.

I mutter words of encouragement as I stand and position myself with my back towards the stairs, squat down and grasp Sawyer's shirt. Due to my possibly dislocated shoulder, I'm unable to even use that arm, so I can only use my good one.

I lean back and pull.

Nothing happens.

He doesn't even move.

I try again, anchoring my feet into the floor and leaning as far back as I can. The body slides about an inch and stops. I slump to the floor, already exhausted and on the verge of passing out from the exertion. There's no way I can drag him up a flight of stairs. No freaking way.

I scream and kick his body as tears spill from my eyes again.

A cold shiver runs down my spine as I stare into the darkness ahead, remembering the times I used to spend down here. Sawyer would show me his rare wine collection. Bottles and bottles of imported, expensive and highly collectable wine, all lined up in date order; the oldest of the collection starting in the far corner, with the newest nearest the stairs. But even the closest wine rack is at least twenty feet away from my current location.

Wait ...

An idea pings into my sore head.

If I can't drag him up the stairs and call for help then I need to go with one of the other options, which means I need something sharp or heavy.

Where's a sword when you need one? Ah yes, it's upstairs laying on the floor where I dropped it.

There's only one thing in this cellar that I can use as a sharp instrument, but it will involve me dragging him to the nearest rack. If I do that, I won't have much light, as the beam from the upstairs hallway doesn't reach all the way into the corners. There're no heavy objects down here, so my only option is to cut off his hand with something sharp. I cannot even bring myself to think about slicing his stomach open and seeing all that ... *stuff*. I'd never be able to put my hand into his stomach and— I gag just thinking about it.

I can deal with a bit of blood.

I stagger to my feet, grab him again and attempt to pull him around in a circle so I can drag him backwards into the darkness. It will be easier than pushing him. I'm not sure where the strength comes from, but, little by little, inch by inch, he turns.

I take a few moments to compose myself and start pulling backwards again. At first, he doesn't move, but then ...

Yes!

He moves.

And the more he moves the easier it gets once I get some momentum going. My legs burn with lactic acid, my lungs heave, my head spins, but I keep pulling with every ounce of strength in my body. I scream as the momentum starts to fade, as the power in my legs and one arm gradually reduces.

And then he stops.

I kick him as I slump to the floor, puffing and panting. The darkness is creepy and it's quite cold in this corner compared to the rest of the cellar. I begin to shiver, but it's not from the chill.

I think I'm close enough to the rack to reach a bottle now. I reach out my hand and squeak as my fingers brush the cool, smooth surface. I can't quite get a grip on it ... just a few more inches, but my injured arm is already outstretched behind me. It feels as if I'm going to rip my own arm off if I stretch too far. The pain is unbearable as I lean a few inches further away, clawing at the bottle to wrap my fingers around it.

I grab it.

Relief washes over me but is quickly replaced with anger as the bottle slips through my trembling fingers and smashes at my feet. The liquid gushes over my shoes and splashes on my legs. There's now glass everywhere.

I crouch down and carefully feel around in the dark for a big enough piece, but the bottle has smashed into thousands of tiny slithers.

'Shit,' I mutter.

I touch Sawyer's hair by accident and take a quick deep breath to steady myself. A sharp sting pierces my ring finger as a shard of glass decides to make its home there. I wrench my hand away and suck the injury.

I need a new bottle, but it requires leaning even further into the darkness. Adjusting my stance, I grab Sawyer again and heave him a few more inches. Then I reach for another bottle. This time, I keep my fingers firmly around the neck.

How am I supposed to smash a bottle and not have it break into tiny pieces? I need a large piece, big enough to hold on to while I ... while I ... *do what needs to be done*.

I raise the bottle above my head and pause.

How the hell has it come to this?

Before I can change my mind, I smash the bottle against the side of the wine rack. The impact is more brutal than I was expecting. It ricochets through my whole body. Cool liquid spills across my hand and down my arm. I'm left holding the narrow neck of the bottle, which amazingly hasn't disintegrated. It might just be large enough to work, but I won't know until I try.

Is it even possible to cut through flesh and bone with a piece of glass? Where's Google when you need it?

I run my trembling fingers across the sharp edge, but then reality hits me like a punch to the stomach.

Now what?

Now I must cut off his hand.

Well, obviously I'm not going to cut off my own hand.

But, even so, the thought causes my stomach to roil. The thought of slicing and sawing through flesh and bone ... I shudder. The only saving grace is that it's so dark I won't be able to see all the blood.

I fumble around until I find Sawyer's arm and follow it down to his wrist. The idiot cuffed himself so tight there's no way I'd be able to slide his hand through the metal circle even if I did have a heavy object like a hammer to smash his fingers to pieces.

Am I seriously about to do this?

I'm grasping the piece of glass so hard and shaking so much that I can't even control myself.

I hold my breath and start to cut ...

My mind is breaking. I'm not myself anymore.

Who am I? Am I a monster now? Am I a killer?

I'm still holding the shard of glass as I reach the top of the stairs to the wine cellar after leaving the mutilated corpse of my abuser behind. My feet move of their own accord, one foot in front of the other without me thinking about it. As I reach the doorway to the bar area, the room shifts in and out of focus. The walls close in and then zoom away at lightning speed.

A large crack appears in my vision ...

I enter the room where Bryan is – *was* – he's gone; a puddle of blood remains and nothing else, which means he was conscious at some point while I was downstairs doing ... the unthinkable.

My brain is working at a slower speed than usual, but everything around me feels as if it's on fast forwards. I should be running for help, looking for the discarded phone, but I'm frozen in place. Blood covers both of my hands and is dripping onto the floor. I can hear the tiny splashes as if they're great big buckets of blood.

Red spots dance in front of my eyes.

I'm no longer Ashleigh Carmichael.

I'm broken and I don't understand what's happening to me. Where is Bryan? Why did he leave me? Had I stayed downstairs a bit longer would help have arrived? Why didn't he come and save me?

'Ashleigh?'

At the sound of my name, I barely even react. It takes me several seconds to turn on the spot and look into the face of a man who shouldn't be here.

'C-Curtis,' I whisper. It's the only word I can form. He looks a lot better than the last time I saw him; cleaner at least, but why is he here?

'What the hell happened to you?' He steps forwards, but I raise the glass shard.

'Stop.' I'm struggling to form any sort of coherent thought. I'm afraid that if anyone comes near me, I might explode.

'You need help. I need to get you out of here and away from him.'

'Just stop ... please ... What's going on? How are you—' My sentence is cut short by Bryan running into the room at full speed. He shouts like a general on the battlefield as he charges into Curtis and tackles him to the ground. The thud that echoes around the room sounds like a rumble of thunder.

My eyes can barely take in what I'm witnessing as the two men brawl like they're in a fight to the death. Bryan gets kicked in the face. Curtis gets punched in the ribs. Blood and saliva fly as they continue their abuse against one another. I feel powerless as I stand, rooted to the spot, shaking like a leaf that's clinging onto a branch in a strong wind. I need to help one of them ... but who? For the first time my brain is confused about who's in the right and who's in the wrong.

I make my decision.

It could only ever be one person.

I look down at the glass still clenched in my bloody hand. I've been squeezing it so hard that the sharp edge is digging into my palm. I look up at the two brawling men. Curtis has Bryan pinned on the floor with both his hands wrapped around his neck. Bryan's face is bright red. His bulging eyes are rolling backwards, the whites streaked with red veins. He doesn't have long left.

'Curtis ... stop! You're killing him.'

Curtis laughs. 'That was the plan all along.'

'No!' I run towards Curtis with the glass raised above my head. He sees me, stops strangling Bryan and turns to me, ready to defend himself.

'You're making a huge mista—'

I launch myself at him, but because he's awkwardly kneeling on the floor, he is off balance and stumbles to the side.

I don't think; I just act as I slice the glass clear across his throat. It's as effortless as cutting through soft butter.

It takes a few seconds for Curtis to realise what's happened. He clutches his throat with his hands as dark blood oozes between his fingers, streaming down his neck and chest, the flow getting stronger with every passing second. It even spurts in short bursts in time to his heartbeat.

We lock eyes and he knows it's the end for him.

He knows what's happened.

I've won.

He slumps sideways to the floor as his final breath leaves his body and I watch as the pool of blood expands around him.

It's quite beautiful really, like a red rose blooming in majestic sunlight.

My mind goes dark.

Chapter Forty-Seven

HANNAH
7 July 2022 – 03:45 a.m.

I listen as Bryan speaks, and as each word leaves his mouth, the memories appear in my head. They pop like bubbles. I see my blood-drenched hands and feel the surge of nausea as I cut through bone and tissue and how easily the glass had sliced Curtis's neck open. It had been too easy.

'So … you're saying I've killed two men.'

'It was self-defence,' replies Bryan.

'Was it though?'

'Barbie … get real. Of course it was.'

'I don't know anything anymore. Nothing makes sense.'

'So, you remember?'

'Only bits and pieces, but yes, I remember.'

'And do you remember what our plan is now?'

I spend several seconds searching my memory for what happened next, but that part is still black. I shake my head. 'No. I remember their deaths and what happened before, but nothing of what happened after.'

'When I managed to pry the glass out of your hands, I told you I needed to get you away from that house. I told you I'd do anything to keep you safe, so now we're just travelling around while I get some plans in place. Ashleigh Carmichael is dead. No one is looking for you. I've got you a new ID, a new name, and we're leaving the country as soon as possible. Hannah Holden can start afresh with me.'

'Where are we going?'

'America. I know some people over there who can protect us, or we can just drive around on the open road for a while.'

This is all happening so fast. My brain is still full of fog and confusion. 'I ... I don't want to go to America. I should stay here and—'

'And do what? We're both on the run now. We're in this together. You said so yourself. You're Hannah Holden now. You can start a new life, be anyone you want to be, do anything you want to do. We can be together. Isn't that what you want?'

I turn my head slowly towards Bryan and study him. His injuries have begun to heal, but there is something that doesn't quite add up. There is a piece of the puzzle missing.

'What?' he asks.

'Nothing.' But it isn't nothing. I know he's lying to me.

'You must know that Curtis's and Sawyer's deaths were not your fault. They deserved to die, and, if you hadn't have done it, I most definitely would have. They were dangerous men and now they're gone.'

'And you're not a dangerous man?'

'Only when it comes to protecting you. Ashleigh ... Hannah ... I love you and I promise to protect you until my dying breath.'

A warm ball of happiness erupts in my cold heart.

I gaze at the dark road outside the car window as the white lines whizz past. I know I can't return to my old life, so the only choice is to start a new one. I have connections. I have money, but I can't use any of it (yet) otherwise Ashleigh Carmichael would be found to be alive. According to the news she is dead, and I need her to stay that way because the truth is ... I do have a plan.

I've always had a plan.

Ashleigh Carmichael is gone.

It's time for Hannah Holden to finally come out and play.

Goodbye, Ashleigh Carmichael.

Chapter Forty-Eight

BRYAN
5 July 2022 – 04:00 a.m.

He watched as Barbie and Curtis slumped to the floor. He hadn't seen exactly what had happened as he'd been on the verge of losing consciousness, but he knew she had attacked Curtis and now he was on the floor, blood oozing from his sliced-open throat.

It was over.

Finally, over.

Bryan coughed and took a deep breath, his throat burning from having Curtis almost crush his windpipe. He barely recognised the woman kneeling on the floor in front of him. She was a shell of her former self. There was no spark in her eyes, no shine to her lips, no glow to her skin. He'd done this to her. It was all his fault.

When Bryan had woken up earlier, he'd tried to find her. It must have been seconds later when she'd appeared from the wine cellar, clutching a glass shard and covered in blood. Sawyer hadn't been with her.

'Barbie ... *Ashleigh* ... talk to me. Are you hurt?' He shoved the dead body aside and began running his hands over her body, checking for injuries. She looked like a victim of a serial killer survival movie. She stared straight ahead, her eyes not blinking. She was practically catatonic. 'Ashleigh?' he said again.

'Hannah.' Her voice was weak and little more than a whisper, so he wasn't sure he'd heard her correctly.

'What?'

'My name is Hannah Holden.'

What the hell was going on? Had she changed personalities or something?

'No, Ashleigh … Your name is Ashleigh Carmichael.'

Ashleigh looked at him and he reacted by leaning away ever so slightly. She was scaring him. Her soulless eyes held nothing but emptiness.

'My name is Hannah Holden,' she said again. 'I'm not Ashleigh Carmichael anymore.'

Bryan didn't know what the hell was going on, but this wasn't the time or place to argue with her, so he quickly nodded. 'Okay, fine, you're Hannah. I need to get you to a hospital. Your head is bleeding.' He glanced at the ever-expanding puddle of blood still flowing from Curtis's body. 'We'll take him with us, but where's Sawyer? Where's all this other blood come from? Is it yours?'

'Not mine.' Her answer was robotic.

'Talk to me. What happened? Where's Sawyer?'

'Dead.'

At that moment he noticed the handcuffs dangling from her left wrist. 'Did he chain you up? Did he hurt you?' A shake of the head, but nothing more. He was losing her. She slid to the floor and laid down next to Curtis's body. 'Ashleigh, stay with me. Come on, we need to leave.'

'I like it here.'

'No, I have to get you help.'

'Hannah. My name's Hannah.'

'Right … Hannah. Han … can you help me? I need to get you up and out of here right now.'

'I'm sleepy.' Bryan watched, helpless, as she closed her eyes. He shook her. 'Hannah. Hannah, wake up.' He closed his eyes and breathed in deep. He knew what he had to do but getting her out of here was going to be difficult. And he needed to take Curtis too. He didn't want him being found by the police or anyone else. Too many questions would be asked. Yes, they'd discover his blood on the floor and eventually put two and two together, but that wouldn't be for a while. Bryan didn't want Curtis's body to ever be found. He didn't deserve it. He deserved to disappear. He needed to buy him and Ashleigh, or Hannah, some time.

Sawyer would have to stay here. There would be a huge investigation when he was found, enough to distract the media and police while he and Hannah slipped away.

He bundled Hannah into the car and ensured she was comfortable. Her breathing was light, but her pulse was strong. Her head wound had stopped bleeding, but it was deep enough to require stitches.

Bryan hoisted Curtis onto his shoulders and dumped him in the boot. He'd deal with him later. He could rot in there for all he cared.

He still didn't know exactly what had happened to Sawyer but, considering the amount of blood that covered Hannah, he could make an educated guess. The handcuffs confused him though. He'd have to cut them off her, which he could do with the bolt cutters he had in the boot.

But first, his only plan was to ensure she was safe. Now he thought about it, he couldn't take her to a real hospital. There would be too many questions. He needed to put her somewhere safe so he could tend to her head wound and allow her to recover. Her left arm hung limply at her side. It was possibly dislocated, so he'd have to sort that out too. Maybe it was best that she was out cold for a while. Then, once she recovered a bit, they could make their escape to America. He wasn't sure why she was suddenly calling herself Hannah Holden, but it worked.

A new country.

A new life.

A fresh start.

For both of them.

Chapter Forty-Nine

November 2008

My life changed overnight. The plan to kill my father and take over his company had gone as smoothly as I'd hoped. But then again ... I had planned it well. The tricky part had been to convince him to change his will so that his daughter would inherit everything rather than his paedophile business partner. Luckily, my father had a liking for whiskey and, after adding some Rohypnol to his favourite tipple, he signed the new and improved copy of his will without a second thought. I'd cleverly disguised it in some of his routine paperwork.

I then snuck into the garage and, after bribing one of the mechanics to tell me what to do (not that they knew I was going to use the information to kill my father), I nicked the brake fluid chamber on his precious Aston Martin. I didn't expect the car to explode though – a happy accident. It made for some spectacular scenes and front-page photos in the *Daily Mail*.

It was the aftermath of the crash that I hadn't expected. Yes, I'd planned to inherit the business, but not become a global sensation. Okay, maybe that's stretching the truth a bit. I dyed my hair blonde and the next thing I knew I was famous because my poor father had died in a tragic accident. Everyone loved a sob story and mine seemed to grow arms and legs and explode overnight.

So ... my plan changed again.

But I missed Bryan Matthews. I didn't torment him every day online anymore because there were eyes everywhere. I just liked to watch and study him, watching him from afar.

On one particularly quiet day while I was scrolling, I saw he'd updated his status with 'Bryan Matthews is regretting his life decisions'. The idea popped into my head before I could stop it.

I wanted to screw with him again. I couldn't help myself. The idea that Bryan was suffering somehow was like a drug to me. I needed him to suffer as much as possible before I killed him.

I wanted to split him and Hannah Baker up, but not in the usual way. Not just a normal break down of a relationship; Hannah needed to go ... for good.

So, I sent Mia Redding a message. She was the twin sister of Curtis Redding, the weird ginger-haired ex-cronie of Bryan's. And you wouldn't believe the response I got ...

Hi Mia,

You probably don't remember me, but my name is Ashleigh Carmichael. We went to school together. I know you used to date Bryan Matthews, and I know he broke up with you, but there's something else you should know ... Bryan Matthews is a dangerous man. How would you like to get revenge? Also ... do you know a man called Sawyer Croft?

Love and kisses,

Ashleigh

Hi Ashleigh,

I do remember you. Bryan and his gang used to bully you, right? I'm sorry for what my brother and Bryan did to you. Bryan Matthews is more than dangerous and as for Sawyer Croft ... Well ... he's the worst type of man. Maybe we should meet in person? I have a feeling that you and I are going to have a lot of things in common.

Love Mia x

It was the perfect scenario and the perfect next phase of the plan. I just had to act the part for a while, smile for the cameras, wear tiny dresses and high heels. It wasn't all bad.

I saw Bryan Matthews one last time before I left him alone. It was after Mia and I had spoken and after the tragedy had happened. Honestly, the look on Sawyer's face when he found out Mia had *jumped* from his office window was priceless. It was a shame that girl had to die for my plan to work though. She never saw it coming.

Bryan was working on a car in his father's garage when I walked up to him wearing my most revealing dress. It made my new boobs pop and hugged my butt in all the right places. He looked up from tinkering with his Impala and scanned my body from top to bottom.

'Can I help you?' he asked, a hint of a smile behind his eyes.

'I was just admiring your car.'

Bryan stroked the black beast. 'Yeah, she's a beauty. How would you like to go for a ride some time?'

I giggled. 'Oh, I'd love to, but I can't. I just wanted you to know that your girlfriend, Hannah Baker, is cheating on you with my boyfriend.'

Bryan's mouth dropped open and his face turned red. 'I ... what?'

'I'm sorry to have to be the one to tell you, but I thought you should know.'

Bryan nodded slowly, his eyes sinking to the floor. He then snapped his head up. 'Hey. You look familiar. Do I know you from somewhere?'

Of course, he wouldn't recognise me. Bryan Matthews never took notice of anyone but himself. Anger pulsed through my body, but I just smiled at him sweetly. 'I don't think so, but I get that a lot. I just have one of those faces, I guess.' Not to mention my face was plastered everywhere at the minute in commercials. My modelling career was beginning to take off.

Bryan narrowed his eyes at me. I could almost see the cogs turning in his head, searching for the truth. The seed of doubt had been planted so I left with a nod of the head, grinning as I walked away, leaving him scratching his head.

And that, as they say ... was that.

How to Commit the Perfect Murder
Step Ten

The Perfect Murder (and Getaway)

Well, how about that? The big reveal is over. It may or may not have gone the way you planned, but nevertheless, it's over. It's time to focus on the main event, the moment you've been waiting for. Like me, you may have waited years for this moment. It's probably been bubbling up inside you for so long now that you feel as if you may burst open at any second.

The perfect murder will be different for everyone. I've had many ideas over the years how I'd eventually kill my subject and, in the end, decided on a more hands-on approach. Granted, I could have made it easy on myself and pushed them off a cliff or run them over or even shot them, but what's the fun in that? I'm not saying I want to torture them to death. I don't have time for that. The perfect murder needs to be swift, but effective. Painful, but not instantaneous-death painful. The perfect combination of everything all rolled into one neat package.

The getaway on the other hand ...

Now, that's a tricky beast to tame because it all depends on how the murder goes and depends on how well you've prepared for it. As I said right at the very beginning, those people who murder on a whim almost always get caught during the getaway phase because they haven't prepared.

So ... Do your homework. It will pay off in the long run.

See you on the other side ... and good luck.
You're going to need it ...
Trust me.

Chapter Fifty

HANNAH
1 August 2022 – 12:22 a.m.

It feels strange to finally be here. The past month and all its dramas feel more like a dream, a distant memory, like none of it ever happened. But of course, it did happen because I planned everything meticulously. I'm so proud of myself. In fact, I'm laughing inside at how well everything has gone. Honestly, I am because, despite a few setbacks, the whole thing has gone perfectly and I'm now lounging on a Miami beach, sipping a cocktail with a pair of oversized sunglasses covering my eyes.

In a strange way I sort of feel like the old me, back when I had money and lived my life in the spotlight. Except now I'm the new and improved old version of myself.

Then again, even the *old* me was never the *real* me.

This is the real me.

Hannah Holden. It's got a nice ring to it.

Yes, the name is fake, but she's the person I've secretly always wanted to be. I've waited all these years to be her. I suffered through all those business meetings and the scheduled appointments. I became a social media bimbo and whored myself out for free stuff. I allowed everyone to believe they were brainwashing me and controlling my whole life. Everyone always took me for granted, always brushed me off as some dumb, blonde girl whose job it was to look pretty and keep her mouth shut, and that's exactly what I did.

I played the part well and I played it for a long time. Because, as you know, you've got to be in it for the long haul ...

I consider myself the greatest actress of all time. I faked a lot of things, including the orgasms with Bryan. The phobia of swear words? Fake. The rich-girl persona? Fake. The terrified spoiled girl? Fake. The addiction to my phone? Fake.

It was all a cover, a brilliant and alluring cover. Whether or not it was guessable is beside the point. There was one thing I didn't fake: my memory loss. It was a minor setback, I'll admit, but thankfully my memories came back and I was able to salvage what could have been an absolute catastrophe. I do have a theory as to why I briefly lost my memories. I think Bryan was right when he said that my brain snapped when everything happened with Sawyer and Curtis. I've never said that I'm a cold-hearted killer. I've said all along I'm only human so things like that are bound to influence me negatively, and sawing through bone and muscle is not my idea of a good time. I had a small moment of weakness and overcame it.

The point is I fooled everyone who needed fooling, including ... Bryan Matthews.

Oh, Bryan.

I almost feel sorry for him ... I said *almost*.

Bryan is swimming in the clear, blue ocean and has been gone a while, but I don't mind. He always comes back to me. *Sucker.*

He's been a wiggling worm on a hook this whole time and now I'm the big fish that's about to snap him up, but first I'm going to play with him a little longer. It's fun.

I haven't kept up with the news in the UK regarding Ashleigh Carmichael. As far as I'm concerned, she's dead and so is the man who abused her. I must leave her in the past if Hannah is to have a future. It was always the plan.

Sawyer Croft …

He was always going to be my first target and the first one to die.

Funny twist to the story … He was never supposed to break his neck in the fall down the stairs. He was supposed to have eventually passed out from the drugs I slipped into his whiskey bottle, but then he went and handcuffed himself to me and … well, you know the rest.

I still have awful flashbacks of the time I spent in the wine cellar, of finding myself cuffed to a dead man. That had not been part of the plan, but thanks to step two I was well-versed to adapting and overcoming any situation that arose. So, I pushed him down the stairs and then cut off his hand with a shard of glass. It wasn't pleasant.

I obviously came out of that cellar a bit broken …

Anyway, Sawyer finally got the ending he deserved. He'll never hurt or abuse another girl ever again. You might be wondering what happened to my father's business and fortune. Well, I'd thought of that too.

In my father's new and updated will (that he signed without knowing) was a clause; a clause that said, and I quote:

In the event of Ashleigh Carmichael and Sawyer Croft being unable to run the company, it shall be sold, and the money transferred into the following bank account ...

That bank account is in the name of Hannah Holden and the current balance is a little over five hundred million pounds. The company was sold a week ago after Sawyer's funeral. There've been no questions surrounding this and, as far as I'm aware, no one is on the lookout for Hannah Holden. Even if they are, she's long gone.

Curtis Redding ...

He was always scheduled to die second, but he certainly had his benefits along the way. In fact, I couldn't have done it without him, so three cheers for Curtis Redding! My hero and saviour and puppet on a string. It's a good job he was so disjointed in the head because it enabled me to control him easily. I purposefully crashed into his car, knowing he'd likely take the opportunity to extort money out of a rich girl. Of course, he may not have done, but I had a Plan B. It all worked so well that I hadn't needed it.

I take a sip of my fruity cocktail and sigh happily.

My plan is all coming together in the final stages.

Some may be shocked, others might be impressed, or maybe it was easy to guess the outcome. But I couldn't give a damn because I'm now about to complete my life's ambition, my one and only true goal ... to kill Bryan Matthews. And it's going to be a wonderful experience to behold.

My hand automatically reaches for my notebook, which is tucked under my lounger. The one and only item I cared about and saved from my bag. Within these pages are the secrets to my success. My ten steps to the perfect murder ... or *murders*. Because I'd always planned to kill Sawyer and Curtis, but Bryan has always been my one true goal.

'Hey, Barbie.'

Time to keep up appearances.

A smile crosses my lips as I casually slide the notebook further under the seat. I then shove my shades on the top of my head, stand up and throw my arms around the neck of the man I loathe with a passion. I stick my tongue down his throat, fighting the urge to gag, as he spins me around. Sand and water fly everywhere, and I screech with excitement.

'The water's amazing. You should come for a dip.'

'I'm still working on my tan,' I say as Bryan sets me down on the hot sand. He slaps my bum before plonking himself down next to my sun lounger.

'I was thinking we should probably get back on the road soon.'

I stretch my arms above my head. 'Where to next then?'

'Well, if you're happy to keep driving, then we'll just stick to the coast for now, so Georgia's next, then on to South Carolina.'

'Sounds good to me.' Bryan watches me for several seconds. 'What?' I ask with a laugh.

'I'm not quite sure how you managed to come into my life, but I'm one lucky guy that you did. I love you.'

'I love you too, and hey ... you never know ... Maybe I've been stalking you for years and this was my plan all along.' I add a wink and we share a laugh and a kiss that makes my stomach roll.

Bryan is snoozing in the passenger seat. We have agreed to share the driving. As soon as we arrived in Florida, we bought a car, a black Impala. He kept whining about his old car so, to get him to shut up, I allowed him to buy the damn thing. He knows about the money I inherited, not that he gets to touch a penny of it.

Bryan thinks we're going to be spending the next year or so travelling around America and seeing all the sights, and that's exactly what I intend to do, but not with him. At some point soon I will end his life, but I need to find the perfect location, the perfect moment. I want to savour it as much as possible when it finally arrives.

What once was a little seed of an idea is now a fully-fledged plan in motion and the excitement is building with every second. The thought of revealing the truth to him after all this time makes my stomach dance. Maybe this should have been classed as the big reveal because he's not going to know what's hit him.

'Hey,' I say, nudging him with my hand.

He stirs and refolds his arms across his chest. 'Mmmm.'

'How about we stop at a motel tonight instead of sleeping in the car.'

'Yeah, whatever you want, Barbie.'

'Besides ... there's more room in a bed to do what I've been wanting to do to you ever since we first met.'

At this, Bryan's eyes flick open, a stupid grin on his face. 'I like where your mind's at.'

And I laugh because he has absolutely no idea that after I've had some fun with him, he's never going to breathe again.

Insert evil laugh.

Chapter Fifty-One

HANNAH
1 August 2022 – 23:04 a.m.

The motel I choose is perfect; a small, remote building off the main highway somewhere in Georgia. We like to keep to the smaller roads where possible, not that I'm worried we're being followed, but because I love seeing the rural sights and it's hard to do that from a main road. It is strange driving in America, but at least now, driving another Impala, the driving seat is on the correct side of the car in relation to the road. My confidence with driving has come a long way since that day I drove away from my London home. That girl seems a distant memory now. Of course, she was never real. She was merely my persona that I'd adopted over the years to keep my true intentions camouflaged, but Ashleigh Carmichael had worked out well for me. Sometimes I felt like I *was* her in many ways. At the end of the day, that was my true name, the one my parents gave me, but I like Hannah Holden better. Hannah is free and confident and more like the type of woman I want to be.

We dump our bags on the floor. I scan the small room. Yes, this will do nicely for Bryan's last moments. It's dingy and insignificant – just like him. He deserves nothing better. The wallpaper is peeling from the walls, the curtains are crooked and there's a weird smell that I try and ignore. It may or may not be a dead animal rotting somewhere under the uneven floorboards.

Bryan grabs me, causing me to shriek in alarm, and spins me around, pulling my body up against his. I can already feel his erection growing. A surge of excitement and arousal surges through me, but it has nothing to do with Bryan and his ugly cock.

Tonight is the night.

'So, Miss Holden, what is it you want to do to me so badly?' He kisses and nuzzles my neck as he begins to peel my clothes off. It doesn't take long because I'm only wearing a pair of tiny shorts and a camisole top. No bra. I like to let the girls be free sometimes.

'You'll see,' I whisper as I shove him hard in the chest. He falls back on the bed and bounces.

After we've finished, Bryan leans against the headboard, one arm resting behind his head, the other stroking my hair as I rest my cheek against his chest, listening to his breathing. I count his breaths.

One, two, three, four …

He has no idea a lump hammer is hiding underneath the bed. I placed it there earlier while he was using the en suite. I'd seen it lying carelessly on a side table when we bought the car from a garage a few weeks ago and it looked so enticing I picked it up and slipped it into my bag while no one was looking.

It's the perfect murder weapon.

I can't wait any longer.

It's go time.

First, let's set the scene.

'Do you ever think about Hannah?' The question clearly hits the mark and throws Bryan out of his post-coital coma. I feel his body tense. 'Hannah Baker,' I add, in case he misses the point.

'Sometimes,' he says, sounding a bit weary.

'Do you ever feel guilty for what happened to her?'

'You know I do. We'd had a silly argument a few weeks prior when I accused her of having an affair. I couldn't let it go. Things spiralled out of control after that. I tried to apologise, but she was hurt by the fact I didn't trust her.'

'Was she actually having an affair?'

'I don't think so.'

'What made you think she was?'

There are a few beats of silence as my heartrate begins to climb. I do my best to steady it in case Bryan can feel it against his body.

'A woman approached me and said Hannah was having an affair with her boyfriend.'

'And you believed a stranger over your girlfriend.' A statement, not a question.

'It just planted a seed of doubt in my mind. My mum cheated on my dad a lot because he was abusive towards her. It pulled our family apart. I didn't want that to happen with me and Hannah, but it did anyway.'

I stroke his chest as I say, 'I'm so sorry.'

He kisses the top of my head. 'But that's all in the past now.'

I allow the silence to build again. My heart is beating so hard and fast I'm surprised Bryan can't feel it shaking the bed. 'You don't speak about your mum much. What happened to her?'

And there it is ... Bryan's heart misses a beat.

If he admits it, then my plan has worked even better than I could have ever imagined.

'I ... I don't like to talk about her.'

'Why not?'

'My dad ... He ... Hannah, what I'm about to tell you is something you can never repeat to anyone.'

I adjust my position and lift my head from his chest, looking him in the eyes. 'You can trust me. We've been through hell and back again. Whatever it is, I can take it.'

Bryan kisses me on the head again and then I settle back down on his chest. He takes a deep breath. 'My dad killed her, and I helped him cover it up and get rid of the body. We transported her body in the back of the Impala and then buried her at the bottom of someone else's grave.'

I resist to urge to laugh by clamping my lips together as tight as possible.

I knew it ... I mean, I was never able to prove it, but I knew something bad had happened to her because one day she disappeared. Bryan told everyone at school she'd left, but I knew there was something he was hiding. It also explains why he seemed to know what he was doing when getting rid of Curtis's body.

'I'm sorry,' I say slowly, avoiding his gaze so I don't give away the fact I'm about to burst into hysterical laughter.

Keep it together, Hannah.

'My dad assaulted her almost on a daily basis, so it was only a matter of time until he went too far.'

Okay, enough about that. Time to move on. It's not that I don't care about his mother being murdered, but I have more important topics to discuss.

'So did you bully kids at school because of how your dad treated your mum?'

'Maybe,' he answers, then lets out a long sigh. 'I bullied a lot of kids.'

'Why?'

'I don't know.'

'There must be a reason.'

'Why are you asking me all of this?'

I shrug and snuggle closer against his chest, running my fingers through his chest hair. 'I'm just curious. I want to know everything about you.' This clearly does the trick as Bryan relaxes underneath me.

'I guess it was my way of dealing with the stress of my home life. I watched my dad hit my mum. I watched her cheat on him. Then he killed her. He never laid a finger on me though and we had a good relationship, but for some reason he took out his anger on my mum. In fact, he hated almost all women. From a young age, I believed that's what men did, so I started doing it myself to kids at school and it felt good. I don't condone what I did, but I didn't know any better. I got in with the wrong crowd too ... Curtis being one of them. He was weird. He looked up to me and eventually became a bit obsessed. He followed my every move, and I realised I could control him. He basically did anything I told him to do.'

'And you liked that.'

'At first I did, yes, but then he became a bit creepy, like a stalker. I started dating Mia and then something bad happened and I kept trying to keep my distance, but he became even more obsessed, so when my dad said we were moving away, I was relieved. It was a chance for me to start over and put my past behind me.'

As he's speaking, I notice his heartbeat doesn't change. He's so close to the truth. I just need to push him a little more and wait for the penny to drop.

'Who else did you bully at school?'

'Just some other kids. I don't really remember.'

'Did you bully just boys or girls as well?'

Bryan tenses underneath me again. *There it is.* The seed of doubt is blossoming. I've got him right where I want him, but I need him to remember and say it out loud. I need him to admit what he did to me and what he put me through.

'Hannah … Why are you asking me all these questions?' There's tension and wariness in his voice. He's nervous.

I lift my head from his chest again and look at him. His face is pale. I speak slowly. 'Because I want to know who you really are.'

We lock eyes and I hold his stare without blinking. Then his left eye twitches.

Bingo.

Bryan shuffles his body back against the headboard so he's sitting upright. I allow him to move and kneel next to him on the bed, my naked body on full view. I have nothing to hide. I want him to see all of me, to know exactly who I am.

'Hannah, you're scaring me. What's going on?'

I want to laugh with glee at the sight of his face. It's contorted into a strange, confused frown, but with a hint of a smile, as if he thinks I'm making some sort of sick joke that he doesn't understand. He's still refusing to admit it.

'You know what's going on.'

There is a ten-second pause and then he gulps hard. 'It's you ... isn't it?'

'It's me.'

'Fuck—'

'Say it.'

Bryan gulps again. 'You're the girl I ... the girl I ...' He's not going to say it, is he? No, because he's weak and pathetic, just like all abusive men are.

Fine, I'll say it then!

'You raped me, Bryan. I'm the girl you raped back in school!' I shout it loud enough to make him flinch.

Bryan's face turns an ugly shade of white. He starts trembling and lunges to the side of the bed and vomits onto the floor. I watch him for a few seconds. I could easily reach down and grab the hammer and smash the back of his head in right now, but he hasn't suffered enough yet. Besides, I'm enjoying myself far too much to end it now.

I wait patiently until Bryan has finished hurling his guts up. He turns to me.

'Y-You can't be.'

'Don't do that,' I snap, shaking my head. 'Don't pretend you don't know it was me.'

'B-But ... it can't have been you. Her name was ...' He stops, as if someone has just stolen the words from his mouth.

'That's right, you snivelling piece of shit. You don't even remember her name, do you? You don't even know the name of the person whose life you ruined. She was just a nameless face to you. Well ... here she is Bryan ... in all her glory.' I spread my arms open, showing him my nakedness, unashamed and proud.

He opens his mouth to respond, but I hold my hand up. 'Don't say anything. Not yet. Allow me to tell you the story, and I need you to listen carefully because it's a wonderful story really. It's sick and sad and awful, but it is wonderful.

'Twenty-two years ago, you started going to a school called St Marks Primary. You were the most popular boy there within a day, even though you began to bully everyone. One day, you bullied a little girl into giving you her lunch. After that, you and your cronies – one of them being Curtis Redding – made that little girl's life a living hell. Every day you tormented her because she liked to read and because she had no friends.

'Then, at the age of fifteen, you got her drunk at a school summer party. You drugged her too, then took her upstairs and raped her. Yes, it was rape Bryan. She was too drunk and out of it to even form any words. Your friends were outside the door, egging you on, Curtis included. You all laughed when you emerged from the bedroom, but before you left her you whispered something in her ear. I want you to tell me what you said to her.'

Bryan has the audacity to shake his head. 'I ... I don't remember.'

'Liar. What did you say to her, Bryan?'

Bryan blinks several times. 'I said ... I said if she told anyone what happened I'd kill her and then rape her dead body and feed it to a pack of dogs.'

I raise my eyebrows, quietly surprised that he had the guts to say it. 'That's right. Well remembered.'

'I ... I don't understand. You've been pretending and leading me on all this time? Why?'

'Isn't it obvious?'

'For revenge?'

I laugh. 'Bryan, if I wanted revenge, I would have left you alone after I caused the car accident that killed Hannah.'

Bryan wipes his mouth with the back of his hand. He is edging ever closer to the edge of the bed away from me. I can't let him get too far. He's on the defensive now. He's bigger and stronger, and if I give him too much leverage he could easily overpower me. I slowly lower my hand to the floor and reach under the bed for the hammer, hiding it under the sheets as I shift closer to him.

'Y-You ... it was you? But Curtis was the one who—'

'No. It was me. I followed you that night. I knew you were drunk.'

'It was you! You're the woman who told me Hannah was having an affair. That was you!'

'Yes! You do remember me. To be honest, I just wanted you to crash your car that night, maybe hit someone, maybe injure yourself, but what happened was even sweeter. You killed your own girlfriend. I was happy with that for a while, so I left you alone. I knew Curtis had his weird obsession with you, so I allowed him to make your life miserable. You could say we were working together, but he didn't realise it. I couldn't have done it without him.

'I wanted you to suffer more, but I had to take over my father's business and make something of myself. I had to build myself a persona so that no one would suspect me, not even you. When you first met Ashleigh Carmichael that day you just assumed she was a blonde bimbo with boobs for brains. You took advantage of her, like you took advantage of her all those years ago.'

'No!' Bryan dives towards me and grabs my hand, squeezing so tight it hurts. 'No, I never took advantage of you. At first you were an annoyance that I didn't need, but then I wanted to help you, to keep you safe, to save you.'

'That's rich coming from a rapist.'

Bryan lets go of my hand as if he's been burned. 'I ... I didn't mean ... I regret what I did, every fucking day, I swear to you, and if I could take it back I would. After that happened, I tried to be better—'

'Did you?' I snap. 'Or did you become worse?'

'I tried my best. You don't know what it was like for me. It was true what I said about my dad. He abused my mum and killed her—'

'Like you abused me! How is what your father did to your mum any different than what you did to me?'

'It's not! I know it isn't, but I was a messed-up kid. I didn't know any other way. I changed. I did. When we moved away, I made a promise to myself to change.'

'Men like you never change. Just look at Sawyer. Look at Curtis. They both got what they deserved.'

Bryan holds his hands up defensively. 'Look, I'm sorry for what happened. I know there's nothing I can say to make you forgive me, but Ash – Hannah – we can get past it, right? I'll do anything, I swear. I just want to make things right. Tell me how I can make things right.'

I shake my head. I pity the man really. He's been completely in the dark this whole time about my intentions and now his whole world is falling apart around him. My heart is beating so hard in my chest I fear it might explode any second and it's physically exhilarating. The long build up has been worth it. Every moment I doubted myself, every stupid business meeting I had to sit through, every posed photograph I took for my social media pages, every time I had to smile for the camera or act a certain way ... It's all been worth it, just to see the look on his face, hear the panic in his voice.

'That's the thing, Bryan. You can never make it right. You can never take back what you did. I don't care if you're sorry or if you feel bad about it. You still did it. You still raped me. You still bullied me and made my life hell. You're still a horrible human being, and the worst thing is you didn't even remember me until just now. You didn't even know the name of the girl you raped.'

Bryan stops shaking his head and stays perfectly still. We lock eyes again and then I see it … His eyes turn dark, as if a demon has just taken possession of his body.

Oh no …

I'm wrong …

I've been wrong all this time—

Bryan lunges at me.

I reach out for the hammer, but it's too late.

He pins me down on the bed, straddling his legs over my hips. His cock is erect and pushing into me through the covers. I thrash and fight as he grabs my wrists and holds me down with such force, I fear he might snap them in half.

'I always knew who you were, you fucking bitch,' he hisses through gritted teeth. 'All this time you thought you were playing me. Well, surprise *bitch*, I've been playing *you* instead.'

I yelp as he releases one of my wrists and slaps me hard across the face. My head snaps to the left and I taste blood in my mouth, which I spit up at him. He barely even flinches as he slaps me again. I freeze, deciding to save my energy. He stares down at me and I stare up at him.

'Don't you have anything to say, Ashleigh?'

I hold his gaze. I will not give him the satisfaction of hearing me beg or cry or shout for help. The plan still holds … I just have to adapt and overcome … again.

Bryan grins at me as he rearranges the covers so that my naked body is on full display. He hovers over me for a few seconds then punches me straight in the face. The room spins and black spots dance as he flips me over and holds me down.

I grip the bed sheets tight.

I can't move.

I can't speak.

I'm close to passing out from the punch. He is pinning my face into the bed so I can barely take a breath. I wiggle as much as I can, my arms flailing out to the side to grab hold of something ... anything. And that's when I feel it through the thin sheet.

The hammer is beside me on the bed.

Bryan hasn't noticed it.

This is my moment.

I slide my hand under the cool sheets whilst hoping that he's too preoccupied to notice. My fingers brush the handle of the hammer. A small whimper escapes my lips as he thumps me hard on the back with his fist.

I clench my teeth so hard that my jaw aches as I slowly curl my fingers around the handle, ensuring I get a good grip.

I can't mess this up.

One wrong move and it will all be over for me. I need to get it right the first time. I know for a fact that if he got hold of this hammer, he would beat me to death with it and then rape my dead body, like he said he'd do.

I realise I can't do anything while I'm being pressed face-down into the bed. I must wait until he turns me around.

Jessica Huntley

After what seems like hours, but is probably only a couple of minutes, Bryan grabs my hair and pulls me up off the bed. He growls in my ear and then licks me.

'I'm going to fucking destroy you by the end of this.'

I don't shudder.

I don't respond in any way except to grip the handle tighter. He drags me up to standing by my hair. The covers drop and my hammer-holding hand is on full show, but he clearly doesn't notice. He spins me around to face him, pressing his hard dick into my stomach.

I smile at him, and it causes him to frown back. 'What the fuck are you smiling at?'

'Goodbye, Bryan Matthews.'

With one fluid motion I raise the hammer and, with all my strength, strike him across the head. I hear the crunch of broken teeth, the snap of a shattered jaw as his head collides with the lump of metal. He falls sideways onto the bed, blood spraying across the nearby wall and the bedsheets. It's a work of art.

I lose my balance on the soft mattress, so I straddle him, pinning him down, holding the hammer above my head with both hands. He isn't dead, but he's severely injured; too injured to fight back. He can't even use his arms to protect himself. He coughs and spits out blood and teeth, covering my bare breasts.

'I would ask if you had any last words, but seeing as you can't talk ...'

I slam the weapon into his face.

I have just enough time to see his eyes widen in terror before the hammer disintegrates his skull.

I don't stop.

I can't stop.

Every ounce of rage and terror this man has instilled in me over the years comes rushing out all at once. This is my moment and I'm relishing every fucking second.

When the last morsel of strength has left my arms, I lower the hammer to my side and survey the damage. His face is unrecognisable. It's merely a mass of skull, blood and brains. I'm breathing so heavily that my chest is heaving in and out and I can't seem to control it. I take a deep breath, but that doesn't help. Am I having a panic attack? Is this what one feels like?

I lurch to the side, swinging my left leg over his body and scramble off the bed. I barely make it to the toilet before everything in my stomach makes an appearance. I didn't expect to react like this, but then again, I'm only human.

Maybe it's because I'm relieved it's over.

After all these years of planning and waiting and faking it, I've completed the ten steps that will enable me to move on with my life.

Now ... the next phase begins.

Chapter Fifty-Two

HANNAH
2 August 2022 – 06:45 a.m.

I take a long hot shower and, as the water rinses away the blood and brains, so does it wash away any remnants of whatever that was earlier. I'd spewed my guts up for half an hour, but I feel better now, cleaner and composed. My body aches all over. I feel bruised in between my legs, and every time I take a step, I wince.

I wrap a towel around my body and pad out into the bedroom. I stare at the monster on my bed and tears prickle my eyes. No, I will not shed a tear over him. He doesn't deserve my tears. I angrily wipe them away and begin to get dressed.

I'm ready to tackle what comes next. I have a plan, but it means getting away without being caught. That's the hard part though, right? Getting away with it. And, at the end of the day, it's what this whole endeavour has been about. There would be no point in killing Bryan Matthews if I couldn't enjoy the aftermath.

But what a mess to clean up.

I could just leave him for the motel cleaners to find, but even that would be too good for him. I don't want his body to be found. I don't want the police looking into his death and wondering who he is. Bryan Matthews needs to disappear forever.

I lock the motel room (leaving the 'do not disturb' sign on the doorknob) and drive to the nearest hardware store, which is quite far away, a little too far for my liking. I buy a saw and heavy-duty bin bags.

I drive back to the motel and spend the next few hours dismantling Bryan Matthews piece by piece. I saw off his dick and put it aside. I have a special plan for that.

Once the boot of the car has been loaded with the bin bags, I return to the room and bundle up all the sheets. I steal some cleaning supplies from the cupboard in the hall and get to work. Honestly, it's a laborious task and I curse his name through every second of scrubbing and washing, but eventually the room has no trace of blood left. The sheets are beyond saving so they get chucked in a bag in the boot too.

I check out at the front desk. The receptionist is a young woman with frizzy black hair and is wearing large hoop earrings.

'I hope you enjoyed your stay,' she says politely.

I nod. 'I did, thank you. It was very memorable.'

'Where's your man?'

'Ah ... he's just popped out for a bit. I'm meeting up with him later.'

I hand her some cash and a large tip, which she takes with a smile. 'Thank you. Where are you off to now?'

I shrug my shoulders. 'Wherever the road takes me, I guess.'

As I slide into the driver's seat, I feel a tingle of excitement, but also sadness. It's a strange feeling because I'll never see Bryan Matthews again. I never have to think about him anymore. My whole life I've imagined killing him, and now that I have, I can't help but feel a little empty somehow, like there's something missing.

I glance at the appendage resting on the passenger seat. It's securely wrapped in a bin bag. I laugh out loud as I accelerate out of the motel car park and onto the road.

I keep driving for hours. Whenever I see a suitable location, I stop and dispose of one of the bin bags. One of them goes into an incinerator. One sinks to the bottom of a pool of wet cement at a building site. One is tossed on a bonfire in the middle of nowhere. One is weighed down with rocks and plummets to the bottom of a deep lake.

But the last one I keep hold of for a while. I eventually come across a pack of stray dogs roaming the streets of a secluded town. I watch happily as they devour Bryan's cock, until not even a scrap remains. It didn't take long. It wasn't that big.

There's a smugness to my smile as I recall his words to me. He once told me that he'd rape my dead body and then feed it to a pack of dogs.

Well ... it may not have been his whole body, but I think I've proved my point.

Now my focus must be on starting a new life.

I don't plan on staying in America for long. It's a big country for sure, plenty of places to hide, but is it really where I see myself settling down? What do I want from the rest of my life now that my sole focus, my one reason for living, has gone? For the first time I can look to the future with hope and anticipation.

I can dare to dream of what comes next.
Here's to a future without Bryan Matthews.

Epilogue

One year and six months later

The hot Maldives sunshine is like pure rays of heaven and happiness. There's no other way of explaining it. The white sand beaches sparkle like diamond dust and the crystal blue waters are so clear you can see to the bottom and watch fish swimming around. It truly is the most beautiful place I've ever seen.

I've witnessed some breathtaking views during my travels over the past decade. I visited the Grand Canyon and flew over it in a helicopter, marvelling at its sheer size and wonder. I saw Niagara Falls and watched as a rainbow appeared across the sky and was reflected in the spray of water. I've travelled across Europe tasting fresh pasta in Italy and hand-picked grapes in Spain. I've been to China and seen the Terracotta Army and walked on the Great Wall of China.

Yes, I've been a busy girl and have been living life to the fullest. I've enjoyed meeting strangers, laughing and getting drunk, dancing the nights away. I've never stayed too long in one place though. I kept moving, breaking a few hearts in the process, but I couldn't risk settling down; not yet.

This was the plan all along.

I'm nervous about approaching her.

It's the first time we'll meet face to face in years, but now feels like the right moment. She doesn't know I'm here yet. I don't know how she'll react to me finally tracking her down and turning up. Maybe she doesn't want to see me anymore and be friends. Maybe she's changed her mind.

I'm sipping a strong cocktail from a coconut shell through a pink whirly straw, trying to summon up the courage to talk to her. She's behind the bar, serving drinks to customers, a pink flower tucked behind her right ear. Her skin is gloriously tanned, her hair dark and wavy and thick.

She hasn't noticed me yet. I doubt she'll recognise me as I've changed a great deal over the years, just like she has. Gone is the self-obsessed teenager. I'm now a confident woman with a pixie haircut and tattoos up my arms. I keep my eyes locked on her while she works. She's beautiful and unrecognisable as Ashleigh Carmichael. Now she's Hannah Holden; the woman who saved me from my abusive brother and two rapist ex-boyfriends.

Then she spots me and walks over. 'Can I get you a refill?' she asks.

I smile as I lower the coconut. 'Yes, thank you.' I really shouldn't, as it will be my third, but there's something about the way she expertly makes my drink that I find mesmerising. I watch as she sets it down in front of me.

'I was wondering when you'd show up.'

'You recognise me?'

'Of course. It's nice to see you again ... Mia Redding.'

Leave a Review

I hope you've enjoyed reading How to Commit the Perfect Murder in Ten Easy Steps.

If you have, please consider leaving me a review on Amazon and Goodreads, share a review on your social media pages and tag me, share my book to any book clubs you may be a part of or recommend my book to friends and family.

Reviews are massively important, especially to self-published authors. They help find other readers who may enjoy the book and spread the word to a wider audience.

Sign up to my email list via my website to be notified of future books and receive a twice-monthly author newsletter.

www.jessicahuntleyauthor.com

Fancy another gripping standalone thriller by
Jessica Huntley?

Connect with Jessica Huntley

Find and connect with me online via the following platforms.

Follow me on Facebook: Jessica Huntley - Author - @jessica.reading.writing

Follow me on Instagram: @jessica_reading_writing

Follow me on Twitter: @jess_read_write

Follow me on TikTok: @jessica_reading_writing

Follow me on Goodreads: jessica_reading_writing

Milton Keynes UK
Ingram Content Group UK Ltd.
UKHW040625290324
440173UK00001B/15

9 781916 827011